Led Astray

Jeffrey,

Thanks for all your help and insight

Donal P Anderson

Dig Dawg Publishers
P.O. Box 119
Hanson, MA 02341
www.DigDawg.com
The Dig Dawg name and logo are trademarks of Defense Investigators Group, Inc.
www.D-I-G.com
Printed in the United States of America
First Printing: June 2007

Copyright © 2007 Donal P. Anderson
All rights reserved.
ISBN: 0-9794879-0-0
ISBN-13: 978-0979487903

Visit www.amazon.com to order additional copies.

DONAL P. ANDERSON

LED ASTRAY

A NOVEL

2007

Led Astray

"There is no hunting like the hunting of a man…and those who have hunted and like it never cared for anything else thereafter."

—Ernest Hemingway

For Dawn

ONE

Everybody wants to know something about somebody, whether it is any of their business or not, and some are willing to pay for that information. Asher "Led" Ledbetter counted on it to make a living; he was a private investigator. He had thought of the line, *The truth may set you free, but the cost of it is hourly—plus expenses*, but never actually had a conversation with anyone where he could use it naturally. He considered at one time putting it on his business card, but the newness of the job had long ago worn off and with it his inclination to be clever.

He hadn't set out to pursue this type of work. He had no former police training, military background, or criminal justice degree. His last job had been as an attendant at Thoreau's self-storage facility watching people's over-bought belongings and dislocated effects. Amongst the mundanity of ripped sofas and old boxes of yearbooks moved in and out of the metal units, there were the glimpses of the renters' lives. The renter of a recently deceased parent, for instance, stored the parent's framed jigsaw puzzle, along with Hummel figurines and some straight-back chairs. The recently evicted stored appliances, wall sconces, and any other household fixtures that could be removed. And there was the obviously convicted, the woman who said she was storing her brother's motorcycle and wanted to know about a discount for a five-year rental. That was before the renter in Unit 27 got a new girlfriend that didn't like snakes. That was before the boa constrictor wrapped itself around the propane heater, died of carbon monoxide, dried out like jerky, and burst into flames. That was before the metal building melted into a black twist of uselessness.

Out of work, Led simply answered an ad for a private investigation agency and it seemed like a good fit.

And so, through providence more than design, he found himself sitting in the conference room and watching the small screen of the laptop play the security camera footage. It was a bird's eye view of a tall, dark-haired young woman. She appeared to be attractive, but the angle was unnatural for judging features. The top of her head was nicely shaped; that was definitive, the rest was implied. Though the angle might have been bad for scoring a beauty contest it perfectly recorded her mashing a bunch of grapes on the floor in the produce aisle before lying gently on top of them. Prone, she was better observed— his suspicions had been right, she was a dark-haired beauty, even in a green work apron and baggy white shirt, staging an accident. Two other employees ran to her aid as she apparently called out in professed pain, but without audio he was only guessing.

Randall Crawford, the senior claims adjuster, stopped the video. "So you can see why the store manager thinks this might be a fake."

"She was pretty careful going down. Did she even get her clothes dirty?"

"We are going to deny it, of course, but need you to do a day on it and see what she's doing. She asked for time off and the manager said no. Then she had this…accident."

"Quite a performance," Led said.

"There's this one and something else I need you to help me with."

Led waited.

"This is nothing to do with the company, this is for sort of a friend of mine, Richard Tuttle. You'd bill him direct. He wanted to know who we used for investigators. I said one of the best. But they weren't available, so I mentioned you."

"You're all heart."

"He's going through a divorce and some child custody issues. He wants to know what kind of guy his wife is seeing. Who she's exposing his children to." Randall was nonchalant in his persuasion. Doing the soft sell. "It's just straight surveillance."

"I don't like doing domestics."

"I know, but he's a golf buddy and a good size account here at the company. He owns Mobile Medical Tech. It would be a favor to me."

"I know who he is. I saw him once at a charity event, the one with the pink ribbons," Led said, playing with Randall, taking the role of the underestimated, where he was the most comfortable.

"Breast cancer?"

"Yeah, that might have been it. It was a few years ago. Tuttle was there, giving a speech and a big check."

Randall smirked. "I can't picture you at a breast cancer charity event."

"What? I don't have a social conscience? I made a donation."

"You never struck me as a philanthropist."

"What does that mean?"

"Someone who donates money," Randall teased.

"I know what a philanthropist is. Why can't I be one?"

"You gave money?"

"Probably half of what I had in my wallet."

"Five dollars?"

"More like ten."

"Because you felt it was a great cause?"

"I had to get one of those ribbons to blend in," Led said, smiling. Randall knew him pretty well. "I was working, getting tape of a waiter."

"A waiter? It wasn't one of my claims?"

"No, it was an auto claim."

"So you know Richard Tuttle?"

"No, we weren't introduced. He was pretty busy talking to some of the speakers."

But Led definitely remembered Richard Tuttle. Tuttle was the type of man that went out of his way so people would remember him. His manner was excessively smooth and could be summed up by looking at his overly white teeth. Tuttle had opened his speech with a self-deprecating joke and naturally smiled as he appreciated being part of such a noble cause.

Led knew he never would want to have a beer with the man, but now he had to suffer with him as a client.

TWO

Led zoomed in on Judith Tuttle's fine-featured, angular face. She was maybe in her mid-thirties, five-foot-six and one-hundred-twenty pounds, pretty. But even through the viewfinder, she looked upset. Despite the highlights in her shoulder-length brunette hair, and her lipstick and fingernails matching, she looked like she was falling apart. In a white linen jacket and salmon-colored blouse she stood impatiently at the back of the opened minivan with her arms folded.

Here came his client, Richard Tuttle, in his silver Audi. Judith glared as his vehicle parked beside her van. The trunk of his sedan popped open to reveal luggage, and the two adults helped three young children get out of the back of the Audi and into the minivan.

Tuttle had said he wanted video of everything. So Led videotaped the entire process. This was useless video; it wasn't going to benefit Tuttle in any child custody case. Led had informed him of this. Tuttle said he didn't care, so Led recorded. He recorded them transferring the bags, recorded them yelling at each other, and recorded as they tried to stop the van—with their three children inside—from rolling down the embankment of the parking lot.

The oldest son, a six-year-old, was seen as he opened the latch, and pushed his four-year-old sister out of the side door of the moving vehicle. He watched momentarily as his sister hit the ground feet-first, tried to run, lost her balance on the uneven turf of the hillside, and tumbled several times with no particular execution of form or style, just a flop and a roll.

He disappeared back into the van as it bounced along.

Then there was the jolt of the abrupt stop—the pop of the airbags.

The driverless minivan had crinkled its bumper and grille around a small birch tree, stopped from its free descent down the embankment with its three—and then two—unwilling passengers.

The parents ran down the hill with their arms flailing in an effort to maintain their balance and navigate the thorny bushes grabbing at their skin and clothes. The girl on the ground was bleeding profusely from her nose. She wiped her face with her hand, smearing the blood and creating a wound of indistinguishable origin by the time her mother got to her. She was crying, but not for her own discomfort.

"I don't want them to blow up!" the girl begged.

"Are you okay, sweetie?"

"I don't want them to die," she sobbed.

Her mother ran her hands over the girl's head, mussing her hair and further spreading the blood. Apparently convinced by her own quick inspection that the girl's skull was not showing or her brains draining through, her motherly triage instincts forced her to get up and run to the van to check on her other two offspring.

The oldest boy lay there with the wind knocked out of him. His breath only entered as short bursts, like air out of a squeaking balloon a little at a time. His mother touched his leg, said his name.

The youngest boy sat still in the child safety seat. Waiting. It wasn't until his mother's pale face leaned into the van that he screeched. He had been observing idly up until now, but if adults were scared it must be time to cry.

"Everything is okay, Mom is right here," she said to comfort him, but kept her attention still on the gasping oldest boy. "Josh, are you alright?"

Breathing with near-full lung capacity again, he sat up and nodded. His mother kissed him on the forehead. She unfastened the youngster from his child seat and helped both of them out of the van.

"I didn't want us to blow up," the oldest boy said. "But I couldn't get Brendan out of his car seat."

"I know, sweetheart. You were very brave. Sit with your brother while I go check on your sister."

Tuttle was with the girl, helping her to her feet. He tipped the child's head back in an attempt to slow the blood from running out of her nose as she cried. Then he got a golf towel out of the car and held it to her face, careful not to get blood on his own clothes. He tried to get her to hold it herself, but she cried, saying she couldn't, that her arm hurt. The two boys and their mother walked over.

"He didn't want us to blow up," the youngest said, explaining the van eviction.

"She didn't tuck and roll. She should have rolled like Tony Hawk did when he fell off his skateboard," Josh said. "You have to tuck and roll."

Asher Ledbetter, ever the professional investigator, was still running the video camera with one hand as he dialed 911 on his cell phone with the other. He told the police where he was and that they should probably send an ambulance. With domestics someone was always getting hurt, and it was never the guilty one.

With their backs to each other, the two parents stood with distance between them, placing their own calls as they consoled the children in the grass. The police and the ambulance were quick to show up. Soon the children's maternal grandmother arrived in a gray sedan. She only spoke with the children and their mother, walking in a big arc to and from her vehicle to avoid any contact with Richard Tuttle.

Led continued to videotape the entire mess as the two parents stood talking with a police officer. "You almost killed my kids!" Tuttle hollered. "I should call my attorney right now. That's reckless endangerment—"

"I didn't do anything," she said loudly. But she had no anger in her voice, just exhaustion.

"You left the goddamn van running!" Tuttle almost sounded happy. "You really screwed up this time."

"You are an ass," she said definitively.

"I got a witness sitting right over there," Tuttle said as if laying down a hand, a full house, kings over queens.

"You got a witness?" the police officer asked. "Where is your witness?"

Led saw them point at him. He was supposed to have been the discreet observer. This was why he didn't get involved in people's private matters. Insurance companies and corporate clients never pointed at him.

The police officer was motioning him over. Everyone was looking at him. So he got out of the jeep, still holding his video camera.

He hit pause.

"Who is this?" the police officer asked Tuttle.

"Ledbettor. A private detective I hired to protect my children."

"You have some ID?"

Led already had his black leather identification case in his hand.

The cop held it almost at arm's length so that he could regard Led and his picture at the same time. "Asher Ledbettor...you go by Led?" His tone indicated he thought it was a dumb nickname.

"Sometimes," he answered. "People call me what they want."

"She left the children in the van unattended," Tuttle said.

Tuttle's wife went to her injured daughter on the stretcher. She looked at Led disdainfully, but with acceptance that he was just another one of her husband's hired hands brought in to make her life miserable. "The parking brake failed because you won't give me money to get it fixed," she said, climbing into the back of the ambulance with her daughter.

The grandmother left in the sedan with the two boys.

"I'll check on you later, babe," Tuttle shouted into the back of the ambulance, never leaving the side of the police officer writing notes. "She has my children in a van that's unsafe."

"Sir, the van is registered to you. If you feel it needs maintenance, maybe you should fix it."

"It's her van," Tuttle said. "She can fix it."

"You saw what happened?" the officer asked Led.

"Most of it." Led flipped out the camera's side screen. "Here, look for yourself."

The woman and the man were talking at conversational levels, but due to the distance there was no volume. Even without hearing them it was clear by their increasingly wild gestures things were getting heated. It was only a minute before the full-fledged yelling. The small speakers and screen on the camera replayed the action for those that missed it the first time.

"You're a bastard," she was heard to say. "You don't care about anyone but yourself—not even the kids!"

"I'm sick of you bitching at me in front of my kids," Tuttle replied. "Trying to turn them against me...I know what you're doing."

"Give me the goddamn keys," she demanded.

"I paid for it," Tuttle answered righteously, pushing her buttons.

"That's bullshit," she said.

The cop looked up from the screen at Led. "So much for the children's impressionable minds. Can you fast forward to how the van rolled down the hill?"

"Sure." Led held the fast-forward button as he and the officer watched the pantomime in eight-quarter time, the exes gesticulating with their arms and bobbing their heads, back and forth like birds preparing to mate. Or peck each other's eyes out.

"Here it is," Led said, letting it play at normal speed.

"—have someone over," Tuttle said as he reached to grab her arm and she jerked away. She walked to the passenger's side of the van, shutting the sliding door hard.

"What I do is none of your business," she said, walking around the back of the van and leaning in close to his face to spray venom. "You left us. Remember? You left *us*."

"Watch," Led said to the cop. "Here's where you can see it start to move."

Led had noticed the van's movement before they did, looked up from his camera to be sure...but before he could decide if he should yell to them, blowing his cover, the crunching gravel under the tires drew their attention.

"Oh my God!" The woman ran to the van, banging futilely on the back window.

"Shit!" Tuttle got to the van before it reached the edge of the pavement, managing to open the driver's side door. But instead of jumping in, he only stuck his right foot inside, in an effort to hit the brake. Hopping on his left foot as he went, he fell and rolled out of the way as the van started down the grassy knoll.

"At least she won't be going out tonight," Tuttle said as the police officer viewed the tape.

"*Riiiight,*" Led said, dragging out the lone syllable, unsure he'd heard his client correctly. He waited for Tuttle to add something about how glad he was his children were all right. He didn't. "Well, looks like I'm done," Led said.

"Can I have the tape?" the officer asked.

"It's his," Led apologized, motioning to Tuttle. "He's the client."

"No," Tuttle responded. "My attorney will want that."

"I can make them a copy," Led offered.

"Then make them a copy. Fine. They will charge her as unfit."

"Right now I'm not charging anyone with anything," the police officer said, handing Led a card. "But I would like a copy of the tape. Can you get it dropped off at the station?"

"Not now," Tuttle interjected. "Make it for them tomorrow. Right now I want you to go over to the hospital and follow her when she leaves. Just to make sure."

"You're not going to the hospital?" Led asked. He wasn't surprised.

"I would, but I have plans," Tuttle said on his way to his car. "And I don't want to be around that bitch any more than I have to."

Led stood still, refusing to walk after him. "But she knows you've hired a PI, and she knows who I am at this point."

"She's stupid. She'll probably think you went home after all this." Tuttle got in his car and shut the door. The discussion was over from his end.

"It's your money," Led said.

A case like this wasn't a matter of reason. It was a matter of brain imbalance, one lobe kicking the shit out of the other, all pure emotional flailing. At times like this, he questioned his own motivation to continue in this profession as a constant observer to the human condition. From what he had seen, evolution didn't stand a chance against the temptations of people to self-destruct their lives. He loved the mechanics of his job but worried that the fumes of futility might some day cause him irreparable harm.

She didn't go to the Cape. She went home with the girl, with her arm in a sling. The lights in the condo went out at ten-thirty except for the blue glow of a television. Led stayed until eleven-thirty. Nothing more transpired. Private cases were a circus without a tent.

THREE

The shower and coffee did little to counter his lack of sleep. Routine substituted for alertness. Led gathered his car keys and took one more sip of coffee hoping to jump-start his mental facilities.

He was reminded of his second reason for staying away from private cases: they didn't go together with the early morning demands of insurance fraud investigations. Trying to cover both ends of the spectrum didn't leave enough time for sleep. Sleep deprivation, however, was merely an inconvenience, not a deterrent; working with it had become second nature, an achievable state just a little closer to consciousness than not, keeping the vehicle in the right lane and the videotape rolling.

He sipped at his coffee as he drove, thinking about Tuttle and his family, wondering how it fell so far apart and what those three children whispered to each other when their parents weren't around. This was what Led's interaction with others, too, had become: all work-related observation, speculation. Except for waitresses, if he was talking to someone it was probably about work or on a case. And why not? He observed more drama in one week than most people—outside of cops and reporters—encountered in a lifetime. And he wasn't mired in the emotions of it. He could skate along on the surface of other people's lives.

He wondered if he'd be feeling the same rancor about private cases this morning if he'd been working for Tuttle's ex-wife instead of Tuttle. He wouldn't have done anything differently; he was as objective as ever, just documenting what he saw. But she would not have given him that look when she walked by, like he had just done something wrong.

DONAL P. ANDERSON

He was just working.

At 5:38 a.m., he neared the three-story condo unit of the new insurance claim investigation. Beyond the home was an empty spot on the same side of the street, but it was tight. A black Honda had parked too far forward, and a white utility van in front of it not far enough.

He cut his wheel hard as he backed up, his rear right tire going up on the curb. *Damn.* He looked around. No one was paying any attention to him this early in the morning. There was only a woman in a terrycloth housecoat standing on the strip of grass between the sidewalk and the street, holding one end of a leash. At the other end was a fluffed-out mop of a dog.

He pulled forward and cut the front wheel the other way so the rear tire slid off the curb. He hoped he hadn't pinched the sidewall, but didn't get out to look; the more movement around his vehicle, the more attention he'd draw. He listened hard for the sound of a tire hissing, trying to determine if the jeep was listing. He couldn't tell. He'd have to take his chances and deal with it later because anyone could be looking out the window from any of the other surrounding multi-family buildings.

It was still early. Those who had to get up for school or work were preparing for their day. The rhythm of the morning was starting to beat. No matter how busy it might get, any disruption to the syncopation of the traffic coming and going, the people exiting their homes and the storefront openings, would stand out like a cymbal crash at a piano recital.

He watched to see if the woman with the dog would notice that he didn't get out of the jeep, but she had a plastic bag on her right hand and was busy trying to catch her dog's excrement as it fell. Catching it hot was apparently less trouble than picking it up off the ground. A bit of a twist to the five-second rule.

He had tried to take a dog along for the ride before, back when he was married, before his ex-wife kept it. There were times when a dog on a leash was the perfect reason to be walking in a neighborhood. No one ever asked what you were doing. They could

14

immediately see. You were walking the dog. Neighborhood residents would pat the dog, engaging in idle chitchat, as he bent and twisted the conversation in ways even he didn't think possible until it was over. That was why he felt it was best not to plan out too many details of what he was going to say. He preferred to let the lies flow from the moment.

"What's his name?" someone would inevitably ask as if scripted.

"General."

"Hey, General. What a *good* dog."

"It's short for General Flea. Like flea bag."

"Oh, he's not a flea bag. Are you, boy?"

Then he'd start to work it. "Have you lived here long?"

"Almost eight years."

"Do you know who lives in that house there?"

"The Norrises."

"I used to have a friend that lived in that house when I was in third grade. His name wasn't Norris. It was Keith Barton."

"I don't know any Bartons in the area."

"I hung out in this neighborhood all summer that year. My aunt lived a couple streets over. She moved and we never came back over here. When you're a kid, a couple miles might as well be a different country. It still seems like a nice neighborhood, though."

"It is. Quiet and no problems."

"I was in the area and hadn't been in this neighborhood in over twenty-five years. I guess when you get older you start thinking about people, times, places. The people that live here now, do you know them?"

"Some. They're nice. A man and his wife and two little girls, younger than my kids so they don't hang around with each other."

Then he'd surprise himself with the stories that would flow. "They ever mention finding a time capsule buried in a Saltine Cracker tin in the backyard?"

"No! What was in it?"

"Important stuff when you're in third grade. A bunch of plastic dinosaurs and matchbox cars is all I can remember putting in there. Some pictures we cut out of magazines, Marlboro Cowboys. I doubt we buried anything we really wanted to keep. Does Mr. Norris work? I'd love to talk to him to see if he ever found that box."

"He was working as a warehouse manager, but I think he got hurt at work. He's now just helping with his wife's store. She has a pottery shop. If they aren't home, try down at the Barn of Pottery in the Tedeschi's strip mall."

"Thanks."

"Good luck with the time capsule."

"For all I know Keith Barton dug it up that fall and took my dinosaurs."

Conversations like that had flowed because neighbors were comfortable talking to the guy with the dog.

But for all the benefits, he didn't want another dog. It would be like breaking in a new partner, and he didn't want to be bothered. It wasn't fair to a dog to expect it to stay in the car all day, boiling hot or freezing cold. It was enough to subject himself to it.

He slid from behind the steering wheel, lifting himself up and over the armrest between the two front seats, settling into the back seat. The brown leather on the armrest had a worn spot that served as testimony to the frequency of this drill.

With his tools of the trade—a cup of coffee and a video camera—he was in his suburban blind, the back of a jeep with black curtains in front of dark tinted windows, positioned to document anything that occurred. He had arrived early enough that no one should have noticed that he never exited the vehicle. Pedestrians started to walk down the street; commuters to a city bus stop, children to school. None even glanced at Led's black Jeep Cherokee. From the outside, it looked like any other vehicle parked on the street. They didn't know what they couldn't see. This was his office.

His workday had begun.

The file information had a decent enough description of the subject, a dentist claiming he couldn't work due to an auto accident.

When the townhouse's garage door went up he identified the man dragging out the trash barrels. There was nothing remarkable about what was happening other than his supposed knee injury required that he wear a brace. The video captured the man's life like a documentary about the morning habits of white middle-aged males in North America. There he was making two trips from the garage. No knee brace. It wasn't like he just caught the guy running with the bulls in Paloma, but it was a good start to the morning. There was activity.

The dentist was in his forties, with a bit of a paunch and in need of a haircut as his thinning hair was starting to hang over his ears. He got into his black two-seater convertible, but kept the top up. He drove away with Led following discreetly behind.

In the parking garage at the New England Baptist Hospital, the dentist parked on the third level. Led found a spot and waited for the dentist to get out of his car. The dentist was doing something, checking his laptop or going through papers, it was hard to tell and taking quite awhile.

Led sat in the back of his jeep with his video camera already recording, watching only the top of the dentist's head in the car. A car parked beside Led's jeep, and he allowed himself a glance as a good-looking blonde woman got out, opened her car's backdoor, and bent over to retrieve paperwork from the backseat. How could he not look a little more? Something about her pose—maybe the style of the knee-length skirt, or the way her blonde hair was pulled back—made her look like a logo on a WWII fighter plane. Though he watched her it was only with occasional glances. He could not allow himself the pleasure as he waited for the dentist to get out of his car. Besides, he had the benefit of seeing beautiful women all the time. Some of them he was investigating and some not. Being the paid voyeur that he was, he just watched them walk in and out of his camera range.

The woman gathered a bundle of overstuffed folders and waited in the glassed-in kiosk for the garage elevator. She stood next to a petite Asian woman and a tall, thin black male with graying hair and beard stubble and carrying a cane, who were talking in a familiar way. They might have been man and wife, based on the way she tucked in the liner of his back pants pocket. They were too far away from Led to hear from inside his jeep—until the Asian woman screamed.

Led saw that the black man was now lying crumpled on the floor of the kiosk. The Asian woman knelt and began to shake him and the blonde who had parked beside Led tossed away her armload of folders and ran to the fallen man. Checking his breathing and pulse, she straightened his arms and legs and tipped his head back as she started CPR.

Led waited to see if the dentist was going to help, but the man was oblivious to the commotion and continued to write on some papers, probably with his radio on. Hesitantly Led put down his video camera, climbed out of the back of the jeep and jogged over to help. He tried to dial out on his cell phone as he entered the kiosk, but it didn't work three levels down in the concrete parking garage. The Asian woman was crying hysterically.

Led approached the blonde woman doing CPR. "Are you all set here?" he asked. "I'll go get help."

"Yes," the woman said in between breaths into the man's mouth, counting out chest compressions. "...two...three...go..."

Led rode the elevator to the lobby and ran at full speed to the information desk. Despite his rapid approach, barely stopping before slamming into the oak counter, the young, clean-cut man in burgundy blazer in the booth was stoic in his response.

"May I help you?" he asked.

After Led explained the situation, the clerk calmly called the ambulance as if sending down a bellhop to pick up bags. When he addressed Led again it was only to say, "Someone will be right there."

Led had expected paramedics to ride back down with him, but no one came as he stood waiting for the elevator. He rode down to level three and could hear the siren in the garage by the time the door opened. The ambulance was winding downward with stretcher and emergency personnel.

LED ASTRAY

The Asian woman beside the fallen man held his hand, sobbing words of hope in some other language. The blonde on her knees looked up for the ambulance between breaths into the man's mouth.

Led felt like he should be doing something more and was self-conscious just standing there. With no useful purpose he stood with his arms folded across his chest. The ambulance stopped and the driver got out with a large medical box. The other paramedic opened the back and unloaded a gurney. Led held the glass doors of the kiosk open for them.

There was little more that he could do now that medical support had arrived. He walked away from the commotion and returned to his jeep, climbing into the back. This was a day when the odds went his way. The dentist was still sitting in his car, uninterested or unaware in the commotion. By the time he folded his paper the ambulance was gone with the heart attack victim and his wife, and so was the woman who had administered CPR.

The dentist opened his driver's side door and sat with his legs out as he put on a Velcro knee brace. Then he walked toward the elevator with an accentuated limp. Led went on videotaping. Once the elevator doors shut, Led climbed out of the back of the jeep and shoved the video camera into a nylon bike messenger bag with a mesh front. This was how he'd concealed cameras since they were the size of small microwaves, back when the bag had to be the size of a suitcase. He had smaller setups, but he preferred to stick with the reliable. In the long hallways of the hospital the dentist would be too far away for the covert camera, and the regular camera out in the open would panic some hospital administrator worried about a violation of privacy.

The camera was set to manual focus and medium zoom. Led rode the elevator to the fifth floor where the dentist sat in one of the chairs in the hall, not far from the office door where he would be seeing his orthopedic physician.

Led sat, too. When the dentists' name was called, Led watched him limp into the office like he had a peg leg. Led got up from his chair and wandered down the hall a few feet to lean against the wall.

Led needed to document as much of the performance as possible, to show that the dentist had a strong propensity to exaggerate his injury.

The surveillance position was fine. He was feeling comfortable with the surroundings, nonchalantly blending in with wandering patients and the people who brought them here. In the hall of yellow walls and fluorescent lights, even the healthiest people looked jaundiced as they walked past a few at a time. Standing, instead of being cramped in the back of the jeep, he was thinking about it being an easy day. Finish early, go home, do some laundry, get some sleep...

There was commotion from one of the offices, and shrieking, and then, as if class had ended in a high school of the infirm, an entire orthopedic office emptied into the hallway in a frenzy. A mass of wheelchairs, crutches, and canes surrounded Led. Medical staff and patients, some wet from a burst pipe in the ceiling, some swearing, some laughing, were all in his way. Led stood focused on the door of the office. The spraying water did not appear to be affecting this end of the hall, but the crowd around him obstructed any angle he might have had with the camera bag.

In the midst of the commotion, the door he was watching opened and the dentist exited, startled to see the hall crowded with patients and arriving maintenance staff. He turned sideways and slid along the wall to navigate his way to the elevator. Led got on the elevator with him. When the doors started to close, a hand grabbed the black bumper, causing it to reopen. It was the woman from the garage, the blonde.

"Hi," she said as she got in, apparently recognizing him. "Quite a day around here."

"Yep," was all Led said in reply. He wanted to talk to her. Who wouldn't? But he couldn't get caught in a conversation. She seemed to give a shrug, turning to face the elevator door beside the dentist. Her hair swung as she turned.

It looked soft.

The doors opened and the dentist walked toward his car. Led flashed a smile back at the woman. If there had only been time. He opened the bag as he walked in hurried steps, removing his video camera, opening the back door of his jeep. From inside he videotaped the dentist limping back to his car.

The dentist sat in the driver's seat with his legs again swinging outside of the car so he could remove the knee brace. Then the blonde woman trotted up to him, clicking through the garage with her heels on the concrete.

"Excuse me," she said as she approached the dentist.

Led's first thought was that she had figured out what he was doing—that she was going to alert the dentist. He listened hard to their reverberated voices in the concrete parking garage.

"I think I locked my keys in my car," she said. She and the dentist spoke as they walked back to her car, parked right beside Led's. The dentist walked without his brace, cane or limp. He looked through the windows of her car and tried to see the ignition. Then he walked around the car and tried all the doors. He apologized for not having a "slim-jim" with him, or a coat hanger, and just as he was about to call a tow service for her, she found her keys in the bottom of her pocketbook.

"Wait," she said. "Here they are. I feel so stupid!"

"That's alright," the dentist replied. "It happens to all of us."

"Well, thank you. Thank you so much for coming over."

"Not a problem," he said, backing away toward his car. "Glad you found them."

She stood by her car looking in his direction, apparently waiting until he looked back, when she waved the tips of her fingers. He raised his hand, embarrassed to have been caught taking a second look. Led took video of the dentist sauntering back to his vehicle with full natural strides of attempted virility.

Then the blonde looked at the tinted windows of Led's jeep. There was no way that she could have seen him, but it seemed as if she was looking him in the eye. She gave a wave of her hand and smiled, then got into her vehicle and pulled out of the parking spot.

The dentist followed the woman and Led followed the dentist.

Led didn't know who she was or why she had done what she did, but he was fascinated. She was pretty. Had she manipulated the situation so Led could get video? Give a guy a reason to help a pretty woman and he feels good about himself, especially if it's quick, easy, and doesn't cost anything.

He wanted to thank her, to talk to her. But his self-imposed duty called for him to follow the dentist now. At the last moment, he wrote down her license plate number, just before he pulled away. He surprised himself, not even sure why he had done it. He attributed it to just part of his consummate information gathering. Just in case.

He followed the dentist home, sat outside of the brick-faced house.

He looked at the woman's license plate written at the top of his yellow pad. It was easy enough to look up her name and her phone number on his laptop, but should he? It had nothing to do with work. He wouldn't hesitate to look up a nun's gynecological records if it was case-related, but this was personal. What if she didn't want him to know where she lived? He could end up looking like a stalker. A woman like that had guys coming at her from every angle, every day.

What the hell. So he'd be one of those guys. Add him to the list. The name on the vehicle registration was Callie Walker, and he didn't find that there was any Mr. Walker at the same address. He left a message on her answering machine.

"This is Asher Ledbetter. Thanks for the assist today in the parking garage. Call if you'll let me buy you a cup of coffee sometime." He left his cell number.

He'd thought about apologizing for looking up her information, but why draw attention to it? It shouldn't come across as being a threat, he was just thanking her. This way it was up to her. She probably had a boyfriend anyway.

The call on his cell phone twenty minutes later came in as C. McBride. His mind raced, thinking it was a witness on one of the files he was working on.

"Led speaking. May I help you?"

"I'm looking for Asher Ledbettor. This is Callie McBride."

"This is regarding?"

"Callie McBride. From-the-parking-garage-McBride."

"Oh, I didn't recognize your name. I thought it was Walker."

"Walker's a previous name. I'm recently back to McBride."

"I want to apologize for not speaking to you in the elevator, but I was working."

"You were a little odd, the way you disappeared as the paramedics arrived. Then when you didn't say anything on the elevator, I thought you were just rude. But I saw the video camera on your way back to the jeep," she said, in a sweet voice but no-nononsense tone. "I figured it out."

He was starting to think she had called him back to cut into him for his lack of social graces. "Did you hear how the heart attack man was doing?" he asked somewhat sincerely, mostly trying to talk about anything but himself to find something they had in common. At the moment they only had the parking garage.

"Heart attack man? I tried to check but I didn't get his name. The paramedics had him stabilized pretty quickly. Did you get your man? The one you were so focused on?"

"Yes," he said, a little disappointed she was back to that. "Thank you."

"I appreciate the offer for a cup of coffee," she said. "But for all the work I did, I think I should at least be worth a dinner."

"Sure." He fumbled for his pen, usually so available for taking case notes. "I think your assist warrants dinner," he added, stalling. "Where and when can I pick you up?"

He wrote it down and hurried off the phone before saying something stupid that would change her mind. He looked at himself in the rearview mirror. He couldn't believe he now had a date tonight. It was the last thing on his mind when the day started.

He didn't feel tired anymore. He would go spend a few hours on the case in Dorchester before getting cleaned up.

Or at least that was the plan.

FOUR

Richard Tuttle hung up the phone on his not-soon-enough-to-be ex-wife. She was still going on and on about his daughter's arm. The kid was going to be fine. Kids break their arms.

His wife's picture on the desk had long been replaced with a picture of himself standing with three golf partners down at Hilton Head: a pro-bowl football player, a NASCAR driver, and the governor of Pennsylvania, all clients.

Tuttle was one of the first to see the fault in the thinking that mobile medical screening was a niche market that supplemented hospitals and doctors' available procedures. The premise was simple, and he knew it by rote from the presentations he gave to investors. Why wait for someone to get sick before selling them medical screening? That type of thinking limited your client base. Besides, sick people weren't necessarily the ones with the money, or the ones willing to pay a premium for convenience. His company saw the opportunity to provide medical screening to anyone with the ability to pay. It didn't matter if they were ill or needed the test. Mobile Medi Tech didn't sell medical tests—it sold *peace of mind*. Insurance companies and businesses would pay to screen corporate officers and professional athletes for the same reason.

An expert in his professional life, Tuttle's private life was less successful. Richard Tuttle was not much of a family man, and he would be the first to admit it. His corrosive marriage was in its seventh year and in near-total decay; divorce papers were filed, and support payments and child custody were a battle. Meanwhile Mobile Medi Tech was in its fifth year and about to go public; the government filings to offer an initial public offering were already underway, and everything was going smoothly. Tuttle would be worth millions. He tried not to count the money ahead of time, but he could already feel it. He anticipated the day and lived at the edge of his income. His financial partners tightly controlled his salary, and his not-soon-enough-to-be ex-wife was costly. He couldn't stand the thought of the court telling him he had to send her a check every month; at least for now it still felt like it was out of his own kindness, and he could make her squirm for it if he was in the mood. He knew she was probably being told by her attorney to be patient and wait until Mobile Medi Tech went public. But maybe by then he would have something on her, something that would allow him to get custody of the children and not have to pay her child support.

A nanny would be a lot cheaper than what he was paying out now.

His money was hard-earned, and he planned to keep as much of it as possible. It was a high stakes game where his business savvy gave him the advantage over her and her attorney. Beating her out of every dollar almost gave him as much of a sense of accomplishment as signing another big client.

For Led's next case of the day, even his friend Randall Crawford wanted an investigator that could blend into a Brazilian neighborhood. The younger, more enlightened insurance adjusters were careful how they phrased the question: "Do you have an investigator that fits into the neighborhood?" Only the older ones who remembered Boston before the forced busing of the 1970s had the candor and innocence of social correctness to come right out and say what they meant: Do you have a black investigator for Roxbury? A Hispanic for Lawrence? An Asian for Quincy?

They didn't understand that on talent alone Led could make himself unnoticed in a commune of one-legged albino women. Even talent aside, Led was often mistaken for a resident in most of the neighborhoods he worked.

Physically there are some people who are predisposed to have an advantage in certain occupations—height for basketball, long fingers for playing piano. Led's physical advantage was that he didn't stand out. He didn't look like any particular ethnic group. Actually, it was not that he didn't look like any; he looked like almost all of them. For private investigation, it was like being a swimmer with webbed toes. A little something extra.

His looks blended in with just about any ethnic group in the Boston area, except maybe the Southies with their translucent Irish pallor. His skin was a light desert brown and his hair was black, but in a white neighborhood he looked like he had an enviable tan. His nose was large but not flat, with a slight bump, so maybe he was Greek or Italian. In a black neighborhood he may have been just light-skinned or mulatto. Or was he Hawaiian, or Samoan, with his large frame and roundish face? Actually, he might have been Indonesian. His hair had a wave to it, so Mexican was a possibility. He could not grow any real facial hair, only a few spotty whiskers, so maybe he was Native American.

About the only thing that you could be sure of was that his ancestors were not Scandinavian.

A Brazilian case in Dorchester fell in the realm of routine. Led had worked so many cases in Dorchester, he knew the people as well as if he had belonged to one of the three parishes. This was a community always bracing against a changing immigrant population, a force reflected in the neighborhoods of triple-decker homes that lined the residential streets, carved out at the turn of the last century—when land was propagated by stacking families one on top of the next, before steel allowed them to be stacked higher yet in apartment buildings.

The triple-decker had been New England's dubious contribution to residential architecture: a pragmatic answer to housing immigrants and factory workers, not good, but good enough. At the time it was easy for many to dismiss the homes' shortcomings, as their occupants were immigrants and factory workers anyway. The narrow buildings had flat roofs, wood frames, and back porches.

From the beginning they allowed extended families to live nearby but not with one another.

The claimant's green three-story with white trim had a recessed, very wide stained-glass-and-wood-paneled door on the left, with a projecting bay window on each side. There were few other signs of the original ornamentation, except the round columns in front and the roof cornices. The building was now covered in low-maintenance vinyl siding molded with lines of fake wood grain. The brick foundation had been painted red, as if the original brick hadn't been red enough. The building was in good shape with all the right pieces but was now utilitarian covering up what had once been a vibrant style.

Led was investigating Fatima Bettencourt, the staged slip and fall. With only one door emptying out for the three floors, he watched for any woman of the claimant's age that came out.

Led did not move.

As much as he would have liked to have taken a sip of his coffee, it was still in the front of the jeep in the cup holder. He looked out of the side window between the blanket and the darkened glass. For the last fifteen minutes two black men spoke on the sidewalk beside Led's jeep. Only the thickness of the glass separated Led from being close enough to smell their breath and tell what they had for lunch.

When the front door of Fatima's house opened, Led slid up front and started his jeep. Both men startled like wildebeest at a watering hole. They walked down the sidewalk talking, looking back bewildered as to how they hadn't seen the driver get into the vehicle.

The lion was among them.

Fatima came out of the front door and bounded down the front steps to the sidewalk. Her long dark hair bounced and flowed. She was wearing a pair of jeans and a tucked in T-shirt. Nothing about her gave any indication as to where she was going. She carried a large shoulder bag, not quite a suitcase, but larger than most handbags. It looked like black leather, aged and worn enough that the distress cracks were visible even from his surveillance position a half-block away.

It was 3:10 p.m. according to the time on his video monitor screen. Fatima unlocked the driver's side door of her dark gray Toyota Camry and tossed the shoulder bag to the passenger seat before entering. Led waited for her to pull out into the street and turn at the intersection before following behind.

She drove quickly but was obeying the traffic laws, mostly. At the first intersection on Blue Hill Avenue she accelerated to get around the slower moving van in the right lane. She cut back to the right lane as the Honda in front of her waited to make a left turn.

Led was able to keep a better eye on her because of her constantly changing lanes. It wasn't long between those intervals when she darted from behind one vehicle in front of another.

He was careful that she did not get caught in a lane that stopped while he was in one that kept going. Keeping up with her was not the most difficult task—not passing her was. If she did get caught in a lane, he would either have to pass her or take deliberate and not necessarily discreet measures to also get stuck in the traffic behind her.

Finally she made her way through the rush hour throng to the expressway north. Now it was easier. He only had to keep aware of the exits. She seemed to know where she was going, so there shouldn't be any last-minute maneuvers. She had been using her directionals from the time she turned off her street. There would not likely be any surprises. Still, he took nothing for granted, getting into the right lane every time she approached an exit, until she passed it, when he'd cut to the far left to catch up.

Sometimes as he squeezed into a line of cars he felt apologetic, knowing the other drivers were thinking *asshole*. But there was nothing he could do other than raise his hand as a wave of thanks, a gesture that had gained acceptance in the Boston area as a vaccine to the virus of middle fingers.

FIVE

Somewhere up ahead of Led and Fatima in the traffic on Route 93, riding north in the third of four lanes at seventy-three miles per hour, a 1997 silver Saturn tried to get off at exit 40 at the last possible moment. In fact, the last possible moment had already passed before the car attempted to cut hard to the right.

The vehicle went perpendicular to the traffic flow, but it still moved north, only sideways, as it skidded for a moment. Then the tires bit hard onto the pavement and the car rolled over, launching it into a new orbit. The Saturn tumbled down the road, bouncing along and throwing off debris like an asteroid breaching the atmosphere. The manipulating forces of the mechanized controls that provided steering, brakes, and traction all succumbed to the righteous laws of physics that applied fairly to everyone. The bumble ball of metal and poly-carbon panels stopped on its driver's side. A glitter of glass and plastic covered the black pavement.

Five vehicles were part of the initial accident as the Saturn went rolling away. The Saturn was never hit by another car but set in motion a series of events that sprung like a roomful of mousetraps on a ping-pong ball.

To avoid hitting the Saturn as it moved right, the driver of a Toyota hit his brakes and swerved left into the side of a white Town Taxi. With a Toyota suddenly trying to get into his cab, the cab driver slammed his brakes. Momentum carried the conjoined vehicles off to the left. Next to join the scrum was Randall Crawford in his beige BMW, who was just at that moment calling home on his cell phone to see if the mulch had been delivered.

He later learned that his wife, answering the phone, heard him shout "Jesus!"—but not to her. He dropped the telephone and grabbed the wheel with both hands as his BMW struck the left quarter panel of the Toyota. His wife heard the pop of the airbag and the crinkling of auto parts. She called out his name: "Randy!"

But Randy was busy, and before she could say it again, his BMW was struck from the rear and his phone flew somewhere onto the floorboard amongst the brochures of two landscape companies. Crawford was bruised across the chest where the airbag had exploded from the steering wheel. His skin burned from the punishment of the full body block the airbag had thrown to protect him from the steering column. His shoulder was cut where the seatbelt had grabbed him, and the back of his skull throbbed where he had been hit by his briefcase, thrown by impact like a forward pass straight to the back of his head.

The medical RV that had hit the brakes at sixty-five miles per hour would have needed one hundred and fifty feet to stop before hitting Randall and his BMW spinning across the lane in front of it. It had one hundred and five.

The RV crunched up and over the BMW as if it were driving over a discarded soda can. Not gracefully, but without trepidation, it drove up and across the back left tire like a predator eating its prey. Just as it looked like it was going to digest it, the RV lost its momentum and collapsed on its right side, with the BMW still in its grasp under the front tire.

That was the beginning. Like ice flow in a river, the traffic tried to continue through sheer force, to find a way around, further jamming any potential for orderly progression and stopping other vehicles trying to push northbound. The traffic ebbed, as it could no longer navigate the wreckage. The channel of passage was blocked.

The wave of stopped vehicles reached Led.

Fatima was only a few vehicles ahead of Led when the lines of traffic frayed. He watched as her car went sideways, narrowly missing the back of another vehicle. But his focus shifted closer to the rapidly closing distance between his own vehicle and the Mercury Topaz in front of him. He hit his brakes, skidded slightly to the left, corrected, and skidded a little to the right as he tried to stop from a speed of seventy-plus miles an hour. The anti-lock brakes vibrated the entire jeep. Traffic all around stopped like the end of a carnival ride, leaving the bumper cars scattered about with nowhere to go and in no particular order.

Led changed the channel to WBZ to catch the traffic report.

An ambulance passed by going south with the lights flashing. The Channel 4 helicopter was in the air as it went overhead toward the accident. Drivers started to get out of their vehicles and stand beside their cars, trying to estimate the delay or gawk at the carnage, or both.

A guy with a beard and ball cap climbed up into the bed of his pickup truck and then up on the sides, trying to get high enough to see the source of the stoppage. Like a sailor in a crow's nest, he reported back to everyone and to no one in particular that he couldn't see anything. There was no smooth sailing. The doldrums went for a few miles, over seven, according to the traffic report. A several-car pileup at exit 40 northbound meant Led was about in the middle of it.

At the accident scene, the driver of the RV, Paul O'Hearn, hung from his seatbelt, caught in its webbing. The seatbelt had done its job and prevented him from being flung through the windshield. Its usefulness now exceeded, it held onto Paul six feet off the ground of broken glass. He tried to undo the seatbelt to get free, but his weight on the belt did not give it enough slack to reach the release that was now behind him. He got his head and right shoulder out from the shoulder strap and then kicked his legs to crawl out from the still-hooked lap belt. Holding onto the steering wheel he swung his feet down, standing on what had been the passenger side window but was now the blacktop of Route 93. Finally oriented as to which end was up, he reached up above his head and tried to open the driver's side door. Though it would click, he could not get any leverage to push the door up. It was now a heavy bulkhead. He tried to put down the power window and found that it still worked. It retracted sideways and he climbed up the center console of radio and GPS equipment, stepping as he went on knobs, cracking LCD screens, and scratching the interior of this vehicle, the dashboard of which only minutes before he would not have even considered setting a sandwich on.

The front tire on the RV was still spinning as Paul pulled himself through the window and sat on the door.

"Are you alright?" Someone asked. It was the driver of a pick up truck that had stopped only a few yards from becoming part of the pile up. Vans, cars and trucks littered the lanes, jutting like teeth of a broken zipper.

"That certainly ruined my day," Paul said, realizing that the back of his left hand was bleeding from a deep cut. "Yeah, I'm good."

"Is there anyone else in there?"

"Nope, just me," Paul said, standing now carefully on the slippery surface that had been the RV's well-waxed fiberglass body.

"Are you going to need help getting down?"

"I don't think so, thanks." Paul looked precariously over the edge of the RV, down the side that minutes before had been the undercarriage.

"Your best bet is climb down off the back where the ladder is."

Paul walked as if on ice, gingerly and with his stance widened, to the back of the RV and climbed down the now horizontal ladder.

Randall Crawford was still strapped into his seat and sat motionless. His head was back and his eyes were closed as he waited to catch his breath.

"Hey, buddy. Are you okay?" someone asked, with an inflection that made the question sound rhetorical. It was obvious that he was not okay. He felt dead and probably looked worse. He opened his eyes.

"What's your name?" A Good Samaritan leaned in the passenger side window.

"Randall," he answered, as he was still putting all the information back together. The back of his head and neck felt like he had crushed gravel in every joint. He was disoriented and just wanted to be out of the vehicle.

"Is there anyone with you?"

Was there anyone with him? No, he was on his way home from work. "No, just me."

"You have to stay still. You could be hurt more than you know. An ambulance will be coming."

"Are you a doctor?"

"My only medical background is from watching a lot of television."

"Can you at least open the door?" Randall asked, feeling claustrophobic and just a little panicked that there was nothing more than entertainment training currently available to help him.

"Sure." The man tried the driver's side door, but it wouldn't open. He put his foot against the vehicle and pulled. The door was twisted on the frame so that it wouldn't move.

The sirens were coming from the southbound lane. Two state cruisers sped down the southbound side and slowed as they drove down the grassy hill of the median and back up the other side to the accident.

"Just stay still until the police get here," the man said. "They'll get you right out."

"I don't want to blow up," Randall said, starting to think the worst. Why shouldn't he? Only minutes before he was thinking about lawn care. Now he was encapsulated in crushed metal in the middle of the highway. There was the slight smell of gas, oil, and antifreeze.

"You will be fine. I'll get someone to get you out. Just stay calm."

Randall sat listening to his own breathing and watching the slow progress of an ambulance as it approached, navigating the errant vehicles in the breakdown lane that had attempted to short-cut out and around the backed-up traffic. Police cruisers blocked traffic further by backing up the exit ramp to get to the accident. Already two officers stood and directed traffic to take the exit, one car at a time, trying to bring order to the lawless world of impatient commuters.

The driver of the Saturn was lying in the road with the vehicle laid sideways across her chest. She was a bluish purple by the time a state police officer checked her pulse. The police officer went back to the trunk of his cruiser and retrieved a small silver bundle the size of a baked potato. He unfolded the crinkling, shiny space blanket and laid it over the driver's head and shoulders, tucking it slightly beneath her arms. There was nothing the paramedics could do for her.

Randall couldn't see the cab driver, but could hear part of his swearing—that he did not own the cab, that he only leased it by the day. He was now going to be out a day's worth of fares and have to deal with the dispatcher. Through half-opened eyes, Randall could still see the car that he had hit, a Toyota Corolla now missing the front right quarter panel and with the front right wheel splayed out with a broken ball joint. The back trunk was sprung from the collision. But both impacts had been glancing and didn't appear to have shaken the young Asian man now standing next to his car.

A middle-aged fireman with a double chin approached Randall's car. He told Randall to sit tight as he used a pry bar to open the door of the BMW. Two paramedics crowded each other as they reached into the vehicle and put a blue brace around Randall's neck. These were young white guys wearing short-sleeved white shirts and blue latex gloves. The two men were interchangeable, it seemed, and he couldn't tell if the one who had fastened the neck brace was the same one who had put a blood pressure cuff on him or was it the one who was coming back with a stretcher? They were young, in their early twenties, but they moved with such methodical measure they must have known what they were doing, so Randall listened to his own breathing and answered the occasional question asked of him.

"Can you move your legs?"

"Yes."

"Where does it hurt?"

"My chest and neck."

"We're going to move you now. Take a deep breath and just allow us to slide you out of the car onto the stretcher. Don't you move. We will move you."

The hands of the two paramedics grabbed his shoulders and his legs firmly as they slid him onto a stretcher. He was becoming aware of the commotion of the blue and red lights and the activity at the other vehicles, but all he could do was look straight up at the blue sky and the circling news helicopter. Now the two paramedics became even less discernable. They leaned across him and tightened straps. His view was up their nostrils. The stretcher extended up on its scissoring legs and wheeled; blue sky became the white mottled ceiling of the ambulance. One of the men in white sitting beside him taped wires to his arm and chest. The door shut and the channel of background noise changed to a muted whir-and-hum of voices and winches, and the beep, beep, beep of tow trucks.

Fatima got out of her vehicle and dialed her cell phone with one hand.

Led was five cars back. His video camera had been thrown from the front passenger seat to the floorboard, but it was still in the soft-sided case and seemed to be fine, making its slight, customary whine as he turned on the power. He could make out some activity from one corner of his eye but kept his camera pointing at Fatima. She leaned against the side of her car as she spoke, holding the phone with her right hand and waving around her left like a drunken conductor.

The emergency crews of police and ambulance started to appear like flies on road kill, a few at first, and then a full swarm.

The guy with the beard walked over to speak with Fatima, but she didn't get off the phone. She only lowered it a little to acknowledge him. The video that Led was shooting wasn't showing her with any physical limitations, but then again she wasn't doing much, just leaning her backside against the trunk. She talked constantly, stopping only to make another call. Before switching her phone from her right to her left ear, she flipped her hair. It wasn't just a little brush-back; her thick mane required more effort than that. She tipped her head forward so that her long, wavy hair fell with it. Then she dipped her left shoulder as if ducking beneath it, using her right hand to reach behind her head and draw back the curtain. No sign of physical limitations there.

Some of the drivers got back into their cars to listen to the radio or read a paper, while others walked among the stopped cars, visibly mad that there had been an accident.

Led didn't attempt to get into the backseat of his jeep. No one was paying any attention to him or the jeep. They were all looking in the direction of the delay. He saw a man and a woman dressed in khakis and matching bright blue polo shirts. There was a yellow insignia on their shirts, too small to read. As they walked right in front of his camera their facial expressions changed to surprise with the realization someone was videotaping. They did a quick shuffle-step to evade the camera's view, like they'd just walked in front of a bride.

What he had hoped would be a quick surveillance showed no sign of ending soon. Time would not have mattered, usually. It had been an abundant commodity. But at the moment he desired a nine-to-five schedule. He was not going to make his date with Callie, but he hesitated on making the call. Maybe at any moment the traffic would let up and he could follow Fatima to a destination and be done. Not that he would ever consider letting the claimant go so he could make his date. All right, he was considering it, but he would never do it.

He delayed the call as long as possible. She answered the phone with a pleasant hello and a sweet expectation in her voice that reminded him how nice it would have been to have seen her. This was exactly why he never planned anything in advance.

"Looks like I'm going to be working late," he said. "I've been sitting in dead-stopped traffic on 93 for the past hour. There's some bad accident."

"I didn't hear anything about it," she said. "I just walked in."

"Can we do it some other time?" he asked, expecting a yes, but no commitment as to when.

"Tomorrow night good?" she asked.

"Absolutely. I promise I'll leave work early to be sure to make it."

"Alright. It's still a date. Have a good night. And good luck with your case."

"You too," he said awkwardly, realizing only too late that what he'd just said didn't make any sense. She'd already hung up. How much of a dolt would she think he was now?

He was stuck in his lane of traffic for almost ten minutes longer than Fatima. Her lane had started moving at a slow speed. The lane of traffic where Led was wedged just sat, everyone with blinkers on, wanting to merge, but there was no mercy. The line of cars wouldn't break. After what seemed like thirty cars had gone by, he resigned himself to the fact that he would have to do another day of surveillance to find out where Fatima was going and what she was doing.

He stopped at Frizzell's for dinner and sat at the counter. His wife had gotten the house and the dog, but he got to keep eating at Frizzell's. It was by default. She never liked the place, but then, she had never given it a chance, having only been twice.

Sue stood behind the counter. She called him dear and asked him what he wanted. She was probably only a few years older than him, but she had picked up the owner's maternal mannerisms. Mrs. Frizzell called everyone dear.

He looked at the lime green piece of paper with specials on it. It seldom varied except for the day of the week: Salisbury steak on Tuesday, pasta on Wednesday, liver and onions on Thursday, fish on Friday.

Without asking, Sue brought him a bottle of beer and sat down a glass. He handed her back the glass and said that she could keep from having to wash it. He'd usually tell Sue about whatever case he had worked on that day, but today he didn't tell her about the dentist and the woman in the parking garage. He wanted to keep that one to himself a little longer.

She asked if he heard about the pileup on Route 93.

"I sat in it for a few hours," Led said.

"You gonna get some work out of it? There's got to be a lot of insurance claims in a mess like that."

"Never know. There will be plenty of claims. Whether I get called for any of them is anybody's guess. Could get a couple, might not get any."

He stared at the menu that he knew by heart. He did it for inspiration, to spark a primitive impulse or salivary gland. Frizzell's had a home cooking feel to it in that the main spices used were salt, pepper, and ketchup, and the daily specials almost always came with mashed potatoes or gravy poured over something. He ordered the Salisbury steak and wondered about his date for tomorrow night. He really didn't have the time as busy as he'd been.

Eating alone at a restaurant didn't bother him the way it did some people, seeming all fidgety and needing to read a book or something. He was used to sitting alone for long periods of time. He sat at the counter and engaged in intermittent conversations with Sue whenever she returned to work the register or get a clean place setting.

From the counter he could see in the window the reflections of the people in the dining area. Led people-watched just like everyone, except he'd made a career out of it. But predetermining actions and filling in back-stories was a lot different when a paycheck was riding on it. It always seemed easiest when it was just for entertainment.

Three men at the first table looked and sounded like they were from out of town, talking about a tower placement but mispronouncing Leominster. Led listened to see how they would handle pronouncing the town of Billerica, but they never mentioned it.

He had never seen a claimant in this restaurant. For all the times he had been to Frizzell's he never ran into anyone he'd done surveillance on. He ran into them in supermarkets, in libraries, and at the movies, but they never knew of the intimate time they'd already spent together on opposite ends of a video camera. Some he had worked recently, some years before. The names were not fresh in his mind, but he could usually remember their houses and cars.

Sue brought him his plate of Salisbury steak and a big mound of mashed potatoes. She sat a little plate with a roll on it and two pats of butter. "Here you go, dear. You need another beer?"

"Please."

He considered that he might be stuck in such a routine that it was about the only restaurant he went to that didn't require unwrapping the food before eating it. He finished eating and left money under the plate as he said good night to Sue.

SIX

Many ex-wives may fantasize about getting even, but Judith Tuttle was actually being given the opportunity to turn her ex-husband in to the FBI. Or so she hoped. She wasn't sure what they wanted to know, or how much information she had, but if they wanted to talk about Richard Tuttle she would be glad to spill the contents of her broken marriage.

She was nervous getting ready. She went over her reasons for burning him and weighed them against the reasons for not. This was a big step. Richard had been a decent enough man for several years. Hardworking, attentive to her and the children, but as his company started to succeed, he became almost resentful of her, like she was holding him back to a past that he was trying to overcome. He was consumed with his own stature among the business elite.

When he stopped making as much time for her and the children, she could have accepted it. It wasn't like he was home much to bother them. Maybe she should have just got herself a boyfriend. She had friends who lived like that for years, seemingly happy. Others did it, but she couldn't. It ate at her to see him appear in the paper with respect and prestige, going to events with other women. He could call them colleagues; they were more like call girls. Advisors, consultants, or researchers, he was still porking them. She had her own self-respect. He would pay, too, but since her lawyers had found that most of the wealth was tied up in trusts, she was faced with the prospect of moving to a smaller house and sending the children to public schools.

But then came the call from the FBI. They wanted to talk.

She showered and blew dry her hair, put on a purple sweater that plunged enough to show the gold necklace with the diamond pendant descending into her bosom. It had been a birthday present from her husband when they still liked each other. She had to admit that he had good taste.

As she put on eyeliner in front of the hotel room mirror, she realized that it felt like a date. She stopped and looked at herself, stepped back and turned to profile her own figure. Three kids, but she still looked and felt good, confident that she still could get and keep the attention of most men, if not her husband's.

She thought, *it was like a date*, but the only person that was going to get screwed was her ex-husband, and her own witty use of the double entendre buoyed her mood even further. She would tell them how Richard Tuttle, from the time they met in college, was smart and good with money; he just didn't have any. He was not content simply to build a company and make money; he wanted a legacy, and he had been desperate for financing in the early days. Thus Richard Tuttle might have sought some alternative financing with some more aggressive investors. People he met through his bookie. He referred to them as *venture capitalists*.

Even when they still were in love, she had questioned his decisions, but he told her that these were just businessmen and he knew business better than anyone. All he needed was opportunity. He kept her in a nice home and put the kids in good schools. Life had been good and getting better. Richard said it was like the Kennedys running moonshine; any of his early indiscretions would be absolved once he was powerful enough. One thing you had to say about Richard Tuttle, he always knew what he wanted. He wasn't willing to let morals get in his way, but he wasn't as smart as he thought he was, just more ruthless. If he expected to move on from their marriage to the next best thing, his power appetite might have become bigger than he could stomach.

There was a slight knock on the door; she looked through the peephole at the dark-haired man in an azure blue shirt and black sports coat. He was younger than she thought he would be, maybe in his early thirties, but not too young, and better looking than she had hoped. He held a single rose to identify him as Special Agent Chancellor.

When she let him in he showed his more routine credentials of FBI badge and photo ID. The rose had only been a marker, but Judith accepted it out of his hand and smelled it before setting it down on the bed stand.

"I'm a little nervous and not sure what I'm going to be able to tell you," she said as she looked into the agent's blue eyes.

"We appreciate you meeting with us," he said, speaking in plural even though he was alone with her.

"The FBI colors are blue and white?" she asked, wondering if the blue from his shirt didn't make his eyes that much more intense.

"Yes." He took out a small recorder and set it up on the table.

"Blue is supposed to represent truthfulness."

"I didn't know that."

"That's probably why they chose the color."

"That might be."

He adjusted the recorder a little closer to her. "Are you ready to start?"

"Someone sees you coming in here, they are going to think we're having an affair," she offered up as she considered her own willingness to do such a thing. Have an affair with the agent investigating her ex-husband. It would be devilish.

"We've taken many precautions to provide a plausible cover," he said stoically, still not looking at her diamond pendant.

Yeah, she thought, he was handsome, but having an affair with this Agent Chancellor would be about as exciting as having a German Shepherd hump your leg.

"What do you want to know about Richard Tuttle?" she asked.

Paul O'Hearn wasn't going to go to the hospital because by his self-diagnosis his hand had only been cut; but as some time passed, his thumb began to throb, like he'd pulled a tendon or something. His girlfriend, Cheryl, had insisted that he go and have it checked out as he couldn't use the knife to cut the pork chop she had left in the microwave.

Now he was waiting in the emergency room, filling out the questionnaire he had been handed at the reception desk. He was six-foot-five and two-hundred-eighty pounds, a healthy thirty-six-year-old male with no preexisting medical conditions. He checked the box for "work related," and listed his employer, Mobile Medi Tech.

"Are you all set?" the nurse on the other side of the sliding window asked as he handed her the form back. She flipped over the form to see if he had filled out both sides. "Do you know the name of the worker's comp insurance company at your job?"

"No, I don't. I'll have to find out."

The woman set the clipboard on the counter. "Have a seat and a doctor will be with you shortly."

As he selected an old *National Geographic* with a cover story about glaciers, he overheard a man at one of the two payphones in the corner.

"The tests look fine. I'm sore. I'm just waiting for the doctor to sign something and give me a prescription...Percocet...the television is on here in the lobby but I haven't seen anything...they say what caused it?...I don't know, I couldn't see anything really...how many cars? Shit. No one here said anything about anyone *dying*..."

Paul moved closer to the payphones, meandering around the lobby, looking at a few of the postings on the bulletin board, one warning against deer ticks with Lyme disease, another on how to protect yourself from mosquitoes carrying Eastern Equine Encephalitis. You couldn't protect against everything, he thought. The man on the phone finished his conversation, and Paul leaned over.

"Excuse me," he said, "but I overheard you on the phone. Were you just in that wreck on 93?"

"I'm afraid so. Was it on the news yet?"

"I don't know, I just got here," Paul said. He felt instant familiarity with a veteran of the same event. "I was in it, too. I was driving the white and green medical RV."

"I saw it. It was on its side. So you were okay?"

Paul motioned with his bandaged hand. "I hurt myself more climbing out of it than when it fell over. What about you?"

"Randall Crawford," Randall introduced himself. "I was in the car that you hit."

"Oh, man, I'm sorry. I had nowhere to go. I tried."

"I know. So did I. Don't worry about it, that's what insurance is for. Seatbelts and airbags, you gotta love 'em. You have an airbag in the RV?"

"No, just the seatbelt."

"Were you wearing it?" Randall raised an eyebrow.

"Always. Company policy."

"Good." The man reached out and patted him on the shoulder with approval. It was an odd but friendly enough gesture. "My airbag just about broke my ribs." He put his hand to his chest. "I thought I was having a heart attack. But glad it was there, it's softer than the steering wheel would have been. The belt limits my reach out to run the ticket through at the garage, then I don't bother. But today I was lucky I did, at the last second. On the way home I think I'm going to stop and buy a lottery ticket. What about the person in that first car? Did you hear or see how they made out? It didn't look good."

"No. I talked to a guy who had stopped. Then I got a ride with one of the tow truck drivers, back into town. The worst part for me, besides knowing someone was probably dead," Paul said, "was that several thousand people were sitting in traffic calling me an asshole for having an accident."

"I've done that, got all pissed off that somebody wrecked, made my long commute even longer." He offered his hand, which Paul shook with a hard grip. "What's your name?"

"Sorry," Paul said. "Paul. Paul O'Hearn."

"So you work for Mobile Medi Tech?"

"Yeah."

"Ha."

"You heard of it?"

"I know of the company. Is it good work?"

"It's alright. It's a mobile medical unit. They use it for tests, full of medical equipment like x-rays and CT scan equipment," Paul said. "I'm just the guy who moves around the units and sets them up. But it's okay."

"I know the owner, Richard Tuttle. I work for the company that insures Mobile Medi Tech. How is he to work for?"

"He's okay. I don't deal with him much directly. He's in the office and I'm just one of the grunts. But the job has some perks. I met pitcher Matt Clement."

"You're a Sox fan?"

"Was at game two of the 2004 World Series; Schilling pitching with the bloody sock. It was history with flair. You can't make up stories like that."

"I was at that game, too; one of our clients had seats. It was a little anticlimactic after the Yankees series."

"It was history. Nothing anticlimactic about history." And Paul thought of how this man, Randall, was nice enough, but taking it for granted.

"Your registration on the car, you're from New Hampshire?" Paul asked.

"Meredith."

"Really?" Paul was surprised at the peripheral connections he had to this stranger.

The nurse at the window called out his name: "Randall Crawford?"

"Right here...excuse me a moment."

Randall walked to the window and was handed two forms and a slip from a prescription pad. He borrowed a pen from the counter and wrote. Paul waited by the chairs.

"So do you go to the motorcycle races in Loudon?" Paul asked when he returned.

"I've been. Living in the mist of the mayhem, I get a little sick of the crowd. Do you go?"

"No. My dad used to. He used to tell us how wild it was."

"You should go and check it out. It isn't as wild as it used to be. It's more family friendly."

That's too bad, Paul thought.

"Well, they're done with me," Randall said. "Maybe I'll see you up at the races one of these days."

"It's always a possibility," Paul said and wondered why he and his brother had never gone, except for their mother saying no.

SEVEN

Tuttle wasn't happy when his secretary, Stacey, came in to tell him that Paul O'Hearn, one of his drivers, was in an accident and calling from a payphone. Richard Tuttle didn't like staying late. He thought about dealing with it in the morning, but he had a seven o'clock tee time. Besides, when he heard that the vehicle might be totaled, there was the advantage of getting the claim into the insurance company by tomorrow, meaning he could be looking at a check by the first of next week. The RV was a place of business and he was insured for loss of use, they would be quick about it.

Time was money, and money was how you kept score on success.

Tuttle was a man who made aggressive business decisions, and so as he sat with the forms Stacey brought him, he started to see where he could take a piece of coal and turn it into a diamond. He had not done anything to cause the claim. The accident was real. The fact that he claimed that the new CT scanner had been installed was just a matter of timing. It was supposed to have been installed already. He had the paperwork showing it was to have been installed two weeks ago. Only scheduling issues had it still sitting in the warehouse, saving him about a quarter of a million dollars.

Besides, he had not been in that unit in months; if the insurance carrier did happen to pick up on the difference he would admit he must have been mistaken. There was no downside to submitting the paperwork for the new machine as if it were in the mobile unit. He didn't see it as anything more than aggressive accounting.

Stacey had plans, not that he asked. If Mr. Tuttle stayed late, it meant Stacey stayed late. The man was helpless. She waited for him by playing Scrabble on the computer until she heard him shut his office door and start walking down the hall; then she clicked over to a spreadsheet.

"I need you to FedEx these forms for the eight o'clock pickup," he said, handing the insurance papers to her. "Make me a copy first. Please," he added in an offhanded manner, "and have a good night."

"Yeah, you too," she responded, though he probably didn't hear her as the door was already shut.

Standing at the copy machine as it made the repetitive *urn-chush* sound, she stared at the picture on the wall for the umpteenth time to avoid the flash of white light that leaked out around the copier's closed cover. She was thinking about margaritas, and how she might try the peach one tonight. She was in the mood to try something different. Her thoughts of salt and tequila were interrupted as the copier stalled, a staple jamming the feeder, sucking in the attached page with a crunching of paper. One sheet had been summoned, but two had attempted to go. She lifted the cover and pushed the little blue tab to release its grip, an easy fix. But the crinkled page would not feed through, so she lifted the cover and laid it directly on the glass. Instead of removing the staple, she folded the second page back.

The folded page was the itemization of the Computed Tomography Scanner and the damaged equipment: the heart monitor and the EMG. It stated that all the units were recently replaced and brand new. *That's not right,* she thought. The CT scanner was still the old one. Mr. Tuttle knew that, as he had been the one to have her reschedule the installation for three weeks out.

The rich just kept getting richer, she thought. It didn't matter so much to her; it wasn't like she was going to see any benefit either way, unless he took another vacation and was out of the office for a few weeks.

She finished copying the pages, putting one of the copies in the FedEx envelope for Trust Insurance and another in a manila folder marked "Insurance Claim–Unit 12," as this was the number of the RV. Each had its own reference number so it could easily be distinguished for repairs, service, and scheduling.

Then she filed the folder and left for the night.

It hadn't been on her mind to tell anyone about what she'd learned. It had just come up. She was already late to meet with the girls: Bobbie the receptionist, Tammy from payroll service, and Sherma and Angela, friends she had had known since high school. They usually sat at the same corner table and ordered margaritas, acting as a management summit for each other's lives: lending encouragement, insight, and support, but mostly gossip.

They talked about Sherma's new job at the bank, and discussed how long before she'd lose it as a result of another bank merger. Angela's twin nine-year-old boys were discussed, as they were Little League stars: one a pitcher and the other a catcher. Bobbie mentioned the woman who washed her hair at Salon Ché. Her sister had died in the accident on 93 today. She was a single mom with a little girl.

"What happened?" Sherma asked.

"Don't really know," Bobbie said. "They said she was late for her second job at Wal-Mart."

"The papers thought she fell asleep at the wheel," Angela added.

"Who has the little girl?" Stacey asked.

"Her sister," Bobbie said, reaching for another nacho and stringing melted cheese across the table. "But she has three children of her own."

"That's a shame," Angela said, sipping at her peach margarita.

"You never realize how everything can change in an instant," Bobbie said.

As in any town, "townies" tended to know all about, if not actually know, other "townies." Wilmington was no different. Stacey's coworker, Paul O'Hearn, had been the driver of the Mobile Medi Tech RV. Though none of the girls really knew Paul, they had grown up with his girlfriend, Cheryl. This made him known by proxy.

"How is Paul doing?" Sherma asked Stacey.

"I talked to him right after it happened. He said he was fine, but was going to go get checked out to be sure."

"He's a hard worker," Sherma said. "Has anyone seen Cheryl lately?"

"I ran into her at FoodMaster," Angela said. "She seems to be doing fine. Paul watches her two boys like they were his own. He's coaching the youngest one's Little League team."

"Good for them. They deserve to have a little stability." Bobbie gave the synopsized story of Paul and Cheryl; how Paul had taken care of his brother's family after his brother had been killed. Tammy thought about asking how Paul's brother had died, but the conversation moved too quickly, and anyway it didn't seem that important.

"Small world," Stacey said, "knowing two separate people in an accident like that."

"Paul should get some money out of it, worker's comp or something." Sherma licked the salt from the rim of the glass like it was a melting ice cream cone.

"He should take advantage of any time off they offer him," Angela said. "An accident like that has to be worth some money, too. I know they could use it."

"You have to watch out for insurance companies," Sherma said, balling up a dirty napkin and putting it into her empty glass. "You have to stay right on top of them to get them to pay anything. My company didn't want to pay for the ice damage last spring. The roof leaked, wrecked the ceiling, and they wanted me to pay a $1,500 deductible."

"Oh, this is good," Angela interjected. "Wait till you hear this..."

Sherma continued, "So my husband and a couple of his buddies moved the old pool table out of the garage and put it in the living room under the leak. The table had already been warped. It used to be a nice table. The money they gave me for the table covered the deductible."

"You're terrible!" said Stacey.

"But her ceilings came out nice," Angela laughed.

"You have to do stuff like that with the way they gouge you with the rates," Sherma said, motioning to the waitress.

Stacey thought about telling them she had just seen Mr. Tuttle move the proverbial pool table under the leak by overestimating what was in the vehicle. But you had to know Mr. Tuttle to appreciate the story, so she didn't say anything about it and ordered a frozen peach margarita, no salt.

It was on her way home that Stacey remembered she was out of cream for her breakfast coffee. Stopping at the convenience store, she saw Cheryl getting gas at the pumps. She might have avoided her if she had seen her sooner. She liked Cheryl, and felt a little guilty about not having called her to join them. Anyway, they used to include her; it hadn't been a conscious effort to leave her out.

"Hey," Stacey said. "We were just talking about you guys. I got together with Angela and Sherma tonight." There, it was out in the open. She had nothing against her, nothing to hide. "We were all wondering how Paul is doing, I only talked to him for a moment when he called Mr. Tuttle about the accident."

Cheryl looked tired. "He hurt his hand, but he's alright. It's me that has to listen to his complaining. He's already bitching about coaching baseball with one hand bandaged. I'm just coming back from getting his prescription."

"Do you think he might be out for a while with his hand?"

"Paul? You can't get him to stop working. If they let him drive with one hand, he probably will. He doesn't want Tuttle getting all upset with him being out with lost time."

"Mr. Tuttle? He steps in money the way other people step in gum. He's already got the insurance claim in for the mobile unit. I had to stay late to get it FedExed." Stacey felt liberated, the margaritas fueling gossip she would have otherwise kept quiet about. The camaraderie of the sisterhood she had just shared was still flowing as she let it spill out onto Cheryl. It felt cathartic to tell what she knew. "Mr. Tuttle won't lose a penny," she continued.

"He'll probably make money off of the accident. Paul will tell you. The mobile unit was ready for a scheduled upgrade, but it got postponed. Tuttle is getting insurance money for reimbursement of new equipment that wasn't even installed yet. He still has the new stuff sitting in a warehouse."

"That company is capable of doing anything." Cheryl hung up the nozzle on the gas pump. "I'm trying to talk him into getting a different job. Go back to being an electrician fulltime. The money was good and he didn't have to deal with people like Richard Tuttle."

EIGHT

Before becoming a PI, Asher Ledbettor had worked at a storage facility due to the flexibility needed for his training and competition schedule. He had been an Olympic hopeful and a gold medal contender, America's hope against Korea sweeping the archery event.

A gold medal in archery was not a meal ticket. There were no big name sponsors or recognition, but damn if his ex-wife didn't believe that there was a possibility. She was a marketing major from Bentley and he was going to be her product. He was making some money at a few country fair demonstrations and car shows sponsored by Myra Ford. Shooting arrows at a brand new Ford Thunderbird, always drew a crowd and even if he was able to hit the balloons that rolled by attached to the center of the tires, he knew that people gathered to witness if he missed, politely clapping when he didn't.

His ex-wife was sure that a gold medal would get him a real sponsor, and she dreamed big, writing letters to Target department stores and Arrow shirt company. That had been before Steve "Sting" Tingley discovered he was not going to make the cut due to a lapse in consistency and lack of concentration. Led had taken him out for a beer to talk it over, see if he couldn't help his teammate keep his place. It was a modest gesture at the time.

Sting confided that he suspected his girlfriend Deena of having an affair with someone; he couldn't get it out of his head even though she denied it and he had no proof, just whispered phone calls and vague absences that were supposed to be shopping trips, but resulted in few purchases. If Led would speak with the coach on his behalf, he was sure he could get it straightened out and get back to his competitive mode within a week or two. He and Deena were going to go away for the weekend and when they got back everything should be all right.

Led agreed to talk to the coach, which was how he walked into the supply shed where Coach had his khaki shorts around his ankles with Deena kneeling before him. The coach looked over his shoulder at the sudden distraction of the door opening. "Led!" Coach said, bending quickly to grab at his shorts, in doing so knocking Deena, topless, backwards into the target stands.

Led shut the door and said, "I'll wait out here."

A minute or two of muted whispers from within the small storage trailer, and then Coach came outside acting like he had been simply putting away lime and field markers.

"I was going to tell you that Sting is a little distracted because he thinks that Deena is fooling around," Led said, "but you already knew that, except for the part of Sting thinking it."

"Deena and Sting might have some problems with their relationship, but that doesn't have any bearing on me putting together the most competitive team I can." And Coach actually looked serious as he said, "If he can't concentrate, he will be off the team."

"How about you help his concentration by keeping your pants on around Deena?" Led's blood pressure started to rise and he clenched his jaw and ground his teeth as he continued. "You're his coach. You're suppose to help him score, not score with his girlfriend."

"Are you going to tell him?" Coach asked.

"Are you going to stop?"

"I don't know my intentions at this point."

"Neither do I," Led said as he walked away.

It wasn't his place to tell Sting anything, but he didn't have to. The next day Sting read one of Deena's e-mails and figured it all out by himself. Since that time, Led had thought about how he should have stayed out of it and let Sting shoot Coach in the balls and make him into a kebob like he wanted.

"Bet I can make that shot blindfolded," Sting said, drunk, mad, and armed with his quiver and bow. He was knocking on Coach's door when Led got there.

"I'm calling the police," Coach said from inside the hallway.

"I'm going to make you look like a goddamn porcupine."

Deena called out, "Go home, Sting. You're drunk." That was not going to help.

"Sting," Led said. "Let's go home and get some perspective on this."

Sting started to walk away from the door then stopped and nocked an arrow and shot it at the closed living room window. It crashed through the glass, drawing the attention of a neighbor, who did nothing more than turn on the porch light and look out through the blinds.

Like a demented cupid with arrows of bad intent, Sting started shooting a barrage of arrows at the front windows, breaking all seven. Then he launched one at the front door; a low-octave *wonk* emanated as it stuck.

"Damn you!" Coach screamed from within the home.

"No, damn you," Sting responded. It was a rather unremarkable verbal volley.

Led was pretty sure that if he rushed Sting, Sting would not turn and shoot an arrow at him, but he wasn't really willing to chance it. No one was getting hurt and Sting was almost out of arrows. Let him bust a few more of Coach's windows and go home. Coach deserved as much.

But then Coach returned fire with an arrow from the second floor window. It struck the side of Sting's foot, mostly ripping the sole from his sneaker. Sting sat his bow down and tried to free his foot. Led took the opportunity to push him over and grab for the bow. But as the two men rolled briefly on the ground, Coach must have continued to rain down arrows from on high, as three more arrows permeated the lawn of the suburban home.

"Stop it!" Led hollered, addressing Sting and Coach. "Just stop it!" He pulled one of the arrows from the ground and used the razor head to cut Sting's bowstring. "It's over," he said to his friend. "You made your point. Now let's go home."

With the bowstring cut, Led handed the bow back to Sting who limped slightly, with the sole of his left sneaker flapping like the tongue of a beat dog.

Sting threw the bow at the front door of the house and let Led drive him home.

And so Led quit the team, in disgust and in solidarity for Sting. However, his grand gesture and departure opened another slot; Sting was put back in the line-up, and both he and Coach decided to stop seeing Deena in the best interest of the team.

It was at that point that Led decided not to get involved with other people's problems anymore. His wife's marketing plans evaporated so it was no surprise when she said she was leaving. He had been part of her twenty-five-year plan. A plan that was no longer in place. He didn't plan on making any more plans.

It was 5:57 the next morning when Led pulled up in front of Fatima's residence. Start early, finish early, and don't get caught up with a case even if it means only working until the early afternoon. He owed himself a night out and he had been thinking about Callie enough to decide what shirt he was going to wear. His blue one. It wasn't a plan; it was just being prepared.

No interior lights were on, but her dark gray Toyota Camry was parked in the driveway next to a silver compact sedan. Three white trash bags had been placed in front of the home along with a recycling bin. Led pulled up along the curb and double-parked. He popped the back hatch of his vehicle and walked around behind it. There was no one outside and he didn't see anyone looking out of the windows of the house. He grabbed all three bags and put them into the back of his vehicle. He would look through them when he had time, or when he couldn't stand the smell of the garbage in his jeep anymore.

It was a nasty job, going through trash—hygiene products, rotting meat, and the indistinguishable goo and glop that had been scraped and tossed—especially if it had been sitting in the sun for a few days before pickup. But it was also revealing: there were magazines indicating interests, telephone numbers on scraps of paper, old phone bills and pay stubs. Like tracking an animal by its droppings, tracking humans by their trash gave a time stamped glimpse into what they ate and did, and a little insight into what they might do next.

A truck picked up the rest of the trash from the street. Two men in dark jumpsuits adorned only on the back with yellowish reflective tape worked the cans and bags from the sides of the road, flipping and banging them into the back of the truck with a lot of resulting clamor; the cans were crudely tossed back onto the sidewalk. None of the local residents paid any attention to the routine and the truck worked its way down the street. Once it had gone past, the trash in front of Fatima's home was no longer the only trash missing.

It was at 7:18 a.m., when the door of the apartment opened and Led saw a thin woman with shoulder-length black hair pulled into a bushy ponytail. She looked a little different with her hair back, but it was Fatima. She wore a yellow sweatshirt and black slacks and had the same shoulder bag as the day before.

The stops she made were not unusual—a convenience store, a dry cleaners, a liquor store—but it was the limited time she spent in each as she entered. She went to a Gulf gas station and handed the attendant something out the window, but never gassed up. Led's first thought was that she was dealing drugs, but then he noticed that she carried a white envelope with her when she entered the news stand and then her second coffee shop. No, it looked like she was probably working for a bookie.

Fatima parallel parked on the side of Central Avenue in Everett. To remain discreet, Led drove past and went down the street to turn around. When he returned he saw she was parked between the Cut Above hair salon and a multi-family residence. There were apartments above the hair salon. Fatima had already exited her car while he was turning around. There was no way to be sure which building she entered, so he kept one eye on the Camry.

At 8:20 an Asian male approximately thirty-five years old walked away from the left side of the salon and entered a black compact sedan, departing the area alone. Fatima was not observed and Led set his camera back down.

With so much time having elapsed, Led got out of the jeep and walked past the front windows of the salon, but he could not see Fatima inside. The windows were dark except for a lighted display. He returned to his jeep and waited.

At 8:46 Fatima slammed open the front door of the salon and ran toward her car. Led wasn't prepared for such a volatile exit and scrambled to get the camera up to the window and turned on. Fatima's face was covered with blood. She fumbled with her keys before unlocking the doors. As she got into her car, a big man with a down-turned mustache sprinted from the salon, gesturing wildly and grabbing at her arm. She pulled away, refusing to speak with him, and shut the car door.

Led kept the camera on the man as he ran across the street to a Dunkin' Donuts. Then Led panned back to Fatima. She sat in her car with her head forward, almost touching the steering wheel. She was using her cell phone. The man ran back to her car with napkins from the coffee shop; he tapped on the passenger side window and she leaned over to unlock the door. He partially got into the passenger side and began to wipe the blood off her face as she sat crying.

Led continued to obtain video; as long as Fatima was no longer being hit, he felt no obligation to get involved beyond his current position of observer. If he did, it would alter the scene. He was like an anthropologist, not wanting to contaminate his study with outside influences, or so he convinced himself.

At 8:59 the Everett City Police and an ambulance showed up at the Cut Above hair salon. Three police officers surrounded Fatima's vehicle. One stood at the driver's side talking through the window as the other two pulled open the passenger door and asked the man with the napkins to get out of the car. As he started out the two officers grabbed his arms and put a pair of handcuffs on him. He seemed resolved to his fate as they led him over to the closest police cruiser and put him in the back.

Two paramedics from the Metro Ambulance helped Fatima out of the car and had her lie down on the stretcher as they checked her vitals. Led could see the backs of the men in their dark jackets with yellowish green bands of reflective tape across the back. How much it reminded him of the trash men's jackets earlier in the day... a metaphor? Linking the two ends of the spectrum, those who pick up refuse and the broken—no, nothing that symbolic to it. They were just men trying to do their job, without being hit from behind by some inattentive driver.

As the police did their thing, Led noticed that someone was standing by the door of the salon watching—a man of considerable bulk with a shaved head. He had not been there when Fatima first ran out, but the man seemed interested in watching the commotion. A few pedestrians briefly stopped to look until they saw that all the action had already occurred. The man in the doorway stayed, however, peeling an orange, working his fingers around the fruit to free the peel in one piece.

The stretcher was placed into an ambulance and driven away. The man by the door was still there under the small awning, leisurely eating the orange one slice at a time, killing time.

Led got out of his jeep and walked over to speak with the police officer that appeared to be in charge. "Excuse me," he said.

"You gotta keep moving along," the officer told him.

"Officer, I'm an insurance investigator and I followed that woman here earlier."

"You did?" the officer asked, accepting Led's ID case and just as quickly returning it. "Did you see them fighting?"

"No. What happened?"

"Her boyfriend hit her. He had a ring on his hand and he cut her face pretty bad above her left eye. I'm not a doctor but from what I could tell she's going to need stitches."

"He admitted it?"

"Oh yeah, just as soon as we pulled him from the car, the son a' bitch said, 'I didn't mean to bust her up, just getting her attention, she was pushing me. She knows she shouldn't be pushing me.'"

"Did they say what they were fighting about?"

"No."

"You see the boyfriend go in?" The cop made no pretense at writing the answers down.

"No, I first saw him after she ran out bleeding."

"When she isn't bleeding she's probably a real looker." The officer smiled as he said it. "Don't know what she's doing with that guy. This a private case?"

"Domestic? Nope. Insurance, but I never know what else I could be walking into."

"You and me both."

"Do you know what they do above the hair salon?"

"No idea." The officer shrugged. "Could be anything in this neighborhood."

Led walked back to his jeep as the cruisers departed. The man was gone from the front of the salon; there was only the deflated orange peel on the ground where he'd been standing.

Having lost Fatima for the second time, Led went to the dumpster behind the strip mall and went through Fatima's garbage. Wearing a pair of latex gloves he dissected the bags, removing every item one piece at a time. The only thing that he could tell was that she ate a lot of Hot Pockets and drank Diet Coke.

Not all trash was treasure.

Perkins had finished his orange and drove to Somerville without Martinez. They were neither mob guys, nor were they in a gang. They were free agents, but their best client was Uncle Charlie.

They were disparate forces of violence, Perkins and Martinez. Perkins was a lumbering bear of a white man with a shaved head and a big barrel chest. His arms hung out away from his sides. He was five-eleven, an ill-defined mass of muscle. But if Perkins was a bear, Martinez was a Puerto Rican bull; taller, leaner, more kinetic with cut muscle and sinew stretched over a six-foot-five frame. He was more self conscious of his appearance, wearing silk shirts and tailored jackets and frequently checking his dark curly hair and moustache in any available reflection.

They first worked together when Perkins was working the door at the Sans Solei in Jacksonville and Martinez was personal protection for a third-rate white Southern rapper, Seed-E. They kicked a kid to death; Perkins remembered it a little differently than Martinez but let Martinez's story stand as the official record. There was a small handgun and threats to the performer; however, Perkins still remembered the guy carelessly stepping on Martinez's shoe and then being too drunk or high to have the sense to apologize. No one found the body so there was no investigation to dispute Martinez's version.

Whatever incendiary events might have caused it, it was one of those moments where two people met through providence and realized they worked well together: Jagger meeting Richards, Crick meeting Watson, or Bonnie meeting Clyde. It was instant chemistry, kindred spirits. When they had realized that the kid wasn't moving anymore, neither one said anything. No, they looked at the body lying limp with blood coming out of the ears and, as if they had done it a hundred times together, one grabbed his feet and the other grabbed his arms. They threw the body in the touring van, drove to the construction site on Duval Street, and tossed the carcass into the large dumpster that was half full of construction debris. They covered it with pieces of scrap aluminum ductwork and plywood, but the coup de grace was when they thought of tossing a port-a-john in on top of the body. They both thought of it at the same time. Dumping the Sani-Stall into the dumpster sealed the deal. No one was going to go dumpster diving. The smell of anything was just the shit from the toilet, and the dumpster would be hauled off out of the sun and dumped into landfill when the general contractor couldn't deal with the stench any longer. The Lennon and McCartney of homicidal sociopaths had just written, "Love, love me do."

Martinez got Seed-E to add Perkins to his posse and it was good to be together as a team, but a year later with a record deal that fell through the performer Seed–E decided to become the car salesman Seth Eichell and go to work for his father's Toyota dealership in Houston. That had left Martinez and Perkins to find work as personal protection for a variety of minor celebrities; it might have been while working for Corbin Bersen that they met a Boston bookie called Uncle Charlie. He had a need for some light administrative support that could keep them busy nearly fulltime, so they moved to Boston.

Unlike Martinez, who spent every cent he made on clothes, drugs, and women, Perkins planned for his retirement. He was the responsible one. He tried his hand at opening a donut shop before selling it and buying an old cranberry bog and some acreage for a paintball course. Shooting people for fun and profit and letting them shoot each other was a good side business. The clients were respectful; paramilitary types, kids, and middle-aged men living out a fantasy of war without death. Perkins enjoyed welcoming in new guests and giving out the medals to the winners at the end of a war game weekend. It was that little extra that created repeat customers.

This wasn't the first time that Martinez had got popped, either, leaving Perkins to work alone for a while. It must be that hot Latin blood that made him lose his cool over a woman. It wasn't Perkins' style, but he would never say anything to Martinez about it. It was none of his business.

Meanwhile, Uncle Charlie wanted to send a message to a couple of college gamblers who lost big on betting a soccer game, of all things. And Martinez or no Martinez, what Uncle Charlie wanted, Uncle Charlie got. These college kids were punks with degrees but they were still punks and they were hesitating too long on coming up with the money. At the off-campus apartment in Somerville, a skinny kid in a pair of smiley face boxer shorts and a Clash T-shirt answered the door while eating from a bowl of cereal. He dropped the spoon when he saw Perkins standing there, and tried to push the door shut. Too late, Perkins leaned his shoulder and kicked at the bottom of the door; it pushed the young man back, spilling the bowl of brightly colored puffed rice down his shirt.

"Man, look what you did."

"Uncle Charlie asked that I stop and pick up his money."

The kid held out his hands palms up. "We're going to pay. Just that eight thousand dollars is a lot of money."

"Eight thousand is what you owed after the game; now there are handling charges and you owe ten."

"What the..." The kid tossed the mostly empty bowl into the sink as if he had just been told he was grounded for the week and was going to throw a tantrum.

"Where's the other one? I'm supposed to talk to both of you."

"He's in his room."

Perkins unceremoniously kicked in the locked bedroom door, awakening the other kid who squinted at him from underneath a sheet on a mostly unmade bed. He was not completely startled, as if his door had been kicked in often.

"Get up and get me some cash."

"Sure." The kid stood up, still blinking. "We don't have all of it."

Perkins looked around the apartment of the twenty-year-old kids with their large televisions and game consoles. "Maybe you better sell some of your shit, or ask Mom and Dad to send you some money to live on, if you know what I mean."

The kid got out of bed and pulled on a pair of sweatpants. "I can give you our rent money today, but it's only twelve hundred."

He reached into the top drawer of his nightstand and handed Perkins a wad of five, ten, twenty-dollar bills.

"You know if I don't have all the money I have to break something before I leave here."

"Like our television?"

"Like maybe your thumbs."

"On both of us? Cause I only agreed to go in on the bet at the last minute. It wasn't really my idea."

Perkins was prepared for nonsense. He had heard the skinny kid in the kitchen and could only imagine what he was planning, filled with ideas from television. There the kid was with a golf club and he hit Perkins from behind, hitting him in the shoulder blades but mostly hitting the hallway wall with the back swing.

Perkins shot him in the calf and he dropped, crying, not saying anything coherent, just crying as if testosterone were pouring from his leg instead of blood. Perkins couldn't believe the ignorance of today's youth. Spending too much time in front of video games and the computer. They didn't know anything.

"Your roommate is going to need a doctor, better make them believe he was mugged, got it?"

The kid nodded like a bobble-head on the Green Line and looked at his roommate on the floor. "Do you still have to do something to me?" he asked.

"Maybe tomorrow," Perkins took the money from his hand. "Depends if you have Uncle Charlie's money."

"We just gave you twelve hundred."

"That was just to cover my traveling expenses since you're going to make me come all the way back over here again to pick it up. I ain't FedEx. Pick-up ain't free."

Perkins disassembled the handgun, taking off the barrel and replacing it with a new one he had in the glove box. The entire gun didn't need to be disposed of, just the barrel. People always threw away perfectly good guns. Jesus, to throw away a Sig P220 every time you shot someone. That was the real crime. A barrel of a gun was hardly recognizable to the average citizen, just a piece of pipe with a flanged end on it. As a trademark, Martinez had come up with the idea of dropping it in the end of the metal fence posts that surround the municipal parking lot near a police station. Said it was poetic to place the barrel as close to a police station as possible. By taking a tire iron and knocking the end cap off a metal fence post, he could drop the barrel inside and put the cap back on. No one was ever going to stumble across it with the posts usually cemented three feet into the ground.

'Course, with anything stupid, there were stupid risks. If the post end cap was left off, someone might get suspicious, and that couldn't be chanced. And Martinez had almost got his balls ripped off in Detroit as he climbed over the fence to get the end cap. Then he got stuck coming back over the fence and fell twelve feet. Perkins almost wet his pants laughing at the time; he still snorted every time he thought about the look on that crazy Puerto Rican face.

Now security cameras were everywhere. Used to be a car lot was a safe place, but now no one trusted nobody for nothing. He tossed the barrel off the Tobin Bridge and text messaged Uncle Charlie "1200 wgbt" to let him know that he had got some money and would go back tomorrow for the rest.

NINE

Dale Foley's missing teeth were the result of a training accident with a collapsible baton. He'd swung it in earnest as his sparring partner Rollin threw basketballs for him to hit away. Somehow the baton bounced back with enamel-shattering velocity and left him missing four top front teeth and two chipped lower.

When he was bored he clicked the dental plate with his tongue.

At Mobile Medi Tech, Stacey was finishing up a call as Dale stood in the reception area with coffee and a bag of pastries. He was making that clicking sound.

Dale Foley was a part-time employee for Mobile Medi Tech as well as a constable, a process server, a repo-man, a private investigator, a self-appointed underwater dive team commander, and a volunteer for the Missing Children Network. He was certified to carry mace, licensed to carry a concealed weapon, and was an instructor and distributor of the Fanning Knight Stick. To first hear his baritone voice as he recounted one of his latest cases he was working, with all the lurid details of a child's abduction and battering, he seemed a force of righteous vigilance. But as Stacey learned over time, Dale's enthusiasm was not proportionate to success: he'd never actually found any child. He received all his information from the Internet and added his own theories. Dale lived in a world where chaos could erupt at any minute, and only he, his protégé Rollin, and a few other well prepared people would be ready.

If he was coming into the office, he usually stopped and bought Stacey a danish or a muffin, and he was friendly, assuring her that she would be one of the people who should not be worried in a time of crises. He had included her on his list of protected targets. Dale didn't just seem to prepare for anarchy; he seemed to hope for it, for an opportunity to show his usefulness to someone besides Mr. Tuttle.

He was affable but his stories always started about his current pursuit of an abducted child. He seemed to think it lent legitimacy to his talk about weapons training or his latest technique for thwarting an attack. Stacey saw him once outside of work at the mall, walking around in black paratrooper pants and a green nylon motorcycle jacket; being in his late thirties, with a modestly athletic build and cropped, sandy blonde hair, he looked like Special Forces for mall security.

To avoid him she'd stepped into the Wicker Place and spent ten minutes having a sales associate show her an amazingly ugly elephant-shaped wicker end table. It was better than Dale expounding on the benefits of some new stun gun he bought. Through association with Dale she was afraid that she, too, would be put on some government watch list.

This morning he brought her an apple turnover and cup of French vanilla coffee. He stood at the desk and told her about a twelve-year-old girl named Silvie from Wyoming that he was looking for in the area, pulling out a folded piece of paper with a color photo. Stacey told him good luck with the case and thanks for the coffee. Then she buzzed Mr. Tuttle to let him know that Dale was out front to see him.

Almost two years ago Richard Tuttle had hired Dale Foley to drive him around and offer executive protection because of death threats that he still suspected were from one of his former business partners. Dale was not the most qualified, but he was the least expensive. And though Tuttle never did find himself under attack, he enjoyed having his own low-cost bodyguard and general lackey on payroll. Now, it was comforting to have Dale shadowing around the former Mrs. Tuttle to keep an eye on her and the children.

As Dale entered his office, Tuttle glanced up from his computer and told him to take a seat.

Tuttle knew his hold on Dale. Dale was malleable; he looked for Tuttle's approval on everything. It was understandable. Tuttle thought of himself as a dynamic presence who could persuade or make a deal in a boardroom or on a golf course with men far smarter and tougher minded than Dale. Tuttle considered his ability to lead and gain control of a situation a genetic trait as legitimate as a sprinter's quick-twitch muscles. Other people attested to it all the time. His office walls bore community plaques and letters of appreciation from the Massachusetts Small Business Association, recognition by *Inc.* magazine, and thanks from the Bradford Little League Organization, not to mention about another dozen wood, brass, and Lucite hangings attesting to his benevolent nature and business acumen.

It was easy to see why Dale would clamor all over himself to work for Tuttle. What Tuttle could not understand was why Rollin succumbed to Dale. As far as Tuttle could tell, there was not one thing that Dale said or did reflecting any leadership ability.

Rollin was probably ten years younger than Dale. He rode with Dale and participated in most of his training exercises when not working part-time at Radio Shack. He didn't seem stupid, but he must have had a self-esteem issue. Rollin was shorter than Dale and a little out of shape, layered with what might be called "baby fat" on someone ten years younger, but at twenty-seven made him look just soft and doughy. Rollin seldom accompanied Dale into Tuttle's office, but stayed in the car to protect the perimeter and listen to the radio.

Tuttle looked out of his window and down into the front seat of the white van. He couldn't see Rollin's face but he could see his lap and hands as the sun repeatedly reflected off the pair of silver handcuffs that Rollin was clicking over and over against his palm. *It's easier to lead some people than others*, Tuttle thought, and went back to his computer to review a spreadsheet.

"How did your training go?" Tuttle asked without looking up.

"We did good. They said we were the best tactical team they had seen in a long time."

Tuttle suspected that they had been the only two paying trainees to show up and run around in a corn field in Kentucky, shooting at each other with balls of paint. He was annoyed that Dale and Rollin had left for something so impractical and inconvenient, but he was glad they were back to follow his not-soon-enough-to-be ex-wife. "That's nice."

Dale reached onto Tuttle's desk to pick up an engraved silver pen. He wrote on the back of his own hand in a big, circular scribble. "Writes smooth."

Tuttle didn't answer. He stopped scrolling, scowled, and reached out his hand. Dale gave him the pen and Tuttle put it in his top desk drawer.

"I am going to need you two to watch Judith closely over the next couple of days. One of the kids broke their arm."

"Sorry to hear that. Which one?"

"The girl," Tuttle said, not comfortable talking about his children by name with anyone who worked for him. They might have known, but it seemed the one thing that was personal. "It was an accident, but I want to know if she goes to her attorney this week. I want you to be discreet."

"We're always discreet."

"I know. But try extra hard this time."

Dale nodded. "We'll use a different surveillance vehicle?"

The intercom buzzed. "Mr. Tuttle, Paul O'Hearn is on line two."

"However you want to do it," Tuttle said to Dale. "She's probably still staying at her mother's." He barely paused. "I'll take it, Stacey." Tuttle hit the intercom, leaving the call on speakerphone.

"Paul. How are you? Is that hand healing alright?"

"Soon enough."

"You should take in a game while you're out. I'll try to get you some company tickets."

"I appreciate that. Mr. Tuttle, I'm calling about the accident."

Tuttle watched Dale sit back in the big leather chair across from him. Dale crossed one leg and looked at the heavy waffle tread on the bottom of his black jump boot, extracting a stone wedged there. Tuttle continued to listen on the phone but watched to see if Dale dared to drop the stone on the floor. "Go ahead," he said to Paul.

"When will you get a check from the insurance company?"

"I don't know, Paul."

Dale saw that Tuttle was staring at him and put the tiny white rock from his shoe on the top of the burled maple desk. Tuttle shook his head. "That's something that goes through accounting."

"Can you take me off speakerphone?"

Tuttle picked up the handset. "Yes?"

"Well, I'd like to get a little bonus out of it. Seeing that I was the one that was in the accident and all."

"Paul...you have worker's comp and medical coverage. There isn't much more I can do for you."

"I want a little consideration. For being the one in the accident."

"I'm sure we can get you a couple extra days of sick time. There isn't much else I can do."

"I think there is. I think I want a hundred thousand dollars."

Paul sounded to Tuttle like he was working too hard to be cool, kind of tough with just an air of casual matter-of-factness that the street hustlers worked so hard at perfecting. "Excuse me?"

"You will be collecting extra on the medical equipment, and I want some of it. It's not like I'm asking you for something that's yours."

"I'm not sure I understand what you are talking about."

"You put in for the replacement cost of the new CT scanner, but the new one is sitting in storage."

"Really?"

"The difference between the old and the new is no small amount," Paul said. "Give me one hundred g's."

G's? Tuttle was amused at the term. It sounded like Paul was trying to talk like he was in a Scorsese film. "I'll have to look into this matter. You bring up some interesting issues that I was not aware of. Thank you, Paul."

"So we got a deal?"

"Paul, I'm not sure you have your facts straight. But I'll research it and let you know what I find."

"I'll call you tomorrow."

"If you like."

"Okay, bye."

"Goodbye, Paul."

Tuttle hung up the phone. The left side of his mouth twitched up just slightly as he took his negotiating posture. It was a standard look he put on for others so often he now did it by reflex, a coy grin he used to conceal his excitement over a position of leverage, or now to conceal a feeling of acid reflux.

Dale watched him but didn't say anything. Tuttle turned his chair and looked out the window and down at Rollin with his arm out the van window. He thought about the folder. Stacey had to have read it. He thought about firing her right then, but he didn't want to upset Uncle Charlie. How Paul O'Hearn found out didn't matter as much as how he was now going to handle it. He was not about to be blackmailed or extorted or whatever it was that O'Hearn was trying to do.

Tuttle thought about it as a self-test. Everyone makes mistakes and misjudgments. The great business leaders are the ones who deal with them creatively, make them into opportunities. He wasn't sure what he was going to do in the long run, but first he needed to keep an eye on O'Hearn.

"Trouble?" Dale asked intrepidly, not sure if he had given Mr. Tuttle enough thinking time. From the corner of his desk Tuttle picked up the business card of Asher "Led" Ledbetter and flipped it between his fingers.

"Maybe. I don't know yet."

"Rollin and I can investigate something for you. Get more information," Dale said. "If you want."

"No. I'm going to use someone a little more experienced and professional in matters like these." Tuttle tapped the edge of the card on desktop.

Dale hung his head and fondled the crystal clock on Tuttle's desk. Tuttle could tell the comment stung him, but he would get over it. He needed to toughen up and not waste so much time pursuing skills that were of little use outside of gang warfare and kung fu movies. If he spent half the effort on his wardrobe and the way he looked as he did playing with ninja stars and collapsible batons he might at least have a regular pair of shoes and his own front teeth.

That was it? Paul O'Hearn wondered as he closed the cover on the flip phone. It had not gone as well as hoped. Of course, he didn't know what he had really expected. He had worked for Tuttle long enough to know that the man was not going to just agree. But it could have been so easy, just pay a consulting fee. The accountants would think nothing of it.

Finally, he had a chance to get a little ahead, to set some money aside for the boys to go to college. His brother's wrongful death suit could still be tied up in court for years, according to the attorney, whom he suspected was just running up a bill of expenses. He should have insisted that they use a different attorney.

Mr. Tuttle, trying to act all blasé, like it didn't matter that Paul knew about the insurance scam. Arrogant, like he didn't care. *What else can I do for you, Paul?* His voice never changed. It hadn't gotten excited or cracked. It didn't sound like he was concerned in the least. Paul didn't know what bothered him more, how he had lost his cool or how Tuttle kept his.

The last thing he wanted to do was give Tuttle another reason to feel superior. He went to the refrigerator and got a beer, pouring half the can down his throat before pausing to take a breath. It was still nine-thirty in the morning. He was glad Cheryl was not home to see him drinking already.

TEN

Led was scheduling his day carefully around his date with Callie. The Fatima case ended early, so he was going to do some simple research cases in the afternoon, nothing he couldn't stop when he wanted to, at least that was the plan before he listened to the message on his phone that came in at 11:27 a.m.

"Led, this is Randall at GIA. Call me on my cell; I'm working from home today. I got to have you bounce over to another assignment first thing this afternoon. It's a claimant from that big accident that happened on the North Shore. The insured is all worked up on this one and asked for you personally. Start heading toward Wakefield and call me back, I have a first-hand description of the claimant for you."

General Insurance of America, known as GIA in their ads— *There, because we care*—was an all-lines insurance company writing policies in forty-eight states. If a dollar amount could be put on something, chances were GIA could insure it: life, auto, property, disability, liability, and worker's compensation. But despite the claim of its advertising, like all insurance companies GIA was not in business to pay out money on insurance claims. It was in business to collect premiums. Paying out on a policy was what they wanted to avoid.

Randall Crawford, the senior claims adjuster for General Insurance of America (GIA), was a law school graduate and had passed the bar in New York State. This made him a bit of an overachiever for an insurance adjuster. But he was coveted by his managers because of the added level of protection he provided. If Randall was handling the case, they were getting an adjuster and an attorney's opinion. So he got the claims when the exposure was potentially high. If Randall was calling Led, it was usually something big or bothersome for someone at GIA.

"How are you, Led?" Randall answered the phone.

"Good. Been busy keeping the honest people honest. I'm returning your call about the new assignment, but I also have a couple of updates for you."

"Our girl, Fatima?"

"It looks like she might be working for a bookie but might even be out of work from that for a while." Led recounted what he had seen and added, "I'm just guessing, but she probably needed time off from the market to run numbers."

"I was thinking the same thing, but if I was making good money under the table, why work at a market?"

"Health insurance, considering her taste in men."

"Hold off on that one for now. Let's see what she does with her claim. Nice work."

"You have another update?"

"One you gave me at the end of last week, Lobik."

"Do you have the file number?"

Led flipped through the folders on the passenger seat. "WC078-983605." He could hear the Randall typing on his computer.

"Anything good?"

"Got him working. About forty minutes of video of him moving ladders and putting up gutters. He's working for his brother-in-law who went back to Brazil."

"Great. Get the report in to me."

"There's more. I can't prove it, but none of the social security numbers match up for Mr. Lobik. I think he might be an illegal. I don't know if INS or Homeland Security or whatever they call themselves these days will send him back if they find out."

"I don't want them to send him back yet, not with an open claim. If they deport him we'll own the claim forever."

"You want me to get more video next week?"

"Yeah," Randall said distractedly, typing away as he spoke. "If he's sent out of the country I won't have any control over the claim. Get me what you can."

On the surface it didn't seem right to have immigrants enter the United States illegally and then reward them with a comp check if they were hurt. Led had worked a concentration of claims where there were so many illegal aliens of one nationality trying to collect a comp check and go home that it seemed like there was some type of class being taught on how to do it back in the old country.

Randall had enlightened Led on this before. It was not some liberal law, constructed to hand out money unjustly to the disadvantaged. It was a law of fair trade. The insurance companies weren't hurt in the long run. They never were. They would just raise the premiums to cover the loss. Led hoped that he could avoid another dissertation by Randall on the subject: *the law is a way to keep employers from hiring illegal aliens to do the dangerous work with substandard safety measures in place, thus saving money.* Randall worked for a conservative insurance company, but sounded pretty liberal when he talked about comp laws not having anything to do with the protection of the illegal workers. It was the protection of fair trade. The almighty dollar. It would give a cost savings advantage to one company over another.

"You know how these types of claims just get under my skin," Randall said.

"Sure do," said Led, not knowing what part of it bothered Randall more, the illegal worker manipulating the system, or the fact that Randall was part of a system that manipulated right back.

"I can give you another twelve hundred on the budget."

"Great." Led could still hear Randall typing. "And you got a new one for me?"

"Let me know when you're ready to write this down."

Led pulled over to the side of the road in front of a Christie's Mini Market, flipping to a blank page in his yellow pad. "Go ahead."

"Mobile Medi Tech is the insured. The date of loss was yesterday. I don't even have a claim number assigned to this yet. You'll have to get that from me later. This was a bad one, with five separate vehicles, I was one of them."

"Are you alright?"

"My car is totaled so I'm working from the house. Which is a good thing because I'm so stiff I can hardly walk. But I'm fine. Here's the kicker. I was hit by the claimant on this file. We own the policy for worker's comp for Mobile Medi Tech. Their driver hit me. I want you to go talk to the owner of the company. He asked that I assign the case to you. You need to go see Richard Tuttle."

"Tuttle?"

"He asked for you to help us out on this, too. He liked you."

"I wish I could say the same."

"He's asked that you meet with him. Please. So he leaves me alone."

Led sighed. "What's to be gained by meeting with him? All I need is a name of the subject and a good address."

"Bill me for talking to him. Then go out and do a general activity check. Take a statement from some witnesses of the accident, do some surveillance on the claimant. Let me know what's going on. It was a bad accident, but I saw the driver at the hospital. He looked fine except for a bandaged hand. I don't want it getting out of control. Most of all give the insured the five star treatment so he's happy and off my back."

"What kind of a budget?"

"Let's start with two thousand, but call me, I can give you more if you need it."

"Who's the claimant?"

"Name is Paul O'Hearn. They sent over the Form 110 and then I received a message this morning from Rich Tuttle. He wanted to know if we would be following around O'Hearn, because he thinks the guy is a fraud and will milk this. I haven't told him that I talked to his driver yet. He asked that you come by his office. He'll give you whatever you need for information on the claimant."

"Any medicals?"

"He hurt his hand, but I don't have anything back from a doctor. I doubt he's represented yet. So it's Paul O'Hearn. DOB 3/21/71."

"Do you have an address?"

"I'm not sure. They only have a P.O. Box." Randall gave him the box number, street address, and phone number. "Rich seems to think that he might be out for a while. Get me the police report too, if you can."

"The police aren't going to have any information available yet."

"Probably not. But do what you can."

In the parking lot at Mobile Medi Tech, Led opened the back hatch of his jeep where he kept two mismatched garment bags and a pair of black wing tips. He unzipped the plastic bag down far enough to see that there were a blue oxford shirt, gray pants, and a navy blue blazer. He zipped it back up and retrieved the green garment bag with airline baggage tags and strings stuck to it. The airline tags were old and should have been removed, but they reminded him of travel that he kept meaning to do. When he unzipped the green bag he found the black sports coat he was looking for. He took it out, closed everything up, and put on the jacket then bent over for a partial view of himself in the side mirror. The dark gray polo shirt and pair of khaki pants dressed up fine with the addition of the jacket. He ran his fingers through his hair twice and considered it satisfactorily combed. He showed his teeth. Nothing stuck there. Retrieving the black leather briefcase from behind the front seat, he popped it open and made sure he had a pen, a fresh yellow pad of paper, and some of his business cards.

Mobile Medi Tech was not marked on the exterior of the building but was listed on the small directory by the elevator. At the second floor, he walked along the sunny hallway that overlooked the atrium. The building was quiet. No one other than a FedEx deliveryman was walking through the lobby.

The solid oak door of Suite 217 opened straight into a small office where a woman wearing a telephone headset was sitting in front of a computer. She gave Led a slight smile of acknowledgement before turning back to the monitor on her desk and talking into the little silver wire that ran from in front of her mouth to her ear.

A doorway to the left opened into a darkened room with a conference table and six chairs. Another doorway was the start of a hallway bathed in diffused, fluorescent light.

He set his briefcase on the floor by a fake ficus tree in a large ceramic pot and walked over to look at a picture on the wall above the copy machine. It captured a dozen men, ironworkers, sitting on steel girders, eating their lunch above a 1930s New York skyline. That had to have been a hell of a way to make a living.

According to the brass nameplate on her desk, the office manager was Stacey Vickers. A white woman in her mid-thirties, short and a little chunky, with brown, shoulder-length hair worn straight with bangs, pulled back behind her ears and the headset. She was dressed professionally for a small office that apparently no one entered: an olive green knee-length skirt with matching blazer and a cream-colored blouse with an ascot-like flourish to the front. She wasn't wearing any makeup, maybe just some light lipstick. She was finishing an exchange with a doctor's office, rescheduling the medical appointments that were no longer going to be made with the damaged mobile unit.

"May I help you?" she asked, turning to Led.

"Asher Ledbettor to see Richard Tuttle."

"Will he know what this is regarding?"

"He called for me."

"Oh, yes. He's waiting for you."

Led followed her down the short hallway, passing a small kitchenette on the way, before turning into an office.

Sitting behind a mahogany desk was an overly tanned white male with premature salt and pepper hair. He didn't look any different than when Led had seen him fighting with his wife in the Stop & Shop parking lot. In fact, he might have been wearing the same teal golf shirt he had on now, sitting hunched over a laptop computer on his desk, his large hands working the keys cautiously as he clicked out a couple more words and used the thumb pad.

Stacey stood in front of Led as they both waited for him to look up.

"This is Mr. Ledbetter from GIA."

"We know each other." Tuttle stood and extended his well-manicured hand. "You like to be called Led, right?"

"That works."

"You were fast. I was speaking with Randall only a little while ago. Have a seat." He motioned to the two high-backed leather chairs in front of his desk. Led sat in one and Stacey sat in the other, to his left.

"I was in the area." Led said, as a routine response no matter from where he had traveled. He was always in the area; as long as he was being paid his area had few boundaries.

Tuttle was backlit by the large window behind him.

"How's your daughter?"

"She's doing better," Tuttle sighed. "Her arm had a slight fracture."

Stacey seemed uncomfortable as she busied herself by looking through notes written on the pad of paper she had in her hand.

Led continued. "I understand one of your vehicles was involved in an accident."

"I'll say. I've already printed you out everything about the mobile unit." He handed Led a light blue folder. The letters on the front were MT-MU. Inside was a pocket folder filled with color copies of technical specs for medical lab machines.

Led thumbed through the pages, but he had no interest at this time about what they contained. Good to have for later, maybe, but not really the point right now.

"Who am I checking out?"

"The driver of the medical unit, Paul O'Hearn."

"What's his injury?"

"His left hand."

Led took out his yellow pad of paper from his briefcase and put the folder he had been handed inside of it.

"He called from the scene and said that the unit had been in an accident on 93. It had flipped over on its side."

"Did he say what happened?"

"Just that a couple of cars collided in front of him and he was not able to avoid them."

"Can I get whatever information is available on Paul O'Hearn?"

"Sure. Stacey, can you get Paul's employee file for us?" Tuttle asked her pleasantly but stared after her as she left the room. It was not a look of fondness, Led noted. It was the same look he had given his ex-wife.

"I'm going to have to start with some pretty basic questions," Led said, "because I'm not sure what it is your company does."

"We provide mobile independent medical diagnostic and wellness screenings." Tuttle had snapped into his salesman persona. "We have twelve vehicles here in Massachusetts outfitted with state-of-the-art technologies."

"Who uses these?"

"We contract with doctor groups, hospitals, and some insurance companies and businesses. By being able to offer diagnostic testing for diseases in their earliest stages, the company specializes in uncovering early disorders such as heart disease, lung cancer, colon cancer, and other conditions years before patients become symptomatic." He sounded to Led like a pamphlet, like he was reciting a speech he'd been giving for years. "Catching the problem early enough, some diseases can be treated with simple lifestyle changes or minimal medication."

"Is this the main company's headquarters?"

"For MTMU, yes. You might have seen our company featured on *Chronicle*, and there was a write-up in the *Boston Business Journal* back in April."

"If it wasn't on ESPN, I didn't see it," Led said. "Other than a doctor saying you need tests, who uses these things?"

"We've had a lot of athletes and celebrities, some business leaders and politicians screened in our mobile units. Usually prior to a performance contract or issuance of a large disability policy."

Stacey came back into the room and handed Led several pages of stapled papers. "This is Paul's employee file," she said.

"Why don't you think he'll be back to work?"

"We had a little heated argument this morning when he called in, and he said that he didn't care because he'd just collect comp for the summer."

"What was the argument about?"

"Nothing, really. I was wanting him to come back to work this week, even if it was to help out here in the office on light duty."

"You don't have a street address for him?" Led asked as he looked at the papers in the file. "There's just a post office box in Charlestown, do you know anything else?"

"Just whatever is in the file. His driver's license should have the address." Tuttle then addressed Stacey, who stood quietly by the door: "You're friendly with Paul. Do you have any other information on him?"

"Not that I can think of," Stacey said.

"I'll figure it out," Led said. If Stacey was friendly with Paul O'Hearn, it was not a good idea that she was standing there as he discussed the investigation. Besides, she wasn't looking at Tuttle when she replied. Something was up between them.

"Where's the mobile unit?"

"We were told it was being taken over to B & B Towing in Tewksbury."

"Anyone tell you when you might get it back?"

"We don't want it back, I'm sure. Once all that equipment takes a hit like that, we would never be able to get any of it to calibrate correctly again. Are you involved in the property damage claim?"

"Nope. Just the comp."

"They're both with GIA, so I didn't know if you would deal with both."

"They'll send someone else out to appraise the damage. Usually takes a few days."

"When can I get a report on Mr. O'Hearn's activities?"

"You'll have to request it from GIA. I'll submit it to them and they will likely give you a copy. Just ask."

"Very good. Thank you again, Mr. Ledbettor."

With copies of the file, Led shook Tuttle's hand and was led back out by Stacey.

"This seems like a nice building to work in," he said.

"It's alright for now," came her reply.

Uncle Charlie, who was neither her uncle, nor named Charlie, had recommended Stacey, straight out of Massasoit Community College, for the job at Mobile Medi Tech just as the company was starting. He was someone her family knew growing up. Somewhere along the way, she had learned that his full name was Horatio C. Fisher, but she always just heard him referred to as Uncle Charlie. He was some type of a silent partner in the Mobile Medi Tech, to what degree and role, she never asked. He never came to the business, and she had not even seen him in person since she got the job, but she talked to him often. She knew that she was expected to tell Uncle Charlie things when he called. It was usually nothing to do with the company itself so she didn't feel she was breaching any confidentiality of her employer. Not that she especially liked Mr. Tuttle and his mood swings, but the money was good, and he was her boss.

No, Uncle Charlie was looking for information from files regarding the medical evaluations of different people, like the Celtics' new forward or the CEO of Gillette. She knew why he wanted to know; he was a bookie and investor. It was the type of information that could help set the line for a basketball game or impact a stock in the market. She didn't see much harm in it. Uncle Charlie referred to her as his risk manager.

When Uncle Charlie called wanting to know about the tests that had been run on the jockey, Dallas McCray, she was still a little agitated about the way Mr. Tuttle had been treating her that morning. He was in one of his foul moods, barely mumbling a few words of greeting. She told Uncle Charlie that they had canceled that test because of an accident with one of the units. And he was surprised that he hadn't been told and asked to speak with Richie.

She intercommed Mr. Tuttle with his personal call on line one and knew that Uncle Charlie was going chew out Mr. Tuttle for something. It was the only time he ever asked to speak with him. Stacey smiled to herself.

"You ever think we missed our time?" Rollin asked Dale as they sat in traffic. "Like maybe should have been around in the good old days of honor and trust?"

"Like in the Wild West?" Dale asked. "People didn't shower and the women were hairy."

"Not that far back, I mean the seventies and eighties before all the foreigners came and tried to take over. The Chinese Mafia, what the hell is that? Jamaican gangs? Shit. Back in the late seventies there was none of that. Mostly Italians but they recognized talent and you were able to advance. These other organizations are all over the place. No American values. No codes of honor or self-respect. Strafing a playground or riding around shooting people for no good reason. Pop some guy putting groceries in his car. Guy did nothing. But it's part of the gang membership. What is *that*? I mean, it'd be different if he had it coming..."

"You want to join the Mafia now?" Dale was amused.

"I don't know," Rollin said. "The others don't have no self-respect is all I'm saying."

"I hear you, but why are you all fired up now?"

"This job. I just don't feel you, or we, are getting what we deserve."

"We get paid. Tuttle pays good and it's fairly steady work."

"It's not about the money. What about appreciation? We get money, but there's little gratitude for the work we do. Long as he pays us, he just pushes us around."

"It's our job. You're just wound up, too much caffeine. Mr. Tuttle is always saying how much he appreciates the work we do for him." Actually Tuttle never mentioned it, but Dale was in the habit of expounding for Rollin's sake upon the gratitude Mr. Tuttle expressed for their diligence.

"I hope so. I just get the feeling he thinks we're a bunch of clowns. He said he's going to use a 'professional' to follow around that driver. What, we're not professionals?"

Dale wished that he hadn't told Rollin that part, but he'd been upset when he returned to the van. Now Rollin was upset. He didn't get upset easily or often. It made Dale uncomfortable.

"Maybe we'll check it out. Show Mr. Tuttle we can be as professional as anyone. Stacey said that the PI Mr. Tuttle put on it doesn't even have Paul O'Hearn's address. It wasn't in the folder and she didn't give it to him," Dale said. "But she gave it to me." And he exaggerated his good fortune by waving the yellow post-it note that Stacey had written on. Perhaps she felt sorry for him, but pity or not, he was glad for the help and bragged about cultivating valuable sources.

Rollin sat with his arms folded but smiled when Dale pulled the van into the parking lot of the Neon Tetra and took a space beneath the "Exotic Dancers" sign.

"I like you're thinking," Rollin said. "But Serenity doesn't dance until the evening."

"You don't want to stop?"

"Of course I do. Maybe she's filling in for another girl."

Dale was glad to get him thinking about something else even if it was a stripper he thought he had a chance with.

A naked brunette with bullet-shaped silicone breasts and Plexiglas soles on her six-inch platform shoes was skipping around the stage to Motley Crüe's "Girls, Girls, Girls," stopping only to pick up a dollar bill that had been placed on the side of the stage.

Rollin let Dale look for a seat as he watched. The dancer had a tattoo on her lower back. In the colored strobe lights it was nothing more than a black inkblot marring what otherwise would have been a lovely ass. He couldn't figure out what the tattoo was supposed to be.

Dale had found a table one row back from the stage and cleared a couple of empty bottles from it by placing them on the next table over. A pixie-sized waitress approached. They ordered a couple of beers.

"I think I should be in the entertainment industry. I got ideas."

Dale shrugged. "You say that every time we come in here."

"I've been thinking about it more. I got a few ideas that would make an artist management company take off."

"You don't exactly work in the industry."

Rollin looked away from the naked woman on stage. "If Suge Knight can do it, so can I."

"Suge Knight went to jail."

"I'm serious, man."

"Alright, what's one of your ideas today?"

"A band is successful when strippers are dancing to their music."

"Not as successful as when a car company uses it in a commercial."

"Same thing, though. The music is no longer the song. The meaning is all in the association. I think I might try to get some local bands to represent and have them play in strip clubs. Get them some buzz that way."

"I don't know, Rollin."

"The Beatles started by playing burlesque shows in Germany. I think Monique is on stage next. She just went in the back."

"Guys don't want to see a band when they have a hard-on for strippers."

"Why not?"

"I don't know. Too distracting all the way around."

"Music videos got both."

"Music videos are for music. Tits and ass are a bonus. Like going to a restaurant, you're there to eat. It don't matter if you got an ugly waitress if the food is good. But if she's hot, then it's a bonus. You go to look at some tits and ass, what can be a bonus?"

"Live music."

"I don't know. I think you should have a band with strippers around, but strippers with a band around? You better do some test marketing before you put too much into the idea. I've read up a lot on it. Before I became a distributor for the Fanning Knight Stick, I did surveys and everything."

"No shit? I didn't know that."

"Absolutely. You got to know what people think of the product, what their daily habits are."

"Who did you ask?"

"Police, martial arts instructors."

The waitress returned with the beers. "Twelve dollars, please."

"Would you go see a band in a strip club?" Dale asked the waitress, shifting his weight to get his wallet out of his back pocket.

"I guess, if they were any good." She smiled.

"Thank you." He gave her fifteen. "That's all set."

"See? Start asking people. Do a survey."

"What is she going to say? She works in a *strip club*."

The waitress walked to another table of men sitting with their bills, mostly ones, in neat little stacks, like they were playing Monopoly with beer bottles for game pieces.

"Do some test spots before investing too much into it; that's all I'm saying."

They finished their fourth beer and the lineup of strippers had already gone through a full cycle. The brunette who'd been on stage when they entered was back. This time she was wearing a plaid schoolgirl skirt and a white unbuttoned blouse, her hair in pigtails.

"We've seen this one," Rollin noted. "Serenity isn't working during the day. You ready? We gotta have time to swing by a pizza joint when we leave here."

"Let me piss first." Dale tipped his bottle back for a last swallow before heading for the men's room.

Rollin sat and folded a five-dollar bill into an origami swan while he waited.

"I'm good," Dale said, returning.

Rollin got up and as they walked out, put the swan-folded five on the stage. The dancer bent over with her ass facing him to pick it up, her short school skirt rising to expose a red thong. Slowly the thong moved to one side in appreciation of Rollin's tip. She raised her skirt in a flirtatious, flapping motion when she stood up.

The tattoo was just a word in some Old English font, with roses entwined: RESPECT.

ELEVEN

Back when the office building of Richard Tuttle's company was still being constructed, on a Tuesday morning in August 2002 as fellow construction workers went to the back of the silver quilted canteen truck for danishes and egg sandwiches, one worker ran across the street to rob The People's First Union. The robbery was done in twelve minutes, leaving enough time to get back on site without being missed by the foreman.

The authorities reviewed the surveillance cameras endlessly and through interviews pieced together most of the events.

A large white man with sunglasses and yellow hardhat pulled low shadowing his face entered the bank with a check in his hand and a deposit slip. He kept his head down, but no one thought anything of it. He was looking at the paperwork he held. His appearance was like any of the men from the office park that was being built. He had an untucked no. 9 Red Sox jersey hanging loose, but upon reflection, it did hint at something tucked in the waistband in the front of his pants. It bulged enough to look like a pistol even on camera.

At the teller window he had taken a deep breath and handed the check and deposit slip to the young teller as she was halfway through saying, "May I help you?" As she read what he wrote on the deposit slip, her ringlets of dirty blonde hair bounced a little as she nervously glanced at her bank manager sitting at the desk.

The man in the yellow hardhat just shook his head, and the teller got the message not to call anyone over. The man was empty-handed but hiked up his pants to give emphasis to the object shoved in his waistband, then nodded toward the note, which read, "Here is a check. I have no ID and it is in everyone's best interest if you don't ask for any. Just cash the check."

 And the check was oddly made out for $9,999.99 as if staying under $10,000 limited additional authorizations or penalties, or was just a misappropriated tribute to Ted Williams.

"Do you want to cash this as all large bills, sir?" The teller was confused and scared. She wasn't sure if she was being robbed, but it felt that way. But she didn't want to be embarrassed by erroneously hitting the foot switch for the silent alarm.

He nodded yes and she counted out ninety-nine, one hundred dollar bills, and then as she was counting out the ninety-nine dollars in twenties, tens, and ones, her left cheek twitched, pulling at the corner of her mouth in an uncontrolled tick.

"I can't do this. Please," she whispered, "I have to ask you for identification or call over the bank manager." She had been so pleasant and calm until this point, but now her eyes were welling up and her voice had gone an octave or two closer toward hysteria.

He tried to tell her, "Forget it, not a problem, keep the $99.99," without speaking, by shaking his head vigorously. No, she should calm down. No, no, no she shouldn't cry. Stop.

"I'm going to be fired," she sobbed, and the manager, a middle-aged woman with uncomfortable shoes, started to walk over to see what the problem was. The robber realized that it was time to leave.

He turned around and kept his head low, walking a few steps at first then bolting like a base runner stealing home. The bank guard near the door was talking with a customer about town politics and didn't focus on the commotion before the man in the yellow hat beat the play and shoved the guard into the pamphlet rack, scattering him and mortgage information all over the tile floor.

In the parking lot, witnesses said that they saw him drop something and the police retrieved it. But it was not a gun that fell from his waistband. It was a metal cast alligator that was later identified as being a custom kickstand from a Harley Davidson motorcycle.

The police responded to the construction site, where a twelve-year veteran of the Wilmington Police Department made a life or death split-second decision to protect himself and fellow officers as he saw a man wearing a yellow hardhat and a no. 9 Red Sox jersey, standing in the unframed window with an apparent weapon; and there was the pop, pop, pop. The officer pulled the trigger of his own 9mm almost before having it fully extended. One shot and the man in the window fell backward. It was over except for the continued, pop, pop, pop of the distant nail guns. In the aftermath, the only thing that was certain was that Mark O'Hearn lay dead holding only a screw gun and Cheryl O'Hearn was now a widow with a large claim against the city.

Led was glad to have a case where he could create some challenges, something to wrap his brain around, to keep him from anticipating his date with Callie. Was she a woman with an edge or was he just hoping? Their brief interaction was starting to feel like something he had observed but hadn't participated in.

With only a cell phone number and post office box, he'd have to be creative and go straight to the source and call Paul O'Hearn to find out where he was living. Easy enough, but first he needed to prepare, set up a cover story, something simple but with enough depth that he could work it.

Flower delivery not to O'Hearn, exactly, but to whomever O'Hearn wanted them sent. Find out who his lady friend was, and then show up with the flowers and ask her all about O'Hearn. Let her gush about him.

Someone gushing is good for a PI.

At the Stop & Shop, Led asked the florist if he could use the phone. He was told no, which wasn't exactly what he expected.

"I used it the other day," he protested to the man in the green apron, who acted like his job was part of some work release program.

"I wasn't working then. That's for store use." He motioned to the phone clipped to Led's belt: "Don't you have a cell phone?"

"Dead battery. I'll only be a minute."

"I can't. You'll have to ask the manager."

"Where is he?"

97

"She. She's on break."

"No problem, maybe you can help me. I need to get an arrangement of crystal lilies."

"Crystal lilies? I never heard of them." The clerk motioned to the display cooler. "What do they look like?"

"Beats me," Led shrugged, and he wasn't lying since he had just made up the name. "My wife told me to pick up a bouquet of them, for her mom in the hospital. They're her mother's favorite."

"We don't have anything called crystal lilies."

"I see that. So if I could make a quick call, I'll find what to get instead."

"Fine," the clerk sighed, handing the phone over. "But be quick."

It had been a pretext, but for a moment it made Led think about his ex-wife. He wondered what she'd think if she knew he was pretending he was still married. Led turned his back to the clerk and dialed Paul O'Hearn.

It was a lot of effort to go through just so O'Hearn's cell phone would display the Stop & Shop number. But Led was thorough when he could afford to be.

"Hello?"

"Paul O'Hearn, please."

"Who is this?"

"This is Chris at the Stop & Shop florist," Led said. "I'm calling to find out where you want the flowers delivered."

"What flowers?"

"The prize flowers."

"Who is this?" O'Hearn asked curtly.

"I apologize. I thought someone already called to let you know your name was drawn. That you won a celebration bouquet."

"I don't need flowers. Thanks."

"Hey—" Led said, sensing O'Hearn was about to hang up. "They're free. You don't have to take them. Anyone you want me to send them to? No sense wasting them."

"How did you get this number?"

The florist walked past Led toward a display of mylar balloons.

"I'm looking at an entry card. It says Paul O'Hearn, with this telephone number."

"I didn't fill out any card."

"Maybe someone filled it out for you? Trying to win the trip to Orlando? The flowers are the runner-up prize. Still nice, though. Your wife perhaps?"

"Mom," O'Hearn said. "Mom probably put my name down."

"Mom. Okay," Led conceded. He had hoped to find where O'Hearn's girlfriend was living, but his mother would be a good place to start. He could see the clerk trying to listen in on his conversation; by his expression Led knew he was perturbed the call was taking so long. "So do we want to send Mom the flowers?"

"They're free? Sure. Send them over to 2B off of Bunker Hill Street."

"Can I put anything on the card?"

"Nah, just send them over."

"They'll be delivered this afternoon. Will someone be there to accept them?"

"Yeah. She don't go nowhere...put, 'To Mom, Love Paulie.'"

"You got it. And thank you for shopping Stop & Shop."

"Wha—? Yeah...sure. No problem."

Led hung up the phone and slid it over to the clerk at his small podium. He waited, watching the phone.

"So do you know what you want now?" the clerk asked.

"I guess I'll take that small vase arrangement with the daisies, the pink tulips and—" The phone rang. "Go ahead and get that."

"Stop & Shop Florist Department," the clerk answered. "May I help you?" He then shook his head. "They hung up," he said.

Good, Led thought.

On the box containing the vase, he scribbled the address with the clerk's marker. He picked up pamphlets for the Everyday Floral Celebrations, the Balloon Bouquets, and Special Occasions.

Walking to his vehicle he dumped out most of the water from the vase.

The call from the florist had distracted Paul.

He was trying to think, if Tuttle wouldn't agree to spread the wealth, then he'd need more leverage. He realized he should have thought it out better first. Tuttle could too easily say it had only been a mistake. Lower the claim. Fire Paul.

Maybe Paul's information wasn't right…he got it from Cheryl's friend. Women talking. He didn't know for sure that Mr. Tuttle had put in a bogus claim. Mr. Tuttle hadn't denied it, but then again maybe his name wasn't on the paperwork…he could claim it was a clerical error. Paul had no proof, and now he'd probably lost his job. He could not afford to lose this job yet.

He had to get the money from Tuttle or at least keep his job.

He might be behind the count, but he wasn't out yet. His softball teammates called him "Paulie Hustle" because he ran the bases with everything he had, never doubting he'd make it safe, never fearing an injury from sliding. There was time to think about the what-ifs when you were brushing the dirt from your shirt.

He didn't have his tools. They were all at the club where he'd been doing a side job. It would have been a lot easier if Cheryl hadn't been such a pain in his ass about him leaving them in her car trunk. She didn't like the rattling sound they made, said it made her think something was wrong with the car.

He reached under the bed and pulled out a plastic cosmetics case that Cheryl kept for household projects. From inside he grabbed a utility knife and two screwdrivers, a Phillips and a flat-head, and a hammer, hardly more than a tack hammer, useless for anything more than putting up pictures or curtain rods.

Still, he might need it.

He went out to the car and tossed the handful of tools onto the front seat, and then headed over to the warehouse. Better to do it now, before they thought to take his name off the access list and cancel his key card.

He went to the unguarded storage bay. Wooden pallets and crates were stacked tightly, but the shipping tags indicated that what he was looking for was wrapped in industrial plastic wrap just inside the door. He loosened some of the drywall screws holding the supportive pieces in place. He cut the wrap, the vinyl bands holding the contents to the pallet snapping beneath his utility knife.

He wouldn't be able to take the whole machine by himself; it was too big. He selected two of the smallest console units and carried them one at a time, and loaded them into Cheryl's car. Only one fit in the trunk. He threw a sweatshirt over it. The other unit he carried out and put in the backseat. He wrapped a seatbelt around it to prevent it from pitching forward and ripping the upholstery. Cheryl would kill him if he messed up her car.

He had to put these things someplace. They were too big to leave in the car. Cheryl would never allow it anyway. Better to put them somewhere else before he picked her up.

The only place close enough was his mom's.

Led headed up and over the famous Bunker Hill where a granite monolith had been erected to commemorate the spirit of a people unafraid of running counter to their neighbors or the law. The monument cast its shadow of history onto the Charlestown housing projects, brick tenement buildings with flat roofs where that tradition of rebellion lived on, albeit maybe a little misdirected.

There were no ornamental details to pretty up the fact that this was public housing. This was the Boston Housing Authority's largest project, mostly white, Irish Catholic families. And though the government may have owned the buildings, the residents controlled the community, nostalgic for an era of relatively respectable crimes like theft and extortion. Before the whacked-out drug fiends with their music videos took the romance out of it.

He parked and set up a covert camera hidden in a pen that would broadcast back to the recorder in the car. Tiny wires were untangled, fresh batteries installed. He retrieved the flowers from the floorboard, carried them into the green stairwell of the building, and knocked on the door for B2.

"Yeah?" someone hollered from within.

"Flower delivery."

"Flowers?"

A heavyset woman with frizzy gray hair opened the door as far as the security chain allowed. The smell of stale and fresh cigarette smoke rushed into the hallway.

"They for here?" she asked. "For who?"

"It should be on the card," he said, reaching into the middle of the bouquet, but not finding it. He flipped through the pamphlets and the sales flyer looking for it. "I don't know what's going on today...I lost my cell phone this morning; I think I might have dropped it going to the truck. Then I dropped half the orders I was supposed to be delivering. The way I've been dropping things, I'm sorry. It's been a bad day."

The woman laughed like a sea lion, deep and guttural.

Then, from the brochures, Led produced a small card.

"Paulie? No shit? What did he do now that he's sending me flowers?" She closed the door for a moment to undo the security chain, before opening it only slightly to invite Led in.

He had to turn sideways to enter. He set the flowers on a Formica table with fake wood grain next to a half-full glass ashtray, a cigarette still burning there.

"My dad worked on the rehab of these buildings," he said. "They came out nice."

"What's his trade?"

"Carpenter, with the Local."

"My son Paulie worked on these too. He's an electrician. But he's only doing some side work now and then."

"I wonder if they ever worked together...."

Led was establishing what he called *temporary commonality*—bonds that occur among people all the time. It was like musical chairs when the music stops and two people sit in the same seat, or when two people share the experience of watching an arbitrary event like a sausage vendor trying to right his cart after being backed into by a tour bus. At that moment they may speak and share information about family, employment, the benefits to society of good insurance coverage because you just never know.

"They're nice flowers. Your husband must have been just thinking of you."

"Paulie is my son."

"Well, that's a nice thing to do. Not many guys send their mother flowers."

"They *are* nice flowers." She smelled them, picked them up, and walked over to the sink, moving a pan and a few plates to the countertop in order to fit the vase under the faucet. "Paulie's a nice boy most of the time."

"Does he live near you?"

"He's just over in Somerville."

"Oh yeah? Whereabouts? I deliver over there all the time."

"I don't know. Never been to his place." She said it and he believed her. It didn't look like she had been out of the apartment much except to buy cigarettes and Twinkies.

"Does he come by to visit much?"

"Not as much as I like, but like I said, he's a good boy. He comes and checks on me."

Led would need her number so he could call later to determine if O'Hearn had stopped by.

"Can I use your phone to call the store? I'm hoping someone found my cell phone."

"I just have a cell phone too." She set the flowers down and walked over to the couch. On the magazines, next to a remote and a pack of Virginia Slims, was a small flip-phone. It smelled like the acidic breath of a dog, if the dog drank black coffee and chain-smoked. He opened the phone and dialed. Lifting the phone to his ear, he tried not to be too conspicuous in holding it several inches from his face. It made him sneeze.

"Gesundheit!" she said.

"Do you have a tissue?"

"Just some toilet paper in there."

Led walked into the first door to the right, the bathroom, dark except for the yellow hue that shone through a ripped shade that was pulled down over the small window. The toilet paper roller was mounted below the window but was empty. There was a half-roll of paper on the back of the toilet. He unrolled several squares and blew his nose as the woman stood just at the door. Not seeing a trashcan, he put the tissue in his pocket.

"Thank you," he said. "They had me move some pallets of peonies this morning. I think I might have lost my phone when I was lifting them from the pallet. It'll be a quick call."

"It don't make a difference. I got something like fifteen hundred minutes a month on that thing. Never use 'em. Nobody I want to talk to for fifteen hundred minutes."

Led dialed his own number and listened to his voicemail greeting.

O'Hearn's mother sat on the far end of the couch that was perpendicular to the fifty-two-inch television. She sat so that she was sitting on her bare right foot pulled up under her. The bottom of her foot was black except for the instep. She picked up the remote and turned down the volume on the talk show she'd been watching with several women sitting around a table. She lit up a cigarette.

"Ed," Led said, leaving the message to himself. "This is Steve. I'm just checking in. I was hoping you found my phone. I just made the delivery over on Bunker Hill, now I'm heading over to Medford Street."

He had her cell phone number now and would be able to call her back later to see if O'Hearn was around.

"Thanks for the phone," he said. "And enjoy the flowers. I left you with some information about our arrangements and gift baskets in case you want to send flowers."

"Not unless someone dies," she cackled. "Hope you find your phone."

As he walked to the door, in walked a big man in a pink golf shirt and a pair of green chinos. He had a round face and reddish brown hair. His left hand was bandaged.

It was Paul O'Hearn.

Led appraised his situation. He was fine. His groundwork was good; he was the flower delivery guy.

The old woman on the couch blew out smoke, squinted. "Paulie," she said. "I didn't know you were coming."

"I'm not staying. I got to leave off a few things. Who's this?" O'Hearn asked. He puffed out his chest a little and straightened his shoulders as he said it, making himself even bigger.

"He's the delivery man. You sent me flowers?"

"Yeah. Sure." It seemed that he was going to take credit for the gesture but quickly decided against it. "I won them, figured I'd send them to you."

"I'm impressed. I figured you'd send them to Cheryl."

"Guess I could have."

"Well," Led said, hoping to get an address, "I could take an order for another bouquet now and get them delivered later today."

"What, do you work on commission?" O'Hearn asked, sounding annoyed.

"No, I work by the hour. And not much an hour I might add. Know anybody hiring?" He was grasping for some temporary commonality but wasn't making the connection.

O'Hearn said no, stood silent, staring at him.

"Well, they're nice flowers," Led said, moving for the door. "Enjoy." It was best not to push it too hard. Above all else keep it natural, stay with the flow. And right now it didn't feel like it was flowing.

"Wait—" O'Hearn said.

Led stopped but kept his hand on the doorknob.

"Here you go." O'Hearn pulled a money clip from his front pocket and peeled off a twenty dollar bill. A small shamrock tattoo showed itself from under the sleeve of his golf shirt.

"Thank you very much," Led said, taking the bill without looking at it. He smiled as he did a quick study of O'Hearn's face. A large, round head, with fair skin and a few freckles, his features were symmetrical but his lips were small in proportion to his head, with its low, straight-across hairline parted to the right. Led didn't plan on ever being this close to him again; he needed to be sure he could identify the man even through the grainy magnification of a video camera's zoom lens. He then waved to the older woman and left, pulling the door closed behind him.

He could hear someone putting the chain back in the lock behind him.

Led walked to his car and looked around for any vehicle that might have just arrived. It was a large parking area...he couldn't be sure, but he didn't remember seeing the silver Chrysler 3000 before. He climbed into the back of his jeep and waited.

TWELVE

Paul O'Hearn didn't think about his brother too much unless reminded in unexpected moments when the apex of sensation sparked the gunpowder of memory. He had been thinking only about Mr. Tuttle all morning, but this day the heat off the black top and the sounds of the traffic resurrected the ghost of his potential and the evaporated days of his youth.

Today, Paul caught the memory of himself and his brother riding on the old car hood as his dad dragged it behind his motorcycle around the parking lot, gravel and sparks flying as they laughed, feeling the heat of friction where they had to sit on their feet to keep from burning their bottoms. He and his brother were going to be famous and rich without ever having given any serious consideration to the means. Together they were the O'Hearn boys, proud of their rough side and imagining themselves the heirs to their father's reputation: anything, anytime.

His father, Bull O'Hearn, had died at the motorcycle races in '79. He was not a racer; he had been a spectator and tried to jump over three picnic tables with his blue smoke Harley street bike. The kickstand caught and flipped him fatally into a tree.

Mom said his dad was reckless and didn't talk about him much after he died, but to his two pre-teenage sons he was a hero who had gone out of this world with glory, not as some old man. He was young, a fighter, and an adrenaline-seeking pioneer before there were X-Games or extreme sports with elbow pads and sponsors.

His father would have appreciated the simplicity of his plan and the effort of shaking up the complacent and taking the risk.

Paul walked out to the Chrysler and lifted out of the backseat one of the units, struggling with one good hand.

"Ma!" he said, trying to open the door, straining as he held the thing balanced on one lifted knee.

"What is this," she asked, holding the door for him. "A computer?"

"No just some stuff for work. I need to leave these here for a day or two. I'll move it by next week."

"Put it in the backroom," she said, referring to his old bedroom. "Do you want anything to eat?"

His old waterbed was still sitting on a dark pine pedestal, with sideboards and a mirrored headboard. The bed held several large storage boxes that were opened and sitting in different directions on the unstable surface of the bed. By the wall was an old elliptical trainer that was being used to hold a green hooded sweatshirt. A stack of old magazines sat by the closet, and the chipped laminated white dresser, where he once burnt in his name with a lighter, was now covered with clothes and an old chrome toaster.

He set it down and picked up a large box of his old clothes, classic T-shirts, Aerosmith and J.Geils Band. He had promised them to Cheryl's boys.

"I can't stay. I have some things to do." The television was so loud he had to speak in his pub voice to be heard from down the hallway. "I got one more to bring in, I'll be right back."

He carried the box of clothes out to the car, slid it onto the backseat and went to the trunk.

The second unit sat deep in the trunk of the car and was too heavy for him to lift straight up and out with only one good hand. He put his right foot inside the trunk to get enough leverage, lifting it out and balancing it on one edge until he could get both feet on the ground and grab a hold of it enough to carry.

His mother opened the door for him as he neared her apartment. "Can I get you a beer?"

"Ma, I can't. I'll come by tomorrow and grab some lunch with you."

"You have your hand with the bandage."

"It's real stiff still, but what are you going to do." He shut the bedroom door at the end of the hall and walked back to his mother. "Thanks," he said, stopping to kiss her on the forehead as he left.

Now he was ready to call Tuttle. Once in the car, he took a deep breath, as if about to jump, and then he dialed.

Stacey answered. She seemed concerned for him but he was too distracted to talk to her. She put him on hold. Tuttle made him wait for what seemed forever, probably for no good reason.

Finally he picked up. "Paul, what can I do for you?"

"I'm calling to make you another offer. I thought about it. I really hadn't taken everything into consideration."

"And what is your reconsideration?"

There it was. He had Tuttle's attention. "One hundred and fifty thousand."

"Paul, you're embarrassing yourself. You heard a rumor about a mistake."

"Yeah, I thought about that. That you might be slick enough to convince them you were mistaken. So I took the new one."

"You *what?*"

"I took the new one."

"You couldn't have possibly taken it."

"Right. I didn't take the whole body scanner; I took just enough of it to make my point. I have the power supply and the imaging unit. You can get them back for one hundred and fifty thousand dollars."

"If it's stolen, I'll report it that way."

"I thought about that, too. And I guess you could do that, but I don't think you will. You would have to explain a lot. If it came down to your word against mine, yours would clearly have more weight, but I don't think that kind of publicity would be so good for the CEO of a company about to go public. It would cost you a lot more than one hundred and fifty thousand."

"Now, now, Paul. What are you going to do with it? Let everything settle down and come back to work, and I'll give you a raise. I'll give you another couple of shares."

"You've been talking about an IPO for a year and a half."

"Timing is important. This little misunderstanding is just a distraction."

"The one-fifty. That's a discounted rate for early payment. It will only go up if you want to dick me around."

"Let me talk to some people. I don't have access to that kind of cash."

"Take it out of the company."

"It's not that easy. Give me a while and I'll see what I can do."

"Two days. I'll give you two days. I'll call you and tell you how to get me the money." Paul started thinking how easy this was all going. Be a little creative, be like The Bull, and soon enough he, too, would be driving around in a big car.

Hell, he might even end up with Tuttle's.

THIRTEEN

Led had been close enough to count O'Hearn's freckles; he now followed from a discreet distance. As O'Hearn came to a stop in the left lane, waiting to make a turn off Route 60, Led couldn't stop directly behind him, so he drove past and watched in his rearview mirror.

With a break in the oncoming traffic O'Hearn turned onto a side street between a pizza parlor and an auto supply store.

Turning around at the next intersection, Led turned right onto the side street. This was a tree-lined residential neighborhood with sidewalks and front lawns, all tucked away behind the façade of fast food joints, liquor stores, beauty shops, and accountants that lined the strip on Route 60, like a Hollywood back lot where cast and crew brushed their teeth and wrote in their diaries.

As Led started up the street he observed O'Hearn walking on the sidewalk and then up the brick steps of a building on the corner. The building had white clapboards and a pitched, shingled roof, looking much like most of the homes on the street except for the commercial grade, aluminum-framed glass door and the small, protruding sign that read "Harbour Club."

O'Hearn used his own keys to unlock the door. Lights went on a moment later.

Led maintained surveillance.

Small clubs like this were common in the area. Some were affiliated with national organizations like the Knights of Columbus, the Elks or the Masons; some had ethnic ties, like the Italian-American or Polish-American clubs; a few were just neighborhood clubs with no pretense to anything more than a place for a man to drink cheap beer, smoke while he ate, if he were inclined, and watch sports with his drinking buddies. It wasn't that women were banned from the clubs; they just weren't typically encouraged to attend.

Led knew the reason. Men spent most of their time either trying to get a woman or lose a woman. In the game of the sexes, a place like the Harbour Club was like a locker room where men went at halftime to get away from the other team and take a breather.

He sat and waited. Quite a few cars were parked going up the slight hill, but he stood out by sitting in the driver's seat for more than a few minutes; someone was bound to look out a window eventually and wonder what he was doing.

If he got in the backseat it would take too long to get back up front to follow when O'Hearn exited. So he slid over to the passenger seat instead. Anyone walking by wouldn't wonder what he was doing. He had created a nonverbal answer: he was waiting for the driver. He was not an unanswered question, so he was not a threat. He worked on his laptop, keeping his peripheral vision on the Harbour Club.

Led waited. He clicked away on the laptop, searching for information on Paul O'Hearn. In Boston alone, the name was too common. He used the social security number to start, to get some addresses linked to it, then searched just by the addresses to see who lived where, what their pasts looked like, the usual.

Culling information was overrated. Clients expected that through the Internet he could get criminal, credit, school transcripts, and employment information on anyone with just a few keystrokes. But it all went back to that adage: garbage in, garbage out. There was more wrong than right information out there. He needed at least three points to cross-reference. Name and date of birth were not enough, but coupled with an address linked to the social security number they'd ensure he was looking at the right Paul O'Hearn.

As a young mother passed, she glanced his way and gave a faint smile. In her stroller was a toddler passed out taking an afternoon nap, his curly hair sweaty and matted to his head. His mouth was open, his arms and legs flopping at his sides in complete repose.

"Not a care in the world," Led said. "I'm jealous."

"When he finally goes down," she said, "he goes down hard."

"I'm the same way," Led said. "He's a cute little guy."

"Thank you," the mother smiled and continued to push the stroller up the street.

He looked back down at the computer in his lap. Not much on O'Hearn. It had been six years since he had a registered vehicle.

A Google search was more informative. Paul O'Hearn, Charlestown, Massachusetts, found that O'Hearn had been interviewed in 2004 for an article about Red Sox fans. Police shot and killed O'Hearn's brother in 2002, the article said, while he was working a construction job. The police had chased an armed robbery suspect wearing jeans and a Red Sox shirt. The suspect ran into the area of construction just as Paul O'Hearn's brother, Mark, came out of the building to see what was going on. He, too, had been wearing jeans and a Boston Red Sox shirt. But it was October, and the Sox were battling the Yankees for the American League title--half of Boston was wearing Red Sox shirts. Mark, however, was carrying a screw gun. He was shot once, between the O and the X. The article had a picture of Paul O'Hearn holding up the Red Sox shirt with the bullet hole.

The Sox finally won a World Series in 2004. O'Hearn mourned that his brother did not live to see it, but felt that Mark somehow knew. According to the article, O'Hearn put a World Series pennant on his brother's grave.

Interesting, but nothing that was going to help determine what O'Hearn's activities would be, other than maybe go to a ballgame.

Led checked the registration on the Chrysler 3000. It went to Cheryl O'Hearn, in Somerville, date of birth 4/19/79. O'Hearn wasn't supposed to be married...maybe it was his sister-in-law. O'Hearn's mother had mentioned sending the flowers to a Cheryl. At the time Led thought it was his girlfriend, but maybe not. She was the right age. Twenty-six. O'Hearn could be using her vehicle. All speculation, but until proven incorrect, he would keep it as the most likely possibility.

He wrote down her address as indicated on the registration.

A gray Chevy Cavalier pulled in beside the building. Though partially blocked from view, he could see that the driver, an old white guy, was doing something at the dumpster. And now he was walking over to Led's jeep. His hair was gray with a few black strands, thinning on the top but slicked straight back to maximize the volume. His posture was a little slumped at the shoulders but he was still a big man and carried himself with the confidence of age if not the vigor of youth. He had a bit of a gut pushing tightly at the front of his short-sleeved, light blue dress shirt.

Which would be more natural, Led contemplated, to ignore the old man as if he didn't exist or just say hello? Sometimes such decisions were made at the last possible second, when time for appraisal had elapsed.

"How ya doin'," Led said, being friendly but not really inviting conversation.

"It's a very nice day."

The man stopped walking and put his large hand on the door of Led's car. He leaned in a little as he looked up at the blue sky, slightly out of breath.

"You with the Harbour Club?" the man asked.

"Not really. I'm just waiting for someone to show up. You?"

"Nah. I was just going to tell you some kids were trying to break in there over the weekend. Early Sunday morning, six o'clock. They were only fourteen or fifteen years old, so I knew they weren't supposed to be there. Trying the door, looking in the windows. They ran off when they saw me. Since my wife died, I get up early and try to find something to do. Go for a walk, take in the world..."

Led continued to look past the old man toward the social club, but there was nothing to see. O'Hearn was inside but there was no sign of him. If he did come out, it was going to be hard to quickly get rid of the old man, but for now he was helping pass the time, and his standing there talking provided good cover for anyone wondering what Led was doing in the neighborhood.

"The morning is a whole different world. The things I see in the morning...you see everything if you get up early. Ever since my wife died I can't sleep, so I get up. Married fifty-one years, seven kids. All of them redheads like my wife."

"Get to see much of them?"

"I got one in Maine. One was just over in Iraq. He was over there, nine months. I'm glad he's back. He's no spring chicken, ya know? He's forty-eight. He went over there just before Christmas."

"You must have worried the whole time."

"Absolutely."

They both gazed in the direction of the building.

Many times it was hard to find someone to talk with, and then occasionally he ran into someone like this man in his gray Chevy Cavalier, driving around like a morning ghost, almost unseen. Led let him talk. The man seemed pleased to have found someone on his time schedule.

"The thing I saw last winter was two cars in front of me, and one was tailgating the other till it pulled over. Then the guy jumped out and ran up to the other car and was pulling on the door handle. Thank goodness she had locked the door, you know. I pulled up and asked if everything was all right. He said, 'I just want to talk to her.' I said, 'She don't want to talk to you, from what I can see. Now, I called the cops, so go on.' He left and I walked up and tapped on the glass and said 'Miss, the police are coming, you can get out of your car now if you want.' She said, 'I can't. I wet myself.' She was that scared of that guy. I've seen everything around here."

"I'm sure you have," Led said, realizing that he and the man made many of the same social observations, the kind that most never did.

The man lifted his hand and gave two taps to the car door. "I'll let you be. I talked your ear off enough. Enjoy your day."

He had to have been in his seventies, but he seemed pretty sharp mentally. It was only socially he'd been shelved, like a worn-out part, having served his family and employers into high mileage.

Led was sympathetic toward the old man, but didn't think he was any reflection of where he himself would be years from now. Then again, the old-timer might have had the same view of himself forty years earlier.

Perkins drove but preferred to ride. It gave him more freedom to observe without the distractions of staying on the road. With Martinez locked up, he had no choice and rented a gold Lexus and headed out alone to square things away with Uncle Charlie. Not only did Perkins have to go collect some past due wagers, he also had to distribute and pick up from regulars: a chick's job, but Uncle Charlie was pissed that one of his girls, a numbers runner, had been beat up. Normally he would have sent Perkins and Martinez out to settle the score and teach some manners. However, this time it had been Martinez who slapped her around. Graciously, Uncle Charlie was going to overlook the inconvenience, but expected Perkins to fill in until Fatima calmed down and came back again. What was he going to say? No? But with the Red Sox hosting a home series against the Yankees it was a busy time for every sports book in town, when the girls would be the busiest. He couldn't protest. Uncle Charlie had an ear for bullshit, probably from so many years of hearing every excuse on why someone couldn't pay on a lost bet.

Uncle Charlie had picked up on something with Mr. Richard Tuttle, nothing definitive, but he wanted to have Perkins check into it, while running some numbers and doing his regular collections, of course. Perkins didn't get stressed, it was not a reflex to his constitution, but he did focus more, and now he had a lot to focus on.

His eyes had not fully adjusted to the dim lighting of the long, deep bar. With only its one window in the front by the door the back was mostly lit by the television on the wall.

"Here you go." Perkins handed an envelope of cash to the bartender. The midday crowd was only a handful of crusty old-timers nursing beers.

"Where's Fatima? Thought she'd be in today," the bartender said, handing the list of new bets he had taken down.

"She'll be around. She took a few days to visit her mother." Perkins grinned to move the conversation along.

"Man, that rack is perfect." The bartender said wistfully as if he were staring at Fatima's chest at that very moment.

"And I think they are real." Perkins added.

"Like it matters," the bartender said. "They are gorgeous whether by God or DuPont."

By early afternoon he had already made three stops on Fatima's list and was now shifting to one of his own jobs. The move was like a dance, step, grab, slam...1, 2, 3 and he bounced the man's head against the side of the produce truck like a tossed cantaloupe. The man turned around, stunned; his nose flowed red. With watery eyes and his right arm raised across his face, both as a defensive stance and also to use the crux of his arm to apply pressure to his nose.

"Alright, please. I have the money." And then jittery and uncoordinated by the pain of his face the man used his left hand to pull his wallet out of his right back pocket.

Perkins watched the contortions as the man tried to keep his right arm on his nose while opening his wallet with only one hand. With dissipated patience Perkins snatched the black leather wallet, took out the cash, counting out quickly, $2,873.

"Wait, I don't owe that much."

"You do now." Perkins tossed the wallet on the ground.

Despite his profession, Perkins considered himself a people person. He liked being around them. Felt that generally he was liked by most he met, if it wasn't work related. The clients of his paintball facility days later would call to thank him for the good time they had. But he could never figure why there was a tendency by so many to try to avoid paying up. It wasn't that he felt sorry for them, he felt bored with the predictability of watching them squirm, expecting compassion when they bet money they didn't have. Where his partner Martinez relished the violence, looking forward to the next smacking, Perkins did it mechanically with less thought than a politician would give to shaking hands. As a small business owner himself, he saw his role as part of the service. It kept Uncle Charlie in business so he could pay his obligations and be there for the next degenerate to place a bet on the next race, fight or game.

If he had the time he would have sat back and watched Tuttle and monitored what he was up to, get a feel for the situation before walking in, but he had to make up for some time. He loved Martinez like a brother, but this was a pain in the ass. To keep things moving, he thought it might be good to talk to Tuttle directly, see what he was forgetting to tell Uncle Charlie.

He asked to see Richard Tuttle, but the receptionist had said she was sorry but he was in a meeting. She didn't have time to run interference as he walked past her down the hall.

Tuttle held a golf putter and was bent over an artificial green in the corner of his office. He straightened and turned around as he retrieved a ball.

The receptionist stood in the hallway and said, "I'm sorry, Mr. Tuttle." And she threw up her hands and shrugged her shoulders in a gesture of *what was I supposed to do?* "I told him you were busy but he walked right past me."

"Yes, well, I just finished up with a conference call," Tuttle said. "How may I help you?"

Perkins motioned to the receptionist and said to Tuttle, "I need to talk to you in private."

"I'm sorry. Do I know you?" Tuttle said icily, not trying to hide his indignation with this man's presumed familiarity with him.

"We have the same uncle," Perkins said, knowing the effect it would have.

Tuttle's attitude instantly became soft-serve. "Stacey, will you excuse us?"

The receptionist pulled the door closed but it was a few moments of standing in the office waiting before she was heard walking down the hall. Then Perkins spoke, "One of your vehicles was in an accident."

Tuttle walked around behind his desk, seeming to relax more now that there was an object between them. "Yes, it was. I spoke with Uncle Charlie about it earlier."

"Right. Right. That was why he sent me out to…to help out."

"I don't understand. Are you a mechanic?" Tuttle asked and he glanced at Perkins' hands.

"No, but I fix things," Perkins said and watched for Tuttle to have his *aha* moment and understand what was going on. "Uncle Charlie got the impression that something wasn't working right."

"I don't understand why he would have thought that."

"He is a careful man. When you deal with gamblers you don't like to take chances."

"We've had the unit get banged up before."

"At this point, more people are looking into your business," Perkins said, thinking that without Uncle Charlie this guy couldn't grow mold on bread, never mind grow a company.

"I see," Tuttle said. He was a calm character; there was no denying it. But Perkins could see it in his eyes that look of trying to bargain. Tuttle was trying to hold back something, but he wasn't sure what Perkins already knew. Then he said, "There is a little problem that could be fixed." There it was.

Tuttle continued. "The driver of the unit has taken some of the equipment and he is trying to sell it back to me."

"What did you tell him?"

"I told him no. I don't barter with thieves," he said with an air of self-righteousness. "Besides, we will be reimbursed by insurance."

It made sense to Perkins. It didn't seem like a big deal; still if Uncle Charlie had asked him to look into the situation and handle it, he would. "Where do I find your driver?"

"What? What for?" Tuttle lost a little of his composure when he realized that this matter was not over.

"I'll see if we can't get this straightened out."

"But the insurance money?"

"Guess that will be like a bonus. Uncle Charlie wouldn't want me leaving knowing that someone stole something that belonged to him."

"I see," said Tuttle. "I thought the same thing, so I already have someone working on this situation." He slid Led's business card across the desk.

Perkins picked it up, glanced at it, and without asking put it in the pocket of his sports coat. "Then we should be able to get it resolved quickly." Perkins was hopeful because he had a lot of stops and desired to be back at the paintball range at least by Sunday to see his gamers at the awards ceremony.

"Stacey out front can give you the driver's information. His name is Paul O'Hearn. I don't know if we have a current address for him."

"I'll start with whatever you have and make it work." Perkins stood and walked out of the office; with a stiff shoulder he was aware that it was the second time in a day that he had turned his back on someone holding a golf club.

Two hours had passed and the most that had happened was a kid on a razor scooter had tried to jump a curb farther down the street. He fell and got road rash pretty good on his knees and elbows. The kid was maybe twelve years old and expelled a combination of swears and tears as he lay on the sidewalk until he realized he was alone and fine except for some bloody scrapes. When no one came to check on him he stopped crying and picked up his scooter. He limped a little at first but got back on it and disappeared down a side street.

When Paul O'Hearn left the building two hours and forty-seven minutes after arriving he was empty handed except for a fistful of keys. He turned the deadbolt on the door and walked up the street to the Chrysler.

Led followed him out of the neighborhood but lost sight of him at the rotary, as the Honda Accord in front of him stopped instead of slowly merging. "What are you doing?" Led shouted. "Waiting on a written invitation? Move it!"

Led sped down Route 1A as fast as he could in the rush hour traffic. He didn't catch up to O'Hearn, so after a few miles of driving in a manner more befitting a racetrack or video game, he drove over to Cheryl O'Hearn's home. Her vehicle wasn't there. He looked at his watch. It was ten minutes before five. He was running late. He broke surveillance, and then several speed limits.

FOURTEEN

Callie's home was a grand old Victorian that had been converted into two condos. She owned the left-side unit. The hardwood floors were all refinished to a basketball court shine, with rugs scattered about the different rooms. The place was nicely decorated in earth tones. The first thing Led noticed were the bookshelves everywhere, filled with hardcover novels mixed in with reference books, old paperbacks from college lit classes commingling with romance novels and old medical textbooks.

She was waiting for him, ready to go, needing only to shut off the radio and grab a sweater from the arm of the couch. They walked to the jeep and he opened the door for her. Realizing his hands were a little sweaty, he wiped his palms on his pants as he walked around the car. It was a long-forgotten feeling.

He sighed a little before getting in next to her.

She sat with her left leg outstretched, her right leg bent at the knee as she leaned on her left hand—a posture engaging and immediately friendly.

"Do you mind if I turn on the air conditioning a little? I don't want to put the windows down. It's too much for my hair."

"Not at all," Led said.

He glanced over at her. Her blonde hair spilled over her bare shoulders. Layered with honeyed highlights, small strands of it streamed in the flow from the car vents.

"So this is the spy mobile? I thought it would be filled with gadgets."

"It's got two cup holders."

"Nice. You've gone all out. No ejection seat?"

"I can't say. But I don't think I'll have to use it."

The talk was awkward but not unpleasant.

"What is this?" She was pointing at that thing among the loose change in the opened ashtray. His mouth guard. The kind a boxer would wear.

He was a little embarrassed, but explained that he was supposed to wear it as he worked. Not because someone might take a swing at his face, but because he clenched his jaw often and grinded his teeth against each other; it was a bad habit he didn't even know he had until his dentist warned him about the abuse he was giving his teeth.

"You can lighten up, now," Callie laughed, sticking her finger in the side of his cheek. "You're with me. I say we go into the North End, Massimo's. What do you say?"

He glanced at her and smiled. "Whatever you like."

He had never been inside Massimo's but had followed one of his subjects there once. Pulling up in front of the restaurant on narrow Endicott Street, he gave the keys to the valet.

Inside the intimate restaurant, they followed the maitre d' past the bar and between the tables to a small one by the window. Callie wore a simple but stylish sleeveless top and a black skirt. Led noticed several men and even a few women maintain conversations but focus their gazes past their companions to glance at her passing by. She was pretty by anyone's standards. Led sat with his back to the wall, his right hand on the windowsill. It was a nice seat that looked right onto the sidewalk as people found their way home, or out for the evening. They ordered appetizers and a bottle of wine.

Led didn't really think about different ways to entertain a date. It was dinner, some drinks, and if he was lucky, sex. All of his skills at morphing into different roles at work, when it came to dating, defaulted into this one, tired and untrue. If he had been doing a pretext and assumed the persona of someone else he could have a different attitude, be more edgy or hyper, but this was his natural state of confusion when a situation was out of his control. He usually avoided any woman that would expect more of him than that. His ego had little use for it. Still, he realized that a conversation with a beautiful woman was like a shiny object to a monkey; he was drawn to it even though it would not likely serve any purpose.

Some people, as much as they would like to, just don't have a troubled past. Their upbringing is all whole milk and laughter. They grew up in some Midwestern town thinking that their parents were nice people and assumed that everyone liked corn fritters.

Callie was like that. She explained to him how the biggest social disorder to occur in her high school was when the cow walked in through an open door and scratched the gymnasium floor, jeopardizing the varsity basketball team's home court advantage in the finals. Everyone talked about it for days, but after an emergency hearing of the school board it was decided not to cancel the tournament, that the repair could be done in time. The janitor who had propped the door open wasn't fired and the dairy farmer wasn't sued. It took a four-hour meeting and a public vote to officially recognize that the cow was just being a cow and things like this are to be expected at a school where the gymnasium bordered the Hathaways' dairy farm. So after a rousing speech of goodwill by Principal Stanton the meeting shifted its effort to fixing the problem. Everyone bantered about their own preference for how to carry out the fundraising for the cost of the repairs. In the spirit of the evening, it was unanimously decided that a game of cow bingo, with the errant heifer being the game's host or hostess as it were, would be the most appropriate and the fifty-fifty proceeds would probably be enough to cover the cost.

The following Saturday on the frozen football field the cow walked about sniffing and attempting to find a blade of grass in the partial snow cover. It was all marked off into a large checkerboard with spectators lining the field to keep the cow in play as they waited for her to place a cow chip on a square; hopefully their square. And when it happened, it was the square that Callie's parents had bought, so they won half the money raised. The floor was refinished and Callie went to college with some extra money. Her dad referred to the incident in his telling as the family being shit lucky, but in her version she referred to it as her cow scholarship.

She didn't consider herself overly lucky, just happy, and she didn't ever really understand how others didn't find life as satiable or endorphic. Led only nodded without question.

Her one-year marriage to Brian ended because he had confused all business and seriousness with the opposite of being happy. She wasn't naïve. She understood people could hurt but didn't understand how they relished it.

"Where is your skeleton?" Led asked. "The shadow that follows you?"

"I've tried to find one as it always seemed that people expected me to have one," Callie said. "But it didn't feel right making one up. I figured a dark past was in my future some day, so why rush it?"

"And?"

"Nothing yet," she said. "And you?"

"I was almost in the Olympics, but I got sidetracked."

"You're an athlete?"

"I was an archer."

"That was an Olympic event?"

"Still is."

"I guess it doesn't have the coverage of the track and field," she said with an apologetic tone. "So are you still an archer?"

"Not anymore." Led shrugged, not inviting any further inquires as he said, "I lost my nerve to do it at that level."

And the intimacy was interrupted when the waiter returned.

Somehow they ended up talking about the North End of Boston, agreeing it had a different feel to it now. The hulking steel structure that had been the elevated expressway was removed only a few years ago. The institutional green of the girders that once carried traffic north and south through downtown Boston was ugly and utilitarian, hardly quaint, but it had become a part of what was the city. She was interested and the conversation was engaging but hardly a topic for seduction. She knew her date was interested in her; he laid his hand on hers on the table as they continued, but he didn't ask questions about her favorite band, or where she liked to vacation.

She found herself talking about the expressway, how it had come at a high cost even before it was in place. Warehouses, homes, and entire city squares needed to be removed to make way for the overpass's centipede legs. Fifty years later, even the elevated roadways themselves were gone.

The expressway had been like ramparts, as the North End used to butt up against its on-ramps. On the other side was the rest of the world. Now there was no physical barrier to protect the old neighborhood. The shadows were different now, too; in the North End at least, there were fewer of them. Now the traffic traveled beneath the city.

"Good or bad, everything is exposed to change," Led said.

Looking at her, he seemed to emphasize that they were, too.

They left the restaurant and stood on the sidewalk, waiting for the valet. Callie held his left hand and leaned into him as they stood in the warm night air.

"Let's not get the car. Let's take a walk. Go down to the wharf."

"Are you warm enough?" he asked.

"I'm fine." She squeezed his hand, playfully trying to throw him off balance.

They walked along the cobblestone and brick, down to Rowe's Wharf. They passed one couple; a swarthy man, maybe, with black slicked-back hair, and a thin brunette in a shimmering cocktail dress. She was having trouble walking on her toes so as not to get a heel stuck in the cobblestones.

As the couple passed, the man's musky cologne and the woman's flowery perfume wafted off, leaving behind a vaporous trail.

"God," Led exclaimed after walking what seemed to be twenty feet past the couple. "I can still smell them."

"It was a little strong." Callie laughed with a bit of a teenage girl's giggle.

"I can almost see the cologne still hanging in the air," Led said.

"Stop!" she laughed. "How would you like people making fun of us?"

"A couple like us? Come on, we're setting the standard."

A slight breeze came off the water, no longer blocked by buildings. They sat on the wall near the gazebo. The brick walkway and landscaping was new, carefully impersonating the brick warehouses it had replaced. The smell of fish and garbage, diesel and sweat were all but gone. Not that they had been pleasant smells. But they were honest smells.

Scripted weddings and anniversary parties were held here before the harbor backdrop. The wharf was where the two small cruise ships docked, the *Spirit of Boston* and the *Odyssey*. Being a Friday night, they were both out in the harbor somewhere entertaining a boatload of people, far enough away to look back at the Boston skyline. It was a dark night, but the reflection of the pleasure boats' red and green running lights decorated the water as they motored past.

Led and Callie sat and held hands. He felt that she was looking at him and found himself involuntarily smiling. He looked into her eyes. They were blue, and under the walkway lights they sparkled. They kissed, their tongues slightly swollen with the wine. He let go of her hand and ran his fingers through her hair, down to the nape of her neck. He held the back of her head. It was a warm and sweet tasting kiss that lasted, so that his mind wandered, thinking about how beautiful she was, how much different this all felt than anything he could remember in a long time.

He slowly pulled away, kissing her nose and forehead. "I could sit with you like this every night," he said.

Callie sat up a little. Her posture made him aware that he was on a first date and was talking too long-term. It wasn't what he'd meant...he was just caught up in the moment.

"It's nice being with you, on a summer night." The more he tried to qualify it the more he babbled.

"Then again, the New England winter makes for some nice snuggling by romantic fires," she added.

"Nothing romantic about chopping firewood."

"Alright," she said in a playful tone. "Where do we want to go?"

"Someplace without a brochure."

"A brochure?"

"The brochures start to change a place, make it self-conscious. I want to discover somewhere...somewhere where people still work with their hands. And I don't mean on a keyboard."

"Where does all this come from?"

"I don't know. One of my bitter moods."

"You're with me and you're bitter?"

"Bitter but better." They kissed again and he felt goose bumps on her arms.

"I'd like to think it's me giving you those chills, but you're cold."

"It would be fine if it wasn't for the breeze."

"Let's go get the car."

"We'll get the car, then I want to do something."

"Anything you want," he said, more than happy not to have the night end too soon.

"Remember," she said excitedly, "you said *anything.*"

"So?" he asked, and his mind skipped to many things.

"So I want to spy on someone. Like you do for work."

That had not been one of them.

FIFTEEN

They drove down Melina Cass and parked off of a side street in an unlit lot.

"We're going to just sit parked in the car on this street?" she asked, sounding a little confused.

"This is what I do. It's not that exciting." He figured he could make his point and maybe they could sit and make out.

When he had tried to take his ex-wife along on surveillance, she brought books to read. But even that didn't last long. She was bored, hungry, and needed to use a bathroom almost as soon as they set up on a surveillance position. Led's job was nothing like a crime drama, she'd said. More like a foreign documentary with subtitles.

"It's not that it lacks excitement," Callie said. "I just thought you would be more active, like with the dentist, following behind him."

He didn't plan it, but just had the idea as some mangy resident exited the building. "There's our man," he said. "Get out of the car and follow him."

"Him...?" She saw the man in the dirty green T-shirt and jeans but was surprised how quickly something was happening. "That guy right there?"

"Right, the one that just came out of the apartment building."

A weathered, white male with shabby clothes was walking down the street toward the package store. Led thought it would give her a feel for what he did. It wasn't actually a case, just one of the area's downtrodden on a Friday night, but it might give her the excitement she was looking for.

"Why do you care about *him*?"

"He was in an auto case," Led fabricated. "Claims he has to use a cane."

"But he's not using a cane," she analyzed.

"No, he is not." He was amused by her enthusiasm, by the streetlights sparkling in her eyes. "That's why we want to watch him."

"Okay," she said, catching him off guard. "I'll follow him. Give me a camera."

"A camera?"

"You want me to get video, right?" She looked in the back of the jeep at the milk crate full of camera equipment.

"Sure." Led reached back and retrieved a small camera setup. "Here, put this in your pocketbook and clip the pen here. Turn it on by pushing down."

"Wish me luck," she said, as she got out of the jeep and walked down the street to the package store the old man had entered. Led watched her and felt happy.

When the man came out of the store several minutes later, Callie walked behind him, passed him, and got in the jeep. The man walked into his apartment building with a bottle in a brown paper bag.

"So how'd you do?" Led asked with a smile.

"I was trying to be all relaxed," she laughed. "I really wanted to get some good video. I was trying to be all nonchalant, standing beside him at the counter, but I couldn't think of which cigarettes to ask for! I was trying to look at him, he was scratching the tickets, and think what kind of cigarettes my friends in college used to smoke."

"You're a natural," he said.

"But the smell!" She waved her hand before her face as if to clear the air. "He smelled like sweat and vinegar."

He laughed. "You think this job is following around only people with good hygiene?"

"I was nervous, but he didn't notice me."

"Oh, he noticed, all right. He checked out your ass as you walked past him."

"No, sir!"

"He did," Led smiled. "I saw him."

"Eww..." she said, feigning disgust that was somehow flirty.

"If he didn't smell, it would have been all right that he looked at your butt?"

"It's what you guys do," she grinned, cocking her head.

"Don't lump me in with all other guys," he said, reaching out to touch her cheek with the back of his hand. "I get paid to stare at people."

She took his hand and kissed the back of it. "Then why did you stare at me in the parking garage? I didn't pay you."

"For practice."

She giggled and turned, looking out her side window, and was quiet for a moment before she asked, "Is he trying to get money?"

Led wasn't sure if she was talking about the dentist. "Who?"

"The man you just had me follow."

"They all try to get money," he said. He reached to brush his fingers through her hair, but she moved slightly—enough so that he stopped.

She looked straight at him. "He isn't really someone you're investigating, is he?"

"Well, I mean...he...he's *like* people I investigate. But no, no, he's not someone I'm investigating."

"He wasn't in an auto accident?" She was still and unblinking.

"Not that I know of...I wanted to make it exciting for you." He felt the warm air of embarrassment blow across his face. "We could have sat here all night and not seen anything; it was more like training."

"You didn't ask me for the video."

"I was just giving you an example of what it was like...."

"Showing a girl a good time?"

He couldn't tell if she was kidding around or serious. "You were eating it up."

"Don't lie to me again," she said matter-of-factly. "Okay?"

He felt like a chastised student. It may as well have been *don't put your hand in fire*. Not an order, just solid information for his own good, stripped of emotion down to pure fact. He didn't feel that explaining himself further was going to do any good.

"Okay," he said simply.

She leaned over, grabbed his face with two hands and gave him a big kiss, and he felt her tongue in his mouth but only for a moment. She sat back in her seat.

"Now, let's try this again. Let me see a real case you're working on."

He wasn't sure if he should have been scared of her. Was she deranged, a beautiful veneer over a cracked personality? He didn't want to believe that. He had only been fooling around; he didn't mean to upset her. If she wanted to see what a case was like, he would take her over to the Harbour Club. Driving down the small residential street, Led observed Cheryl O'Hearn's car. The one O'Hearn seemed to use so often.

"Here's one. I'm looking to find out what's going on in the Harbour Club, and I'd like to know what someone named Paul O'Hearn is doing in there."

"This is really for a case? You're not just saying that thinking that I wouldn't dare go in there?"

He didn't think she would go in. It was not the most inviting place for anyone, especially a pretty young woman. "It's really a case," he said.

"Then why aren't you going in with me?"

"I, unfortunately, went face to face with this guy at his mother's house. He'd recognize me." He saw her staring at the club's door, at the men going in and out.

"You don't have to do this one," he added. "I'll think of something else we can do."

"No, I'll go. How bad can a bunch of men sitting around drinking beer be? Give me the camera."

Led smirked as if he expected her to back out, but handed the device to her. "You're all wired and ready to go," he said.

"What's my ruse?" she asked, putting it in her purse.

"Ruse?" Led was amused at the word, which made his job sound like a carnie's con game. "Go in and ask to use the bathroom," he said, giving her something simple. In and out, nothing that needed a backstory.

"The bathroom—in there?" She scrunched her face, showing him she didn't think he was even trying to come up with a good reason.

It wasn't easy for him to think why a woman looking like she did would walk in there alone. "Go in and tell them you want to put up flyers for a walkathon...for cancer...because of a friend. It'll give you a reason to start a conversation. Look around a little and try to find this guy. Find out what he's doing."

He showed her a still photo taken from the covert camera he had worn earlier. The wide angle of the lens had distorted the image like a fun house mirror or a security peephole. "This is what he looks like," he said.

"I hope not, his head is very...bulbous." She gave a nervous smile.

"You have your phone, auto-dial me if you need me to come in."

"You're too sweet. Don't worry about anything other than that I might become a member. Do you have anything else to add?"

"Preparation plus confidence equals success."

"You're quoting a motivational poster? I was hoping you could tell a girl how good she looked tonight." She shook her head and got out of the car.

He knew she was kidding, but he did wish he'd said that she was beautiful. He thought he'd said it earlier, when he picked her up. He meant to.

He was parked on the mostly residential street, on the same side of the road as the club. She walked down the street with an exaggerated wiggle, for his benefit, looked over her shoulder and grinned.

Callie realized that Led might be more comfortable being underestimated, but she found it a personal affront. Her parents had treated her the same as her brothers, and her Midwestern upbringing made her confident to the core about a lot of things. Her dad insisted that she learn to drive a stick shift and tie a half hitch on the bass boat. She had confidence, but in things that seldom challenged her. So far in life, she felt she had an advantage of being long and smart. She also knew it was all relative. A blue ribbon in Kenosha might not even get an honorable mention anywhere else. She was nervous as she approached the bar. Sometimes what seems to be unflappable confidence flaps.

With the small pocketbook over her right shoulder she opened the large glass door and went in to the Harbour Club.

It was 8:27 p.m., and already the smoke in the club hung from the ceiling like a gauze canopy, almost reaching the floor, the pungent, burnt-spice of cigars and the acidic sting of cigarettes. The bar area was lit with fluorescent lights running in parallel across the ceiling, giving the two men seated at the bar a pallor of mortician's wax.

The jowly bartender had gray, thinning hair. He wore a black shirt with a white logo: *Jack Daniel's Old No. 7.* As Callie entered, he was putting draft beers in front of the men at the bar.

The two men looked away from the television in the corner and at her, neither taking their elbows from the counter.

"What can I do for you, honey?" the bartender asked.

"Sox still on top?" she asked.

"By one. They just gave up a run in the top of the second."

"I'm looking for a part-time job. Going through a tough time, and this place is local and convenient."

"Most anybody working here is a member. Mostly guys. Not that we haven't had women help out. Sully schedules everyone, I don't know if he needs anyone or not. You bartend before?"

"I waitressed at TGIF and did some bartending there."

"This ain't as complicated as that. We got four kinds of bottled beer, two drafts, and two types of wine, red and white. What you see for liquor is behind me. We don't have a blender."

"Is Sully around?"

"Yeah, hold on a minute." He flipped the counter up and

walked through the archway to the darkened larger room. Callie waited in the archway.

The rear-projection television was in the corner to her left, with several men sitting at the tables around it. She'd heard them whooping and clapping before she entered the front door.

The bartender went over to one of the round tables where some men were playing cards, watching the game. He spoke with a heavy-set guy. Everyone at the table looked over at her.

Callie took a few steps back into the bright lights as Sully and the bartender approached.

"This little lady here wants to know if we're hiring."

As he stepped into the light she saw Sully's black hair, slicked back. It was either dyed or a toupee; in any case it didn't match his graying mustache.

"James Sullivan, call me Sully." With a bottle of beer in his left hand, he put his cigar in his mouth to free up his right, extended it for her to shake. Her slender fingers were enveloped in his sausage pack of a hand. He pumped her hand up and down a few times and then held it as he spoke out of the side of his mouth: "We're always looking for extra help."

"We are?" the bartender asked.

"Sure, especially when there are functions like wedding receptions or anniversary parties."

"Could I get anything a little more regular?"

"Probably," he said, finally letting go of her hand. "Have you ever been in here before?"

She shook her head no.

"Let me show you around." He put his hand on the small of her back and motioned with his cigar to follow him into the darkened area with the tables.

The green-tiled walls, chrome trim, and Formica bar merged abruptly with that next room's dark wood paneling. The décor was 1950s diner by way of backwoods hunting lodge. In the next room, a sort of function hall, recessed lighting illuminated the smoke in shafts, looking capable of beaming somebody up.

The ladder-back chairs with black leather seats surrounded large, round tables with chipped, particleboard edges.

"This is our banquet area."

"Nice," she said, confident the darkness hid her rolling of eyes. She looked around the room. There were two card games taking place, but none of these men were O'Hearn.

"As the new club president, I want to increase the revenue by hosting more functions. Get our name out there as an alternative to those pricey places. Give people a break."

"How many will this room hold?" she asked, trying to make idle conversation as a reason to keep scanning patrons' faces.

"We're not supposed to have more than one-twenty, according to the fire codes. But that's a little flexible, people walk in and out, right? Who's counting?"

"Do you think you can get me a shift?"

"If you're willing to help with functions, I'm sure Sully can find you something for a regular weeknight," Sully said, referring to himself by name as if it were a title of importance.

"I don't want to bump anyone," she said, following him into the bar area.

"Don't worry about it. We need a little beautification around here. Don't we, Phil?"

The bartender looked back from the television above the bar. "First you want to give away my job, and then you insult my rugged good looks?"

"Phil," Sully said, "you know you'll always be the best kisser. Your daddy says so." He turned his attention back to Callie. "Saturday nights can get busy, we could have you work with Phil. He can show you how things work. After that I can probably get you in here one or two nights a week. People get to know you, know you're a hostess for the functions, we might be able to get that to take off."

The door beside the men's room opened. Callie recognized the redheaded man immediately.

Led's man came up the stairs carrying two cases of bottled beer. "Hey, Sully," he said. "Those outlets are all set. Without a ground fault down there, Jesus, it's a wonder no one ever bounced off the freezer. Especially the way that basement takes on water."

"It did give a little tingle now and then," the bartender said. "I got zapped more than once."

"Listen, Sully," Paul O'Hearn said, setting down the cases of beer. "I know your family, and they're all as ugly as you are. So this ain't your sister."

"This is Callie. She's going to be working the bar now and then."

"Good idea."

"You work here, too?" she asked O'Hearn.

"I pitch in. Kind of how the club works. Something needs to be done Sully gets some poor son of a bitch to do it for nothing."

Sully snorted, waving the comment off with his cigar.

"You come in here for a beer and they put you to work," O'Hearn said, putting two dollars on the counter as Phil retrieved a cold Budweiser from the chest refrigerator behind the bar. "Then you still have to pay for your beer."

"What's the pay?" Callie asked.

"Minimum wage plus tips." Sully looked at Phil to elaborate.

"I work the bar now and then," Phil said. "I guess not so much anymore. But I make twenty-five to thirty dollars an hour. You'll probably do better."

"Our members are mostly working stiffs, but they're generous working stiffs."

"Do you have anything that you want me to fill out?" Callie asked. "A W-9 or whatever?"

Sully put his cigar in the ashtray. Though severely chewed on, it was unlit. "It's all cash," he said. He took out a business card from his wallet and flipped it over. "Phil," he said, "give me one of those pens off the register. Callie, give me a phone number to reach you at, in case we need to you to cover a shift."

Callie gave her cell number.

"Where do you live?"

"Down in the Caruso buildings."

"Caruso used to come in here as a member."

"The son, not the old man," said Phil, the bartender.

"Right. Tony Caruso. I haven't seen him in a year. Here's my card in case you need to reach me." He licked his index finger and thumb to take another card from his wallet, looking at the back to be sure nothing was written on it.

"James 'Sully' Sullivan," it read. "Owner, Luxury Limo Service, weddings, special occasions, airport service."

"This is your company...nice."

"If you know anyone needing a limo, I got town cars and the stretch Lincoln, and last year got the stretch Hummer."

"Who would rent that?" O'Hearn asked.

"All different people. It's very popular. Bachelor and bachelorette parties mostly."

"Bachelorette, really?" Callie truly was surprised that women would rent a stretch Hummer. It wasn't anything she'd have thought of, but why not?

"They probably rent it more than the guys. To be different. I think the women are wilder than the guys most of the time."

"I guess I can see that," she said. "Well, if you don't need anything else from me, I'll see Phil Saturday night. It was nice meeting all of you."

"See ya," O'Hearn said.

"Have a wonderful night," said Sully.

Phil the bartender raised his hand in an abbreviated wave.

She could see the reflection of O'Hearn and Sully watching her as she walked to the glass door. She walked down the brick steps and turned out of their view.

Led started the Jeep as she approached.

"I was starting to worry. You were supposed to see what was going on and come back out. What did you do, sit and have a drink with them?"

"No," she said, handing him the camera. "I got a job."

SIXTEEN

Rollin was alone as he drove past Led's trailer.

It was two-thirty in the morning, the lights were out, and Led's jeep was parked right there in the driveway. He stopped at the corner of Chinnook Avenue and stared at the jeep. On the car seat was his Army/Navy surplus military knife still in the leather sheath.

It had been the three beers and the steak knife at the restaurant that gave him the idea....

It wouldn't make Mr. Tuttle suddenly change his mind and he wasn't even sure he was going to tell Dale about it. It was going to be a surprise. Rollin had Dale's back when someone messed with him. He was happy to have a mission, one he thought up and was carrying out all by himself.

The Department of Public Safety had an Asher Ledbettor as a registered PI in Salem, Massachusetts. Through a cross-reference telephone directory and a call placed to the house, he'd spoken with a woman. He told her he was Officer Kennedy from the state police; he needed to speak with Mr. Asher Ledbettor. He had been told that Ledbettor didn't live there anymore and to try him over at the Pinnacle View Mobile Park in Londonderry.

Easy enough. Was that professional enough for Mr. Tuttle?

He opened the door of his car. When the interior light came on he panicked for a moment, putting his hand over it and quickly getting out. Shutting the door, he crouched beside his car in the shadows of the overhanging trees. He crept along the jeep's passenger side. He was good at this, enjoyed the thrill of knowing his enemy slept on the other side of that wall. He could have been a commando.

From out of nowhere a big black dog appeared, nosing him in the face.

"Go on—get!" he whispered, pushing against the beast's side. The dog walked on, lifted its leg, and urinated on the front tire of Rollin's car before lumbering back into the night.

Holding the knife with the blade up, Rollin stabbed at the jeep's tire, hitting its thick tread and steel belt. Meeting such unexpected resistance, the knife slid in his hand and cut him. He looked at his hand as best as he could, reaching slightly into the light. It seemed it was only bleeding when he held his palm open, spreading the gash for the flow of a dark shadow, all color gone...

Now he was more determined.

This wound was Ledbettor's fault.

This time he turned the knife around. He stood up and bent at the waist to get a good angle on the sidewall. What if the tire exploded with a bang? *Screw it*, he thought. Just do it. He took a slow practice swing before pulling back and puncturing the sidewall.

The tire sighed. No bang or whoosh but a slow, steady flow of escaping air.

Emboldened by this success, he confidently moved on to the front tire. The knife slid deeper this time, its serrated edge grabbing at the rubber. He wiggled it up and down to extract it.

By the time he was back in his car, the right side of the jeep was sitting on its rims. Rollin was deeply satisfied. His only regret was that he couldn't get Dale back in time to see the look on Ledbettor's face.

Led checked the time on the kitchen stove as he took his last sip of coffee. It was 5:08 a.m. He was amused about his goodnight kiss with Callie, not knowing if he had offended her. She hadn't invited him in, but the depth and duration of her kiss said it wasn't because she wouldn't have liked to. That woman was not like anything just off the shelf; she was a call drink for sure.

It was easier to forget about it and get on with the day. As he started the jeep he could see Mrs. Trethway in her kitchen window, drinking from the *Virginia is for Lovers* mug. Her day of monitoring the neighborhood was just getting underway as she watched him backing out.

The steering was mushy. He could hear a low rumble of flat rubber being rolled across pavement. He pulled back up into the driveway and got out to look at his tires. The driver's side was fine, but he had two flats on the passenger's. He looked on the ground, to see what the hell he had run over.

Nothing.

There was one spare donut tire in the jeep, but not two. He squatted beside the tires to see if it was something a spray can of "Fix-A-Flat" might seal. *Damn it.* No can of aerosol was going to fill the inch-wide gash that smiled at him from the side of that crumpled rubber. The front tire had the same wound.

Mrs. Trethway walked outside in her orange terrycloth robe and foul-weather ankle boots. Her short, thinning gray hair looked like a translucent helmet. She stood in the wet grass with her white, longhaired cat on a leash.

"Morning, Mrs. Trethway. How are you and Princess Grace this morning?" It only aggravated her to hear her cat referred to by anything other than its full name.

"What happened?" she responded.

"It appears that I am on the receiving end of someone's misguided affection. Did you see or hear anything last night?"

"That's horrible! I didn't hear anything. Why would someone do that?"

"My guess is that someone is either trying to sell me tires, or they don't like me."

"Who?"

"Well the list is long...but usually I only upset lazy people. No one that would take the time or effort to do this. So, short answer: I don't know."

"Do you want me to call the police?"

"I would if I thought it would do any good."

"Can't they take fingerprints?"

"There's nothing to take prints from. Whatever was used to pop the tires was taken."

"I feel terrible. What are you going to do?"

"Call a tow truck and spend the day getting my tires fixed."

"No," she said. "Borrow my car."

This was almost more of a shock than having his tires slashed. Mrs. Trethway had never said much more than hello.

"That's very nice, Mrs. Trethway, but I couldn't do that. I have to wait for the tow truck anyway."

"I can come out when they get here; I'm not going anywhere today. I'll ask around the park to see if anyone saw anything suspicious. Take my car."

She obviously relished the prospect of interviewing the neighbors.

"Alright then." He did need to start on the O'Hearn file. He needed a car for that. "I really appreciate it."

It was always better to start surveillance in a housing project early in the morning, when most of the chemically altered and morally ambivalent were getting their beauty rest. Early in the morning fewer people were hanging out in the cars in the parking lots. There were still the sentries and drug dealers, but they were mostly younger ones, with the same mouth and attitude but a little less sure of themselves.

To work in a neighborhood didn't require looking like the residents of the neighborhood or speaking their language. Those were just conveniences. To fit into a neighborhood required confidence; it required assuming a persona that belonged there. When a resident of a neighborhood saw you, who did they assume you were? It was all about the aura you emitted. If crack dealers and whores wanted to think he was a cop when he was in the projects, he would let them, neither confirming nor denying it. They would circle the perimeter, just at the edge of the buildings, like coyotes circling a campfire. Cautious, curious.

Of course, all that was if he had his jeep. But keeping that fire of doubt burning this morning was not going to be easy. If he had his jeep with the tinted windows he could lay low, act at least like he thought he was hidden. There was no such cover in Mrs. Trethway's Dodge Aries, with its baby blue exterior and its bench seats. To get in the back meant climbing over the seat like scaling a fence. Not that it would have mattered—there was no more discretion sitting in the back than in the front, since there was no tint to the windows. He stayed in the driver's seat and flicked at the crystal butterfly hanging from the rearview mirror.

This was insurance work, not law enforcement. There was no arm of justice being served. It was just a paycheck. If a situation got too crazy, he would just leave; at least, that was always the plan. Of course, everyone has their own tolerance for crazy, and he had yet to find his limit.

The biggest concern he had was that the conservative insurance companies he worked for didn't want anything hitting the papers. No matter what happened, it always was written up in the papers that the big, powerful insurance company hired goons and buffoons to stalk honest policyholders. The littlest thing could make it happen. It had happened with his competitors, just a little incident spinning out of control. National Access had one of their experienced guys chalking a tire to see if and when a vehicle moved. The subject's boyfriend saw him doing it and called the police, said someone was putting a bomb under the car. Papers loved that, front-page picture of the bomb squad at work on a car in the middle of East Boston, the investigator facedown on the sidewalk, the insurance company associated with the fiasco.

It didn't take much…a lot of claimants had histories of being in front of judges for civil or criminal matters. There was always that dangerous percentage that knew what hot buttons to push, to get the police flying out to disrupt the surveillance: bombs, child predators, threats with a dangerous weapon. Wouldn't matter if he checked in with the local precinct or not; if the caller embellished the story enough, the cops were coming to check him out.

He had the police called on him a few years back when a claimant in the Bromley Heath Projects said he was seen with a gun. The result was three cruisers and a blown surveillance. It was a video camera, not a gun, but they still had him pulled out and up against the car. Led didn't even carry a gun. To have a concealed weapon when dealing with the local authorities just made them more nervous. Besides, he couldn't carry it into any of the federal, state or court buildings when doing research and good luck to the person that left it in a car and got it stolen. No, carrying a gun—not that he was against them, actually did a little hunting and target practice—would only cause one hassle after another. In all the gatherings of investigators he'd been to, he never heard of anyone having to shoot their way out of anywhere. If the story involved a gun, it was usually about a PI screwing up by letting the wrong person see it, losing it, or leaving it behind in a hotel room.

Cheryl O'Hearn's Chrysler 3000 was parked across the lot.

There was no way to be in a project without everyone knowing there was a newcomer, a stranger. The projects were like a small village. Everyone doesn't necessarily know each other, but they know who belongs and immediately pick up on anything different. Mrs. Trethway's car was different. Who would they assume he was, and why would they think he was there? It was tough to say.

He noticed a light-skinned black or Hispanic woman in a short, black leather skirt. A middle-aged white guy in a minivan had just dropped her off, and now she was hollering at him through the passenger's side window. As he drove off she threw a bagel at his car. That was what it looked like, a bagel. Then she went to the alcove of the nearest building. She stood there for almost half an hour before approaching Led's position.

From a distance he thought she was attractive, but less so the nearer she got, like the distant manatees mistaken by sailors for mermaids. Up close this woman was definitely a manatee. The long hair was like a wig gone askew, as her hairline didn't look quite right. The knee-high black boots were scratched, the toes worn, her loopy earrings and several bracelets bent up like they'd been run over. In fact she looked like all of her had been run over. Though probably still in her twenties, her eyes were puffy and deeply lined, the skin on her neck was papery and creased. She was so skinny that her knees and elbows poked at the skin like a coat hanger in a plastic bag.

She tapped on his side window with a long red fingernail.

"Whatcha want, man?" she asked.

"Nothing, I'm fine."

"I didn't do nuthin'," she said as she bobbed her head side to side, bouncing the large earrings against her face.

"Okay." He stared straight ahead, giving the impression an important event was about to happen.

"You can't just harass people."

"Do you feel harassed?"

"Fuck you."

"Aren't you late for work?"

"Fuck you."

"What did I do, pull your 'fuck you' string?"

"You can't be here, scarin' away my customers. They think you a cop."

"You don't?"

"What cop's goin' to be sittin' here in a car like this? No, uh-uh. You watchin' somebody, though."

"What if I was watching you?"

"You would have come over to me if you wanted a date. What you want anyways?"

"I'm just sitting here writing poetry. Keeping it real."

"Shit," she snorted. "You think you some white rapper?"

"Just getting in touch with the street. You know. My people."

"Your ass is crazy. You costing me money, though. Unless you want a date."

"It's tempting but I'm working, too."

"Who you looking for?"

"I got to see somebody about something. That's all."

"You a repo man!" she said deciding that she figured him out, then turned and walked away disgusted, like being a repo man was less reputable than turning tricks.

O'Hearn was probably staying here on a semi-regular basis. To live in the projects you had to be officially below poverty level, as the city didn't want people in low-income housing who didn't belong there. The problem this created was a whole class of citizens lying and sneaking around to live in a place most were trying to escape. But free was free, no matter how crime-ridden or steeped in squalor.

Family members, boyfriends, and acquaintances were prohibited from staying in subsidized housing for more than a visit. So these people got post office boxes and "visited" on a permanent basis. No one was fooled and none complained, so long as there wasn't trouble.

There's the system that doesn't work, and the sub-system that does.

The hooker walked to the doorway at the end apartment unit and stood with two men, who crawled from somewhere and were candidates for the methadone clinic. They feverishly smoked cigarettes, watching Led exit the car and head for the brick building across from Cheryl O'Hearn's. People talk quickly in the projects, even druggies and whores, and he needed to be sure they were convinced he was watching anyone other than O'Hearn.

A lot can go wrong from the car to the building. His role-playing started as soon as he left Mrs. Trethway's sedan, even though he wasn't sure what the role would be. He was anyone but a PI. He was still attempting to come up with a reason for being there. Any real apprehension he had he channeled into who he was supposed to be at that moment and now he had a look of annoyance and purpose. He wasn't sure what his pretext would be as he walked to the door. He was still trying to pick up a sense of the surroundings, looking for anything to use, a car for sale, an apartment for rent, anything to waste a little time talking to the residents. None of his standards were a good fit. So if he was going to stick out, he was going to exaggerate it, make it so unbelievable that it would have to be true, because any fool could come up with a better story out of the comics and that would be his reason for being there.

He stood in the entryway of a hall that smelled like someone had been steaming old sneakers in urine. After knocking on the first unit, the battered door opened slightly, with a black woman's face looking through the security lock and an eight-year-old boy peeking out, lower. Neither of them said anything as they looked out.

Led began, "I'm glad I caught you at home. I'm here about the comic books that were found. The online bulletin board stated that the collection contained Silver Surfer number 4." Led spoke quickly and excitedly as he settled into the persona and introduced himself. "Tony Carver, graphic novel and comic book appraiser."

Still peeking out past the rusted security latch that kept the door from opening more than three inches. "'Scuse me?" the woman said. She felt he was wasting her time; Led sensed it. She scowled, which caused creases across her forehead and nose.

"I can get you a lot more money. Please hear me out."

"Go on," she said, and he knew that he had her interest and had risen at least momentarily above nuisance.

"I got an IM, that's instant message, last night from Fan4More that I should come over first thing this morning before you tried to sell them on eBay. If you have what it said you have, you have some real valuable pieces. Don't let them go as a bundle over the Internet. I can appraise them for you and help you get more money."

"Why?" she asked, acting as if she actually had some comic books for sale.

"When you see what they're worth then maybe you'll realize the need for someone like me to act as a broker on your behalf to find a qualified buyer, someone willing and able to pay top dollar. I ask for only a ten percent commission to be paid after the sale of the book."

"Hold on." She closed the door and flipped the latch. She then opened the door all the way. She stood and yelled back into the apartment. "Marie, you got any comic books?"

"I have the Sunday paper from last week."

"Momma, I got a comic book," said the boy who had been standing beside the woman the whole time.

"Go get it and show it to the man."

The boy ran from the door.

She had short hair worn wavy and shoulder length; he could see a strand or two of gray hair and guessed that she was in her forties. She was wearing a black tank top and pair of gray stretch bike shorts.

There was uncomfortable silence as they waited for the boy to return. The woman yelled into the apartment again, "You don't think it was Ronnie do you?"

"Did Ronnie find sumthin'?" she yelled back to the other woman again.

"I didn't hear 'bout nuthin'."

"That's all right," Led said, trying to put some closure on the conversation as he saw activity at Cheryl O'Hearn's apartment. A young boy left the building with a backpack. No adults were outside yet.

"Ronnie ain't here," the woman at the door said and yelled back again, "Marie, you talk to Ronnie today?"

"No, he don't have his cell phone no more."

"He might still be at Joe's."

Led had created more of a scene than he intended. He had expected the door to be closed in his face by now.

"Here is the book I got." The boy offered up a comic book that was missing the cover and most of the pages were dog-eared and torn.

"Night Wing. That's a good one."

"You want to buy it?"

"It's in rough shape."

"Ten bucks."

"I'll give you five."

"Okay," the boy said holding out the book.

The woman at the door brushed the boy back behind her. "You keep that. I want to see what they're selling for online."

"Good idea, check it out and compare," Led said as he tried to leave naturally and get back to the surveillance vehicle. "You might get a little more if you really work at it."

"Go put that away. Some place safe." Turning to Led, "I have things to do now," she said in a much colder tone, as if she were suspicious of his offer for the ripped comic book. As if he had tried to take advantage of her and her boy. She shut the door.

"Thank you." He scooted back to Mrs. Trethway's baby blue Dodge Aries, trying not to look like he was running.

Back in the car, Led tossed an empty manila folder onto the dash, casting a white reflection onto the windshield. He stayed in the driver's seat, ready to follow should Cheryl O'Hearn's car go anywhere.

At 7:35 a.m., Paul O'Hearn exited the duplex. He wore black Oakley sunglasses, a blue Red Sox windbreaker, a pair of jeans, and brown walking shoes with a lug tread like hiking boots, but low, off the ankle. There was no bandage on his hand as he descended the three front steps without using the rail and crossed the street, with only a glance to check for traffic.

Led slouched low in his seat, shooting video with the small digital recorder. With the screen extended and tipped it worked like a periscope, allowing him to see out and over the dash.

O'Hearn walked over to Cheryl's Chrysler and used the remote to unlock the door, with the *wheep-eep* sound of the alarm disengaging. In a single, smooth, and uninhibited motion, he opened the door and sat in the driver's seat, giving no indication he was injured.

Led could see O'Hearn through the windshield, talking on a cell phone.

At 7:38 a.m., a woman with wet auburn hair and pale white skin exited from the same door O'Hearn had. She was in her late twenties or early thirties, about five-foot-five and one hundred ninety pounds, in white pants and a sleeveless blouse with a floral print. The silky green top strained against her large breasts and revealed a crease or two of flesh on her back. Her forearms were large-freckled and without any tone, jiggling as she walked. She crossed the street with a hurried shuffle-step, causing many parts of her to bounce noticeably out of unison.

She went around to the passenger's side of the Chrysler and got in.

Led started the borrowed sedan but kept the camera going.

O'Hearn could be seen checking his mirror before pulling out and heading west.

Led had to cross the eastbound traffic to follow. With only moderate traffic he was able to pull out, leaving only a Waste Management truck and a blue Jetta between him and the Chrysler.

Following another vehicle always seemed easy enough when the surveillance started to go mobile. There was always optimism stirred with a whole lot of trepidation. This was what got the blood flowing, what made it feel like hunting. Stalking the prey. So much could go wrong. There were no rules, except to be active and reactive to whatever came along. The green trash truck in front of Led provided some cover; he stayed up tight behind it. Checking his mirrors, O'Hearn would not see him, but the truck also blocked Led's view of O'Hearn. As Led watched for the truck's brake lights in front of him, he was also looking down every side street they passed, making sure the Chrysler hadn't turned suddenly.

He'd been following for a few minutes when the street made a bend near Tire World. Allowing some space between his car and the trash truck as they went around the bend, he could see that the Chrysler was now four vehicles ahead. The truck was going too slowly. At the intersection with Prescott Avenue, the Chrysler made the light and the truck in front of him moaned on its brakes, coming to a full stop.

It was time to drive like an asshole.

Led pulled up along the truck's right side. Even before the light turned green he started to accelerate, as the crossing traffic's light went from yellow to red. The truck's driver laid on the horn. Led looked in his rearview mirror to look for blue lights, relieved to see none.

There was no fine line between driving aggressively and driving recklessly, there was a smudge. He had no justification for putting others at risk for the sake of an insurance investigation, no special privileges or divine rights in pursuit of a claimant. He tried not to violate any traffic laws, but many were open to interpretation.

Tailing someone was the most underrated skill in the profession. It required the finesse of an athlete playing defense, taking measure of field conditions and anticipating his opponents' moves, zigging when they zigged, zagging when they zagged, and doing it all in time to get the camera rolling again for when they next got out of the car. It required fast reflexes. He still got a pump of adrenaline from it, though he wasn't so aware of it anymore. That rush was now something that happened in the background and didn't carry away his common sense.

Led trained hard to be as good as he was. Years ago, even when not working, he would follow a car for a while, usually someone speeding past him on the highway or running a red light coming out of the mall. An aggressive opponent, someone who could sharpen his skills, he would follow them for a while to see where they went, get a brief peek into their lives: the businessman going to work, the student going to the sandwich shop, the housewife picking up the kids from daycare.

Following someone. It was made to look easy on television, but then again so was heart surgery.

The Chrysler pulled up in front of the Schrafft Building in Charlestown. Led pulled over in the parking lot near the playground, raised his camera.

Only the redheaded woman exited the Chrysler. She walked around to the driver's side, leaned into the opened window, and gave O'Hearn a kiss. Then she gave him a little wave before walking into the building, carrying only her pocketbook.

O'Hearn drove off and Led followed even more cautiously now.

And now he was sure that he was being followed too.

By a van.

The van had New Hampshire plates. The front bumper was

dimpled, the front left quarter panel cracked. Part of the repair had several pieces of gray duct tape holding the grill in place.

There were two men sitting inside it. He'd noticed it, parked to one side of the access road at the projects. He saw it again as he checked his mirror and pulled out. The van stayed several car lengths back. It looked to be in tough shape, like something might rattle loose. Had it been following him since he left his home this morning? Could be a disgruntled subject from a prior investigation except he didn't recognize the vehicle. Now the van was holding back in traffic, allowing one or two cars to separate it from Led's, but was being aggressive in the parking lot, confidently using a multitude of autos for cover, seen but not distinguished...

The driver was now wearing a brown ball cap, a brown satin NASCAR jacket, and wraparound sunglasses. The passenger had a black do-rag tied on his head. It might have been enough to change their appearances if Led had not already picked up on them.

Following him was one thing, but before his tires were slashed again, Led was going to have a word with Speed Racer and the pirate.

Whoever was following him was going to be told to stop.

He drove through the parking lot of the Gas Light Plaza and around the back of the mall, pulling alongside a concrete bunker with a dumpster behind it just outside Young Miss Casuals.

The white van followed moments later. It rolled around the corner of the block of stores, and then not seeing Led's car accelerated to the other end of the mall, looking for the cut-through Led must have taken. Except there wasn't one.

The small strip mall butted against a chain-link fence and a drainage ditch.

Led pulled Mrs. Trethway's blue sedan horizontally across the access road, not quite the menacing effect he had hoped, but it made a point. If the driver of the van was a pissed-off claimant from a prior investigation, this maneuver could get Led broadsided. But he thought about this only after the fact.

The van stopped and the driver rolled down his window and

removed his sunglasses. He was a white male in his thirties, tall and rugged enough to be trouble if he got out of the van. The passenger was younger, with pasty white skin that only looked whiter with the urban head covering.

"Is there a problem?" the driver asked.

"You tell me. I don't believe we've met."

The driver was visibly nervous. Led watched his hands.

"So what are you doing?" Led asked.

"I was supposed to meet someone, and I wasn't sure if they were in front of the mall or had gone behind, looking for me."

"No one back here except me," Led said monotone, sounding very tough, but conscious of the crystal butterfly dangling from the rearview mirror.

"Yeah. I see that. We gotta get back around front so they don't think we missed them. You gotta move."

"What do you guys do for work?"

"Real estate," Dale said, glancing over at Rollin, who nodded. "Property management mostly."

"You have a card?" Led asked.

"Not on me. We have the day off. But you can call me if you're looking for something in the future," the driver said and put the van in drive. "We have to go."

"What number?" Led asked without moving.

"Excuse me?"

"What number. To call you."

The driver cleared his throat and rattled off seven digits. "It's an 800 number."

It was now apparent to Led that he was dealing with one of his own, a fellow investigator. The guy was clumsy but he had a story. Not a great one, but he was sticking to it.

"If you're a realtor, I'm Donald Trump."

"You can't just block a roadway, man. You gotta move your vehicle. I don't want a confrontation."

He didn't want a confrontation, but that was what Led was

going to give him. Like a jacked-up improv player, Led assumed the persona of a lunatic and played it full tilt. "I see you and think: *nah*. Can't be anyone stupid enough to slash my tires one day, and then follow me the next. But here you are."

The passenger stared straight out the window, his mouth cocked to one side in a little bit of a twitch. The driver said, "I don't know what you're talking about."

"Why did you slash my tires?" Led asked. He didn't have any size advantage but felt confident he could get the psychological edge. He could already see the sweat on the driver's upper lip. "Did I investigate a friend of yours or something?"

"Hold on," the driver said. "You're right, I'm a private investigator, just like you. I was following you. But I don't know anything about tires being slashed." He nervously shook his head as he spoke. His passenger looked at him, surprised by the sudden admission.

Led stopped a foot from the van. "You were trying to follow me? Why?"

"It has nothing to do with you really. I was following up on a case."

"So why are you following *me*?" Led caught a glance of the potential weapon the passenger held, a black night stick with a swivel handle.

"You started to work on the same case."

"Which one?"

"Paul O'Hearn. For Mr. Tuttle. Here's my card."

The card read, "Dale Foley, investigations in NH and MA."

Just the mention of Tuttle's name made Led feel the vein in his right temple bulging. "So you don't know anything about my tires?"

"I swear. Come on, we're both in the same line of work. I don't do stuff like that."

Led could see that Dale Foley was fidgeting. He was probably lying but there was nothing he could do to prove it. He would derive some pleasure from reaching through the window and dragging him to the ground, but the satisfaction would only be brief. "How come you're working for Tuttle on the same case?" he asked.

"Mr. Tuttle wanted to double it up. He likes to be sure he has complete control."

"I noticed. So why follow me instead of O'Hearn?"

"It's nothing bad, not like we're investigating you or anything. Just wanted to see what you were doing."

"As of right now I'm done with the investigation on Mr. O'Hearn. I'm not working the file anymore. You can let Mr. Tuttle know that."

"You're not?"

"No, so quit following me. Got it? I know you slashed my tires. And I know who you are. You better hope I don't run over any nails after this. I won't be so talkative next time."

Led moved Mrs. Trethway's baby blue sedan to the side.

Dale didn't say anything but rolled up his window and drove away, clicking.

SEVENTEEN

Perkins started with what he had for information and relied upon his usual tact and tactics as he banged with a closed fist hard upon the apartment door in the Bunker Hill Projects. An old lady opened the door partially and he kicked it, pulling one end of the small security chain from the doorjamb. He looked about quickly for anyone else in the unit.

"Go away!" The woman tried to sound forceful as she said it, but her voice was shaky.

"Paul O'Hearn?" Perkins asked. "Where is he?"

"I'm his mother."

"Does he live here?"

"Sometimes."

The old lady didn't seem like she was trying to give him a hard time, she was just old and stupid.

"Where is he now?"

"I don't know. He hasn't been here in a day or two." She started hacking uncontrollably with a wet cough. He wished she had just started crying, that he was used to. She was vibrating with a hundred years of phlegm.

"Have a cigarette or something."

"Thank you."

He looked around as she fumbled for her lighter and drew on the cigarette with the relief of an asthma patient with an inhaler.

"What's in here?"

"Paulie's room."

Perkins opened the door cautiously and saw only junk. But it was easy to see the out of place medical unit components since they were the only things in the room not buried beneath old clothes or an inch of dust and dirt.

"I'm taking these." Grabbing both units he was surprised at the weight and banged the doorway carrying them out.

"Are there more?"

"Take anything you want."

"I just want more of the equipment that your son left here."

"That was it," she said. "He only carried in those two." She lit another cigarette.

"Tell your son I will be looking to get the rest of it."

"Who are you?"

"Tell him the piper was here and it's time to pay up."

The woman stood in the middle of her living room as he walked out. She'd been scared but he'd seen a lot worse.

The call had come while Led was driving through McDonald's, pulling up to the window for an order of chicken strips. Randall Crawford got to him before he had a chance to get to Randall, which was never a good sign. Tuttle had probably complained about what he said to those two chuckleheads in the van.

"Hold on a minute, Randall...can I get some napkins and extra salt? Sorry about that," he said through a mouthful of French fries. "I should get an ear piece for this thing."

"We got a call from the FBI this morning, Led."

"FBI?"

"A Special Agent Thomas Chancellor, requesting a copy of your report on O'Hearn. I told him we didn't have it yet. You got anything on him?"

"Some."

"He told me to have you call immediately. Didn't say why. So once you see what they want, let me know what's up."

Led dialed as he drove. The voice prompts let him know the call was being recorded.

Special Agent Chancellor kept calling him Mr. Ledbettor. "Mr. Ledbettor, I'd like you to come in and speak with me about some information you may have in reference to some surveillance you've been conducting." His words might have been respectful but his tone was anything but; it was bordering on demanding.

"Why?"

Led's phone clipped, as he had another call coming in. He was going to have to ignore it.

"I can't tell you that until you come in. Are you available now?"

"How long will it take?" His voice was clipped as Led's phone beeped again.

"Half hour, maybe forty minutes. I can be there by two-thirty."

Led looked at the caller ID. It was Callie. His mind wandered ever so slightly. "Where do I need to go?"

"JFK building, downtown. Do you know where that is?"

"Sure.

The phone beeped again.

"I'm sorry. I have to take another call for a second."

"Go ahead."

Though he'd been thinking about her all morning he was surprised to hear her voice.

"You were on the other line?" she said. "I was just going to leave you a message thanking you for a wonderful time last night."

"I usually don't send my dates into bars while I wait in the car. But if you thought that was special, next time I can send you into a bowling alley, or a fish market. Something to keep the romance alive."

"How's your day going?"

"I had a flat tire this morning, and I still have to deal with that." He edited the details down to sound blasé. It wasn't such a great story anyway. So someone slashed two of his tires? It sounded worse than it was.

"What time will you be done today?"

"Probably five, five-thirty."

"Do you want to come over? We can get some Chinese food and watch TV...."

"We would actually be together. Sounds kind of odd for a date, but sure, I'm willing to give it a try."

She said bye with the lightest bit of flirt to her voice, and he thought that this was not such a bad day after all.

He clicked back over to the other line. "Agent Chancellor, I'm sorry. That was regarding something else I'm working on."

Agent Chancellor was all business. "Use the Beacon Street garage."

"What do I do once I'm there?"

"Go through the security screening and they'll call me down. And please bring your notes of everything you've been working on for the last week."

"No disrespect, but I can't give you my notes. I'll need you to get me a subpoena, or have the client give me permission."

"I'll have everything in place. I'll see you at two-thirty."

"Sure." Led put a chicken strip in his mouth. Special Agent Chancellor had all the personality of voicemail, no sign he was amused, perturbed or even interested in talking to Led. Just demanding. *Public servant*. You wouldn't know it. The girl at the drive-thru would be fired for the same tone.

He'd had enough contact with law enforcement to know how it worked; they were conditioned to intimidate. They caused the general public anxiety; no one wanted a police car behind them, no matter how conscientious they were of the traffic laws. Day in and day out, that kind of response had to affect even the friendliest cops. So they put on a tough act and *used* the intimidation. After a while it was no longer acting.

The biggest difference between Led and law enforcement investigators was that Led didn't have a badge. He had to be nice to people, make them *want* to talk. Otherwise, he got nothing. Most retired law enforcement types couldn't make the transition from public to private. He saw it all the time: they couldn't investigate without a badge to flash. Not all of them, there were some that relaxed, understood they had to stop thinking of themselves as separate from those they were questioning. But he only knew a handful.

He parked under the Fleet Center and walked over to Washington Street. Stopping at a Copy Cop, he photocopied every page of the yellow pad with his notes from the morning. He then continued to the John F. Kennedy Federal Building just off of Scollay Square.

Once through the metal detector and patted down, his briefcase passed through the x-ray machine, it only took Chancellor a few minutes before he stepped off the elevator.

Chancellor was square-shouldered, and not as old as Led expected, same age as he was, maybe even a few years younger, early thirties at the most. His voice had seemed older, maybe because it didn't have any superfluous pleasantness to it. With only a "Please follow me," they went to the elevator. The agent walked rigidly, as if he'd just gotten out of the army, his arms swinging in cadence with his stride.

Chancellor swiped his key card and hit the button for the eighth floor. They stood quietly in the elevator. Led looked at the reflection of the agent with his fresh haircut and the white shirt collar slightly showing above the black blazer. He saw his own reflection in the chrome panels of the elevator and stood a little straighter.

Led had crossed paths with the FBI before. They'd wanted information on a case he'd been working but weren't willing to provide any in return. The subject was out on worker's compensation from a moving company and then got a job with a traveling carnival. The subject was chasing the American Dream in his own way, motivated. He had a booth where the object had been to shoot out paper stars with a pellet gun. Led had documented him working over several weeks, had gotten video of him taking cash from the participants, loading their guns, checking their stars, seeing if they shot all of it out and won.

Always just a little bit of the star left.

Unbeknownst to Led at that time, the claimant had also been robbing banks, small local banks, wherever the carnival went. Some people aren't held back by anything from doing what they do.

Led's surveillance of the carnie worker had predated the FBI indictment, so they were very curious as to whom he'd been associating with during the day when not robbing banks. But the Bureau would never tell Led what other activities they were observing with their surveillance crews and equipment, information that might have helped Led's simple worker's compensation case, a little quid pro quo.

More like quid pro no.

"Have a seat. You're a private investigator?"

Led opened his wallet and handed him the ID without saying anything. He looked around at the cubicles, starkly furnished with metal desks. "You guys need some plants in here," he said. "Maybe liven it up a little."

Agent Chancellor handed the ID back. "Do you know a Paul O'Hearn?"

"Paul O'Hearn? I don't know him personally."

"What can you tell me about him?"

"It's a case I'm working on. Worker's comp claim."

"Can I see your notes?"

"Do you have a subpoena? It's my client's product. They paid for this."

"We have a letter from Randall Crawford at GIA." He handed a fax to Led. It was on the GIA letterhead. "Release of information," the subject line read. The letter stated that GIA was cooperating fully with any investigation being conducted by the U.S. government. The release of information was in direct response to a subpoena that had been issued. It was signed by Jeffrey Solomon, Esquire, legal counsel for GIA.

"Well, I guess that covers me," Led said, folding the letter and putting it in his briefcase as he took out his yellow legal pad. "What do you need to know?"

Chancellor only held out his hand.

"Here you go," Led said, handing over his meticulous observations, his recording of notes, times, mileages. Chancellor set the pad of paper on his desk.

"How long have you been working for GIA?"

"We do a lot of work for GIA. Three or four cases a week."

"Who is we?"

"Danko's Information Company. The company I work for."

"This file, on Paul O'Hearn. How long have you been working on it?"

"Since yesterday. The accident just happened."

"You were in his apartment?"

"No."

"No? You weren't at the Bunker Hill Projects?"

"There? Oh, I was there. But that's his mother's place."

"So you were in there!"

"His mother's, yeah, yesterday morning. Nice lady but she needs to do something with her hair."

Chancellor was as stone-faced as a Texas hold 'em player.

"The FBI is investigating this accident? For what?" Led asked, studying Chancellor for any tells.

"I am not at liberty to say. What we need is for you to describe to me what you saw in the apartment."

"Cheap furniture and a lot of full ashtrays. How'd you figure out what I was working on?"

"GIA ran a claims index with the state, so we called them. They confirmed you were working on an insurance claim for them."

"If you can do all that, what is it you need me for?"

"We have a layout of the apartment. What rooms did you go into?"

"Mostly the living room and the kitchen."

"That's a tough neighborhood for someone that doesn't live there to go unnoticed."

"Can be for some."

"Who was there?"

"Just his mother at first."

"Was there anyone else in any of the other rooms?"

"Not that I knew of. I didn't hear or see anyone. Was there?"

"Maybe. Did you see any guns?"

"Guns?" He wasn't surprised the FBI would suspect there were guns in the projects; he just couldn't imagine they thought they were just lying around like dirty dishes. "No. But then again I wasn't looking for any. Were there...guns?"

"Probably. Don't go back in there again."

"It's just insurance work, not worth messing with...with guns."

"So what were you looking for?" Chancellor asked. "You were working on a comp claim."

"Pictures on the wall, diplomas, certificates, pay stubs. Anything that would give me an idea of what Mr. O'Hearn might be up to. You guys aren't usually involved if it's drugs. Being Charlestown...is he robbing banks?"

"Not that we are aware of."

"I don't want to mess up any federal investigation," Led said, trying the humble approach. "I just got to know that this guy is physically active, nothing wrong with him. No physical injury. Something GIA can use to settle or deny the claim."

The agent continued to write notes without looking up at Led. "Describe the apartment for me as accurately as possible."

"I don't know what you want here...let's see...beige carpet, lots of stains and a few cigarette burns. Floral print drapes that don't get opened often, because there was a hangman's noose tied into the pull string, with a frog in it."

"A frog?"

"A little beanbag frog. The old lady seems to collect them, Beanie Babies. They were everywhere: along the windowsill, on the floor in a plastic milk crate.

"So how many people appear to be living in the apartment?"

"Probably just the mother. But O'Hearn stops in often."

"Why don't you think he lives there?"

"The magazines were *People* and *TV Guide*. No sports magazines or anything. Only her shoes, too, two pair: one by the couch and another by the door. No razors in the bathroom, and O'Hearn is clean shaven."

"You went in the bathroom?" Chancellor scowled and wrote on his paper.

"I stepped in for a minute, didn't use it. Wouldn't have wanted to. I just grabbed some tissue, gave me a chance to see if he was there on a regular basis."

"Did you go anywhere else?"

"Just back to my car."

"Your notes say Paul O'Hearn entered while you were there. How did you know it was him?"

"Because his mom called him Paulie, he seemed nice enough."

"Where did he come from?"

"Don't know, just saw him as he opened the door and walked in. Kind of surprised me, actually."

"Why did you tell them you were there?"

"That's a bit of a trade secret," he said, smiling. The agent did not smile back. "But since we're all on the same side here, I delivered some flowers."

"What did O'Hearn do while you were there?"

"Nothing. He gave me a tip."

"How much?"

"Twenty bucks."

"Do you still have the money?"

"I spent it on French fries."

"That's a lot of French fries," Agent Chancellor said, tipping his head slightly and raising his eyebrows.

"I didn't finish all of them."

There was a pause during which Agent Chancellor seemed to be trying to use some interview technique of staring him down, to get him to start talking, fill the space with chatter. Led watched back as patiently as sitting on surveillance.

Agent Chancellor blinked and looked down at his notes. "Did you see any money lying about the apartment?"

"No. Money lying around that apartment would have definitely stood out," Led said.

"Paul O'Hearn was observed carrying items into the apartment, then a big box back out to his car," Chancellor said, looking at the notes. "He then carried boxes into the Harbour Club. Were they the same boxes?"

"Hard to tell. Here's the video. Look for yourself."

Chancellor didn't acknowledge that Led had set the tape on the very piece of paper that he was writing on. He merely tipped the pad, sliding the tape to the desktop.

"So he went to the Harbour Club?"

"Right. He was there yesterday and again last night."

"You spoke with him in the club?"

"Not me personally. Those are notes from the surveillance video someone took."

"Someone else?"

"My girlfriend." He said that and took himself by surprise. What else was he going to call her, the woman from the parking garage?

"What's her name?"

"Callie McBride."

"We'll need to talk with her."

"That's fine, but this is not her profession. She was just helping me out. I don't want her to get involved in anything."

"National security, Mr. Ledbetter. You do care about that, don't you?"

"Like any good American," Led said, smirked a little and added, "Until it's inconvenient."

"Can you have her come in tomorrow?"

"She works a day job."

"It would be easier than having to subpoena her."

"I'll bring her in tomorrow afternoon."

Led left wondering why, Chancellor cared about Paul O'Hearn. Terrorism? *Paul O'Hearn?*

Outside, he called Randall Crawford at General Insurance to give him the latest.

"Fine with me," Randall said. "If they lock him up we don't have to pay him. And if you can get an arrest on videotape, we'll stop paying immediately."

"I don't think you have to worry about the claim, Randall. I followed him from his girlfriend's yesterday, looks like he's working, maybe doing some electrical work at a club in Revere. Anyway, they want me to come back again tomorrow and I'm already at the budget."

"I had a feeling about him in the hospital. Don't worry about the budget. Give them whatever they need; we'll take care of you."

It was a warm summer day, and the heat reflected back off the bricks of Government Center. It was after lunch, the tourists and students were looking up at buildings, taking each other's photos, reading books...

He was anxious to exchange Mrs. Trethway's car back for his jeep with its sunroof. But he was grateful for her help, so at a stoplight he summoned a black man in a red tank top and bought a bundle of carnations from a white plastic pail.

From Mrs. Trethway's reaction, it had been a long time since anyone had bought her flowers.

He wondered how Callie was going to take the news that he had gotten her into the middle of an FBI investigation. Excited or upset, either extreme would be concerning.

"Come on in," Callie called from inside her apartment.

He saw her stick her head out of a door down the hall.

"I'm just finishing some laundry."

"Do you need help?"

"I'm almost done," she said, folding a pair of slacks held under her chin.

He watched her set down something small and lacy that he could only assume was a pair of panties. He looked away out of politeness.

"Put these away for me," she said, handing him a neatly folded stack.

He reached out with his arms extended as if she was loading him up with firewood instead of fluffy towels.

"Wait—" she said, leaning into the towels to give him a peck on the lips. "I'm glad you're here."

"What do you feel like doing tonight?"

"I don't mind staying in with Chinese food and some television," she offered.

"Do you like baseball?" Led inquired hopefully. "There's a game on tonight."

"I love baseball."

"Ever been to Fenway?"

"A couple of times a year since I moved here. But my family back home is all Cubs fans."

"I'm sorry," Led said with deadpan sympathy.

"Be nice. I take my team seriously. My dad was a big fan. Our summers were structured around him having access to a radio to hear the games. He and his buddies sitting around drinking Pabst Blue Ribbon, listen to me, I make it sound like he's dead. Baseball is *still* everything to him. Sometimes I wonder why it matters so much."

"It's communal. Safer than religion or politics. The team you support doesn't change the economy or the chances of life after death. No one has ever been a suicide bomber in the name of the Mets. It's combative, but in a civilized forum."

"Yeah, a *bench-clearing* forum," she said.

"But no matter how heated it gets, there's an off-season and everyone's allowed to start over. Think if that was the way wars were fought." Led heard himself reciting one of his internal monologues he'd created on surveillance and now finally verbalized. "Every year the Native Americans would get to compete against the Europeans for the title to the Americas."

"That's a little silly."

"You're a Cubs fan and you're calling me silly?"

"Watch it," she said, putting away the last of her jeans.

"So what does your day look like tomorrow?"

"Aren't the Sox on the road?"

"Not asking about the game. I wanted to know if you could meet me for lunch. The Salty Dog, we can sit outside. Take a half-day."

"A half-day? For *lunch?*"

"Listen, the case you helped me with last night. I guess the FBI has an investigation going there too. They want to talk with you tomorrow afternoon."

"The FBI?" She walked out of the bedroom and put the empty laundry basket back in the pantry. "Am I in trouble?"

"No."

"Are *you?*" She paused and stood looking at him.

"No, nothing like that. They want to know what you saw. Just basic information. They called me in, too, questioned me about O'Hearn's mother's apartment in Charlestown."

"What do they think he did?"

"I don't know exactly. They don't say much."

"What are you doing in the morning? I could just take the whole day—"

"I have a worker's comp case I should start."

"Wait a minute, you're working on a file that the FBI is interested in, yet you're still doing a worker's comp case?"

"Mercantile Insurance gives me a case or two a week and pays by the hour," he said. "I don't think the FBI is going to be calling in another assignment anytime soon. They don't have much use for guys like me."

As they left the house to pick up dinner, descending the porch steps, Led became agitated. He didn't like the fact that he'd been tailed earlier by the two men in the van: *Humpty and Dumpty.* Now he was crossing paths with the FBI. It all put him on edge. They could have put a bumper beeper on his car. Easy enough to do. Walk up and attach the magnet anywhere on the undercarriage. The older of the two looked capable of anything and the FBI would have the latest and the greatest toys, not that off-the-Internet stuff with the two-mile range. Theirs would be GPS, satellites, computer monitoring...

"Let's take your car," he said to Callie. "I didn't have time to clean mine out."

"If you want," she said, handing him the keys. "But you drive."

At Monroe Street he stopped just past the waterfront. He put the Volvo in reverse and backed up the one-way street, watching as a dark blue Suburban drove slowly by.

Maybe he was being followed, maybe not.

"What are you doing?" She wanted to be in on the game.

"Just checking something."

"On *this* street?" she asked, looking at the church, the elderly housing complex, and the triple-deckers backing up the hill.

"I thought maybe someone was following us."

"Are we? Being followed?" Callie looked around.

"If we were, we're not anymore," Led said, but thought, *Game on*. And he would push back the case he planned for tomorrow, at least another day.

EIGHTEEN

*I*f *it is none of your business and no one is paying to make it your business, then it's best to just stay out of it*, Led thought to himself, but like picking a scab he continued despite the almost certain unpleasant results.

Chancellor threw around his title like it was the weight of experience. If Special Agent Chancellor was interested in what he knew about the accident, Paul O'Hearn, and the vehicle, it wasn't going to hurt to tie up a few loose ends with the insurance investigation. Show off a little. He didn't usually talk to a witness or check out the vehicle on a comp case, but the FBI wasn't usually involved. Before going back to Chancellor's with Callie, he needed a better idea of what was going on.

The accident on Route 93 North invoked four collision policies, five auto liability policies, two worker's compensation policies, one disability policy, and a life insurance policy. The policies were spread across seven different insurance carriers. Very little of the information would be shared until months later, when the information would appear in claims indexes.

Information about worker's compensation claims, liability, and disability claims wasn't shared. The different carriers could eventually be fighting each other in court over who owned the claim, so there was no motivation to share. Even inside the same insurance company, the liability information wasn't shared with the worker's compensation adjusters because it could all end up in a subrogation dispute over which policy had to pick up the tab.

The result was that Led had no central source for information about what claims were being filed with regard to the accident and who else was working them. At this point, he wasn't being asked to do anything other than determine if O'Hearn's activities were consistent with his claim.

Someone named Ken Misheau was the only witness listed so far, meaning he was going to be very popular with all of the different insurance carriers pursuing their own statements. Misheau was listed on the operator's report that had been filled out by the taxi driver. The police report would not be released for weeks or even months if there was an ongoing investigation and there had been a death, making that possibly even longer. All of the drivers were supposed to have filled out operator reports, but only the taxi driver had turned his in so far.

Led called the number on the report and spoke with Ken Misheau, a pleasant enough man, who truly seemed eager to help and a little disappointed that he didn't have, as he put it, "juicier details."

Misheau was the chief financial officer for a chain of cell phone stores. He'd been heading to his store in Lawrence from the one in Medford when the accident happened. He didn't know anyone in the accident and hadn't had any contact with anyone in it since.

Misheau answered every question asked without hesitation and with just a little excitement in his voice. "I was so close to being part of that," he said. "The silver car cut across two lanes and rolled. It didn't hit anything. It rolled right in front of me. I saw the brake lights then I saw the silver car streak across. It almost hit a pickup truck as the car rolled, I don't know how the truck avoided it. My knee still hurts from slamming on the brakes. It was like slow motion as I slid, but so did the RV, and then it bounced up and over the other car."

Misheau was more than happy to be part of an investigation. He outlined how he called the police and jumped out of the vehicle to try and help, humble but at the same time wanting to be recognized for doing the right thing.

Led wrapped it up. "I don't have any other questions, Mr. Misheau. Do you have anything to add to this statement?"

"No, that was pretty much it regarding the RV, I can tell you more about the guy in the car since that was where I stayed until the paramedics arrived," he said. And then almost as an afterthought he asked, "Are you with the other man that called?"

"Well, I'm an independent, working for GIA. Who else spoke with you?"

"I'm not sure...I didn't write it down."

"It could have been one of the companies insuring one of the vehicles."

"No, he was only asking about the RV and driver, same as you."

"I'm just handling a worker's compensation case. It might have been the auto carrier. What type of questions did he ask?"

Led had been doing this long enough that he could tell by the questions asked which side the caller represented. The questions, no matter who asked them, were supposed to be objective; they usually were when asked independently, but when strung together they ultimately culminated in a statement that supported the interviewer's interests. After all, why ask questions if the answers might hurt your cause? Better to let the opposing side ask the questions they want answered on their dime.

"I was in a meeting when he first called. I don't remember him recording the conversation like you did. He just asked a few questions. He wasn't real friendly."

Led thought it sounded like his new comrade, the FBI agent, at least the unfriendly part. But Ken would definitely have remembered being questioned by the FBI; it would have been the highlight of his week. It was probably an attorney or a paralegal getting the information and *then* deciding if they wanted a statement. It was part of the "never ask a question you don't already know the answer to" rule.

"His questions were more about the RV, if I saw the driver remove anything from it or anyone go into it before it was towed."

"You were probably talking to an adjuster for the vehicle's comprehensive coverage."

"I see."

"Well, thanks very much, Ken."

"Quick question, what do you have for a cell phone? In your line of work you'd probably find some of the video capabilities and the GPS features on our new phones useful. You'd never lose your way again."

If you could only guarantee that, Led thought, and politely ended his call.

Parked in the back of the tow yard behind an eight-foot chain-link fence, the forty-seven-foot-long Mobile Medi Tech coach dominated the surrounding trucks, vans, and sedans in various degrees of crunch and rust. There were probably close to twenty-five other vehicles in the small gravel yard. The mirror was missing from the right side and the windshield was cracked into a mosaic, still hanging in place. The passenger side was only slightly marred from its once prone position.

Led stood in front of the closed fence. A teenage Middle Eastern male in a dark blue jumpsuit approached him from the block building just nearby.

Led spoke first. "How you doin'?"

"Good."

"I'm from the insurance company. I need to photograph that white coach."

"Some guy was already here."

"He might have been with one of the other companies," he said, knowing the guy could care less who looked at the RV as long as they got paid for towing and storing it.

"Go in through here."

Led followed him through one door of the building and out another into the gated yard. He went to the RV and with a digital camera began taking pictures. He was not trained as an appraiser. The photos wouldn't be used to assess the cost of repairs, but to aid in determining what kind of impacts had occurred, purely to see if they were consistent with the injuries people were claiming.

The auto appraiser would do his own photos. That was probably who had been out to look at it already. Even though it might have been through GIA, Led learned long ago that insurance works on redundancy.

He took shots that captured a full view of the front and back. He then angled a few down along the side as best he could to show the overall appearance of the vehicle and to provide a reference photo for the close-ups: photos of where the mirror used to be, of the splintered windshield, the scrapes and dents, the busted passenger side window, and the damage up under the front bumper. There was paint from a beige vehicle that had transferred onto the bumper and part of the undercarriage on the driver's side.

He opened the driver's side door and photographed the VIN number, and also wrote it down. He took note of the odometer: 67,336 miles.

It was a nice RV, with a leather driver's seat and a back-up monitor. The dash looked like it belonged in a cockpit, with gauges and switches for leveling the thing when parking it, for opening up its appendages and expansions, for powering up its test equipment.

Out of curiosity he walked around to the back, past the brushed aluminum table resembling a high-tech tanning bed and two machines that might as well have been drill presses as far as he could tell. The floor was littered with health pamphlets, the lavatory area besieged with broken glass from a fallen jar of swabs and liquid soap that had spilled down the side of a cabinet, but otherwise everything looked as if it had stayed secure when the vehicle tipped. The cabinets and drawers were still locked. The only open door read "Technician Only." Behind it were some empty racks and disconnected cables.

A pair of built-in easy chairs sat in the back, at the feet of which a *Men's Health* and a *National Geographic* rested. Led opened the side door. Without the step in place, he had to jump down in order to get out.

His cell phone fell from his belt to the dirt. *Damn it.* It lay in the gravel next to a fresh orange peel that still gave off citrus fragrance amongst the mechanical smells of oil and gas. He thought nothing more of it as he picked up his phone and checked it to be sure it still worked. It showed a full bar of signal strength and a time of 12:25 p.m.

Perkins stopped at the little Vietnamese market across the street and bought some grapes because the oranges looked like shit. So far Tuttle's story checked out. The wrecked medical unit was in the tow yard, but someone had stripped its insides. Perkins didn't know what was missing, but he knew tool marks when he saw them, screwdriver and wire cutters. They stood out even more in the beige shine of the new unit. The empty bay and dangling wires said something was missing.

As he came out and got back into his car he noticed a familiar jeep pull into the tow yard across the street. And then he recognized the driver: a tall, thin man maybe six-foot-two, one hundred-ninety-five pounds with dark hair. He walked fluidly, moving his arms only slightly as he approached the office of the tow yard. It was as if he were stalking a deer, which made Perkins think that the man was at least part Indian. Perkins remembered thinking the same thing when the man was talking with the police that popped Martinez. Yet the Indian wasn't a cop. Perkins could spot cops just by the way they walked; once they wore the belt and sidearm they always walked as if they could feel it was there, even when it wasn't. However subtle, they walked different. The Indian wasn't a cop. But he was checking out the mobile medical unit, so Perkins waited.

He ended up following the Indian back to Chelsea where he picked up a hot blonde number and drove downtown. When they parked and walked into the Federal Building, Perkins let them go. Maybe the Indian was a government employee or just an auto appraiser. Perkins wasn't concerned that it didn't add up. He could live with that, especially on such a busy schedule as he had. Once Martinez was released, things would be back to routine.

"What was your reason for being in there?" Agent Chancellor asked Callie from across his paper-strewn desk.

"To help him," she said, smiling at Led. "To get video of O'Hearn working."

"But what did you tell them you were doing in there?"

"Looking for a job," she said, now smiling at Chancellor, pleased to please.

"They offered her one," Led added, still impressed with her handling of the situation. He relaxed, comfortable being the observer watching this charming woman cast her spell and setting the pompous Fed back a little in his place.

"They offered you a job?" Chancellor asked, raising his eyebrows as he wrote on his pad.

"I didn't really take it."

"That's too bad," he said, looking up.

"Well, I told them I would, but I wasn't really going to go in."

"We need you to go back," Chancellor said, pointing his pen at her, poking at the air for emphasis of each word like he was trying to pop a balloon, "We need you to take the job."

Led shifted uncomfortably in his seat.

"O'Hearn might be in possession of a piece of equipment that has medical grade radioactive material in it," Chancellor continued. "We need to find it before someone has the ability to use it for some other purpose."

"A bomb?" Callie asked.

"A dirty bomb. It can't be made into a nuclear bomb, but it can be used to contaminate a significant area for a very long time."

Led said, "O'Hearn took the thing to his mother's. It was on the tape. That's were you should look."

"We did today."

Led doubted Chancellor. "How?"

"A fire alarm allowed us to send in the fire department along with a few of our men." Chancellor sat back in his chair. "What you had on video was old news. Whatever went in must have gone out."

"I'll do it," Callie interjected. "I can do this," she said, nodding at Chancellor.

Led was surprised by her quick volunteerism, a little hurt he wasn't even consulted. "I don't think they can make you do this," he said.

"That's right," Chancellor said. "We can't. But it would help our investigation and might avoid an incident."

"Sure," Callie said, still sitting back in her chair with her legs crossed.

"Wait—" Led said, putting an elbow on the desk. He wanted Chancellor man-to-man, investigator-to-investigator, but then Callie, too, put an elbow on the desk.

"It'll get me out of the house," she said. "Whatever do you need me to do?"

"Thank you, Ms. McBride. We'll have you positioned with full support."

"I'm going to wear a wire?"

"Yes, we'll be listening. You should be very safe."

"Should be?" Led stared at Chancellor before turning to Callie. "I would prefer you didn't do this, but if you do, know that I will be just outside. I'll make sure you're safe."

Chancellor seemed almost smug. "Mr. Ledbettor, I'm going to have to ask you to not get involved."

"I won't, unless there's a problem."

"No, Mr. Ledbettor. I mean, you are being told to not be in the area. Your presence may compromise the surveillance."

"Compromise the *surveillance?* It's my surveillance you're walking all over."

"I would be less nervous if I knew he was out there," Callie said, placing her hand on Led's. "He has a calming affect on me."

There was silence, Chancellor and Led staring at each other.

"Can you control your emotional outbursts?" Chancellor asked.

"He can't," Callie said, gripping Led's hand tighter. "But that's part of his charm."

"We will remove you from the area if you are in any way a hindrance to this investigation."

Led put his hands up, trying to calm the debate's loser. "I'll help any way I can."

"No," Chancellor countered. "You will not be involved. I'll get you clearance as a civilian observer at the request of Ms. McBride. But that is all you will be: an observer."

They didn't speak to each other as they rode the elevator to the lobby, not until they'd left the Federal Building and were back out on the street.

"Where did all that come from?" Callie asked.

"I'm a little defensive."

"You think?"

"I don't like them using you," Led said with a righteous tone.

"Or you don't like them using your investigation," she said, shaking her head.

"A little of both." He realized that had it not been for her interceding he might have been completely out of the loop.

"This is exciting, don't you think? Like Holmes and Watson."

"You don't realize that some of those guys in that club could be real bad guys."

"No 'badder' now than when you sent me in the first time..."

She had him there. "But we didn't know then. We do now. And the longer you're in a situation like that, the greater the chance of something going wrong."

NINETEEN

L ed dropped Callie off as directed, at the Holiday Inn on Route 1, where she was to meet with her handler to be briefed and prepped. He didn't like leaving her there alone like that. When she assured him she was fine, he suspected it was only to keep him from getting all worked up again, from saying something he shouldn't.

He had two hours to kill before meeting with Chancellor.

He went over to Medford in order to drive past the unit where O'Hearn had been staying to look for Cheryl O'Hearn's car. As he got to the street he noticed an electric utility truck at the corner. It was probably just a repair vehicle, but it could also be surveillance. FBI could pretend they were anyone they wanted to be. If it was Chancellor's crew, and they noticed him, they might bar him from looking on when Callie went into the Harbour Club.

He wasn't going to chance that happening. He drove off.

He was mad at himself for being impatient on the O'Hearn thing. If he hadn't gone into the mother's apartment, O'Hearn would never have seen him, and he could have gone into the club with Callie.

Normally, he'd think of another case, some other location to drive past, another claimant to check on. Do a little preliminary research, fill the gaps in his schedule...but not now.

It was then completely by chance that he saw the gold Lexus. He was almost sure that the registration was familiar. He'd seen it too recently, too often, and there it was parked in front of the Beal Street Market. Led pulled around the block and walked back past the car. It was unoccupied and there was nothing in it that indicated the owner; no parking passes on the dash, no mail in the seat. Only the backseat had two large metal boxes with black handles and cables—computers or something like that. The driver was not around. Cautious, Led looked for anyone familiar in the convenience store, but the small market was empty. A fan propped on a chair held the door open in a vain attempt to let out some of the midsummer humidity. There was not even a clerk when Led glanced in and continued past the window. Then with a bit of a clamor the dark-skinned man wearing a white untucked shirt shuffled quickly from the walk-in beer cooler. He was holding his hand and whimpering as if there had been an accident, but he didn't go for medical supplies or the phone. He punched up the register and counted out large bills from beneath the drawer. A wide-shouldered bald man walked from the cooler and grabbed the money unceremoniously without saying anything. Led stood back around the corner and watched as the Lexus drove away.

Led was glad for the brief distraction. He'd seen the bald man before, but the registration gave no clue as it came back to a rental car. As the afternoon sun clouded over, he turned around and drove over to the mall, where he was supposed to meet Chancellor.

He got out of the jeep and walked under the awning of the ATM kiosk. He missed Callie now, he could imagine already what it would be like if she was gone. She would be only a half mile away from where he and Chancellor would set up, but it was too far. Only two days ago he hadn't been worried about her and she had been fine. Now all he thought about was how unsafe she probably was. Two days ago his mind had been clear, he could concentrate on work, read a paper. If she had never called him back, he had been prepared for it. He had experience with shifting expectations. Defenses had been in place.

Now, it seemed, they were gone.

People are capable of anything. He documented it every day. One day they were suddenly tempted or inspired or prodded into doing something no one, including themselves, ever thought they could. He'd found himself worrying about something happening to Callie, this woman he had met but two days ago...

The clouds started to release a mist that was more than fog but less than rain. Moisture settled in droplets like dew on every exposed surface. It gathered on the awning overhead and dripped to the ground.

Drips of change, people were buckets full of water into which life continued dripping, always adding and splashing away just a little of what was already there.

Once tonight was over, he was going to lighten up, be a little more carefree. Be like Callie.

He stepped out from under the shelter of the ATM kiosk as he saw the dark blue Ford Excursion enter the mall parking lot. A drop of rain dripped from his hair and ran down the side of face as he waited for the vehicle to turn around and pull up beside him. He climbed into the passenger seat.

"Are you ready, Mr. Ledbettor?"

Led looked into the empty backseat, "Are we it?"

"No, the comm team is already in place." Chancellor had an earpiece and spoke into it as they drove off. "In transit, ETA four minutes..."

Led sat quietly.

"I copy, west by southwest, on alternate route bravo, roger." He was reaching into the backseat for a Kevlar vest. "You're going to have to wear this," he said.

"A vest? You're sitting in a car. If someone's going to shoot you, it will be in the head. Unless you're going to make me wear a helmet, too..."

"No, but we might make you wear a gag."

"I'll wear the vest," Led said, amused enough to humor his request now. "Even though I think the only thing it will prevent is a coffee spill on my shirt."

"It's my job not to put you in harm's way. It's merely a standard procedure."

"So how do I look?" Led asked, finishing with the Velcro straps. "Black isn't usually my color. I prefer the autumn palette."

Chancellor ignored him.

"Any chance you have another headset? I'm feeling kind of left out of the loop here."

Chancellor appeared to consider the protocol before relenting. "Under the armrest," he said.

Led opened the armrest and observed a yellow meter device and a small box labeled *dosimeter radiation film*. "What's this—a Geiger counter?"

"We don't know what shape the imaging unit is in. If it's damaged, there could already be radiation leaking."

"Imaging unit? In the club, where Callie is?"

"If we knew it was in there we could just go get it, but if it's already moved along the supply chain, we need to determine who has it and where. We haven't picked up any radiation from outside of the building."

"How much radiation we talking about?"

"You would have to have prolonged exposure to a concentrated amount. You shouldn't worry."

"Worry? I won't expose myself to the radiation in a tanning booth. If you can't see it, hear or smell it you don't know anything until it's already got you," Led said, realizing he had just described his burgeoning affection for Callie, whom he had now put in the middle of this mess.

Callie had dubbed her handler, Agent Kim Clark, "Lil' Kim," not because she looked like the rapper, which she didn't (she was white and rather tall) but because it was the only mnemonic device she could come up with to help her remember Kim's name. She had been calling her Karen by accident, and it seemed rude to not remember Agent Clark's first name; she was so nice.

"You could just call me Agent Clark," Agent Kim Clark said. "But whatever you like."

Callie saw them already becoming friends.

Lil' Kim had wired up her purse and bra, taught her how to place the electronic bugs she was expected to leave behind in the bar, went over the gigahertz frequencies the transmitters worked on.

She set up a diagram of the club based on what Callie had described and what they'd gotten from inspectional services, illustrated where they wanted the devices placed.

Lil' Kim would be in the surveillance vehicle "Comm One" as one of the monitors. If something were to go wrong, she'd be the first to go into the bar, posing as one of Callie's friends.

The FBI, or *Feds*, as she was calling them, had her drive a rented Mercury Marquis. They had briefed her on all the electronics but neglected to tell her how to turn on the windshield wipers and adjust the seat. She drove cautiously from the hotel to the club with the seat too far back and the mirrors askew, imagining all the while how embarrassing it would be to get in an accident.

She parked on the street a block from the bar. She didn't know where Led was, but was sure he was watching her. She glanced up and down the street to check for traffic as she crossed, but consciously didn't focus on any of the parked vehicles.

He'd be out there; she knew that.

A muscular stud in his late twenties stood on the front steps of the club talking on a cell phone.

"The bartender, right?"

"Right," she said, as he opened the door for her.

From the corner of her eye she saw many of the evening's patrons looking her up and down, leaning into each other, making comments, forcing laughs.

Phil, the bartender, looked up from ringing two beers into the cash register. He slapped the change down under his palm and slid it over to the man with the sideburns and narrow beard that just outlined his jaw. The man picked up the bills and let the quarters slide onto the bar.

"You showed up," Phil said.

Callie smiled. "You thought I could turn down a career opportunity like this?"

"Come on back here," he said, lifting the hinged section at the end of the bar. "Let's get you started."

"What's with the bouncer?"

"Sully only wants club members tonight. It's a pay-per-view event. He doesn't need people sneaking in just to see the fight."

Phil showed her the cash register, went over the drink prices. They cost pretty much the same, a shot, a mixed drink, a glass of wine. Beer was a dollar-fifty cheaper.

"Do we bus the tables?"

"Only if we need glasses. We're not their mother."

The bar was busy with three or four guys leaning on it at a time. Several others stood in the lighted area, talking and smoking.

"Lot busier tonight than the other day."

"We get a lot more on a fight night. Why not hang out with friends and watch it for free."

A man in a black dress shirt stood at the bar with a twenty dollar bill on the counter.

"What can I get you?" she asked.

"Two Buds and a gin and tonic."

He left two bucks on the counter as a tip. She put the singles in the coffee can under the bar. The back room was a lot noisier than last time. More chairs had been unstacked from the corner, the tables set up in no particular pattern, some so close together men had to stand up to let others by. A steady stream of drinkers came to the bar.

"Where's Sully?" she asked.

"He might have had some guys driving tonight," Phil answered. "He'll be here before the fight starts."

"We don't charge?"

"Nah, it's a benefit to the members. We get the feed off of one of Sully's buddies. Nothing illegal. It's paid for. Just instead of one person it's fifty, anybody ever have a problem with it, forty-nine of them weren't watching."

She didn't see O'Hearn enter until almost eight o'clock.

Aware of Lil' Kim outside listening for the first time since stepping behind the bar, Callie made a little sound as she cleared her throat. "Hey, it's the electrician man. What can I get you?"

"A rum and Coke."

"So you finished wiring downstairs," she said, scooping some ice into an almost-clean glass, pouring a jigger full of rum and spraying in some Coke from the bar nozzle. "Am I safe behind the counter here?"

"I don't think you'll get shocked, but then again this gang can be pretty shocking. So you better be careful."

"I'll try," she said, thinking he had no idea how careful she was trying to be.

Perkins stared the muscle bound kid in the eyes and the bouncer of the Harbour Club nodded to him in deference as he passed, even though he had never seen the kid before. He walked into the bar and was a little anxious to see the blonde woman again, now behind the bar serving drinks with an old-timer. He was sure it was the same blonde that had gone to the Federal Building. At that point Perkins knew he had walked into some police or federal sting and it was only a matter of time before the shit hit the fan. He feared disappointing Uncle Charlie more than the police, so he decided to have his words with Paul O'Hearn like he planned, and then get the hell out of there. So with the trepidation of a miner sensing a cave-in about to happen, Perkins walked into the backroom and found Paul O'Hearn nursing a drink.

"Excuse me. Can I talk to you?" Perkins said as he grabbed O'Hearn by the elbow, with a forceful but social gesture.

O'Hearn turned. Never having seen Perkins before he was jovial in this setting, relaxed. "Sure."

"In private," Perkins said and stepped several feet away from the other men standing around talking.

O'Hearn walked over to him, clearly not suspecting who Perkins was.

"What is it?" he asked, and Perkins stood silent for a moment. O'Hearn's grin turned to a look of concern.

"You should be a good son and keep your room clean for your mom."

O'Hearn's look of concern melted to rage. "Who the fuck do you think you are, scaring my mother?" Others in the room turned to watch the exchange, even though most of the conversation was muffled by the loud television.

"Hold on there, slick," Perkins said, comfortable in his familiar role as the emotionally placid as his adversary flailed about. "You took some things that were not yours and I took them back."

"Tuttle sent you here?"

"Uncle Charlie sent me here. Tuttle wouldn't know which end to wipe without a hat on his head."

"I don't know no Uncle Charlie."

"And you still don't. But let's just say that the equipment you took belonged to someone else and now they want it back."

"You took it back."

"I have to get it all back. You can either return it all civil like a past due library book, paying the late fee, or I will come to you and repossess it along with a few of your body organs."

"What did Tuttle tell you?" O'Hearn spoke in a loud whisper, conscious of the others in the room. "I don't have it. You took what I had."

"Not my problem. I will be at your mother's house tomorrow night to pick it up. Let's say seven o'clock. And for her sake I hope you're there with it all."

"You come near my mom again and I'll make you regret it."

Right then Perkins should have broken a few bones in the man's hand or face to get his attention and emphasize future intentions. But with the blonde behind the bar all he wanted was to get out of there. As Martinez would have said, *"Muy caliente con Federaleés."* So he backed out the door as O'Hearn stood and sipped from his drink with the cold stare of a prehistoric lizard.

"I'll see you tomorrow night," Perkins said and walked out.

He drove around the block and saw the box truck conspicuously parked on the residential street, undoubtedly with several police inside. He avoided it like a hornet's nest by going around it by two side streets, and there he found O'Hearn's car. Perkins pulled in between a residential garage off the street and waited for O'Hearn, out of the way of whatever the police had planned.

TWENTY

Led and Agent Chancellor were parked before a closed auto parts store. They stared out at the mist that gathered on the windshield. Neither had said much to the other, both being used to the quiet of surveillance and extending to each other the courtesy of not needing to talk for the sake of talking.

Callie had driven by, followed by the surveillance vehicle forty minutes before. Led did not like their surveillance position, established from a point where they could not directly observe the club. But it was clear that his opinion was not going to influence the operation. He wasn't happy, but he was determined not to let any of his wisecracks get him thrown out.

"You get paid extra for nights and weekends?" he finally asked.

"I'm sure you do better than us," Chancellor said.

"I don't even know if Callie and I can bill for this. I get the feeling we're putting in a lot of time gratis."

"The insurance company will pay."

"I'm paid by the hour, on a budget. They hire me to do surveillance on *people*. They don't usually want to pay for doing surveillance on a building...buildings don't tend to get too active."

"You're doing surveillance on O'Hearn."

"We'll see," Led said, doubting any benefit from any of it.

Chancellor had apparently decided to be chummy. "I'm thinking when I retire I might try some private work."

Led had heard it before. Cops weren't interested in his line of business when he needed them most, but let them get their pensions and suddenly they wanted his job.

"You don't want to do private investigation work. Every day your job is solving someone's problem."

"That's what I do now."

"No, see, you're doing your job even if there's nothing to investigate. A slow day is a good day. It means you have it under control. Private sector, if we aren't trying to work an investigation—for less money than some people spend for cable television—we're out trying to hustle more work. When has public law enforcement ever had to go looking for more work?"

"But look at your perks. The expense accounts, the big money..."

"Look at your retirement and benefits!" Led sat forward to watch as another car drove up the hill toward the club.

"Relax," Chancellor said in response to his sudden alertness.

Led just looked at him.

Chancellor looked out the windshield, at the rain starting to hit harder in the dark night.

"Have you been following me?" Led asked.

"If we were, I couldn't tell you."

"I don't suppose you could, but you wouldn't slash my tires, would you?

"No matter how much I don't like you."

Led smiled at that and said, "I appreciate that. Someone did, though, two nights ago. I'm sure it's someone I investigated in the past, someone I pissed off, but I haven't been able to figure out what case."

"Have you seen anyone?"

"There were these two guys that I ran into, but I can't prove they had anything to do with it. But I still get the feeling someone's skulking around my home, and once or twice I just had a sense about it."

"Maybe someone else was following you. Our sources indicate that there is organized crime involved."

"Involved in what? The missing medical equipment?"

"Maybe with all of Mobile Medi Tech."

"Who are your sources?"

"Intelligence is gathered from many places."

Led suddenly realized that Mrs. Tuttle was not meeting a lover; she was meeting the FBI. "You've been talking to Tuttle's ex-wife."

Chancellor didn't flinch. He looked forward, unrevealing, and said, "I'm sure the Bureau talks with lots of people."

"Were you watching him before the items turned up missing?"

"The length of the investigation does predate your involvement."

"Interesting."

"Yes, it can be." And that was all Chancellor added.

"Did the FBI look at the medical unit in the tow yard?"

Chancellor was still for a moment, as if weighing his answer. "I looked at it today. Yes. Standard procedure."

"Today? You looked at it?" Led considered the timing of who was in the tow yard when. "What was with the busted up cabinet? Did you guys go in there and wail on it with a tire iron? It clearly didn't happen in the turn over, and the rest of the vehicle was nicer than any home I ever had."

"We are looking into it."

"So it wasn't you guys. O'Hearn? But he didn't have anything with him when he climbed out." Led waited, but Chancellor sat quiet. "Hey, you don't have to tell me anything."

"I know I don't."

"It doesn't affect my investigation of O'Hearn; just thought you might like to compare notes, since I have been in and around this case."

"I thought we have a copy of your notes."

"You have what I wrote down; you don't have all the suppositions and theories I've been working on. Not that the FBI needs my help. Oh, wait, that's why Callie and I are here. The FBI does need our help. Couldn't get into the Charlestown Projects, couldn't get a cover for getting into the Harbour Club."

"You are trying to bait me into revealing confidential information."

"Nah, I'm just having fun bustin' your balls," Led said. "So are you having an affair with Tuttle's wife?"

"Jesus. No. That would be against protocol." Chancellor was rattled at the insinuation that he would go against department policy.

Led felt better and sat back. Neither man looked at each other, but sat looking out into the streetlights into the night and the rain. There was no trust, only respect between the thinking warriors.

Rollin had sat looking through the green luminescence of night-vision binoculars while Dale watched the end of the street for any vehicle O'Hearn might have left in. When the silver Chrysler drove past, they followed.

As it pulled into a residential neighborhood, Dale had hung back slightly and lost contact with it on the grid of side streets. Now, every silver Chrysler they saw could be O'Hearn's.

Dale and Rollin had been dealing with Tuttle, who had flipped out that Ledbetter quit. He preferred to fire people, and he would consider firing them if he knew they had lost contact with O'Hearn.

Where the hell had Paul O'Hearn gone?

And then they had seen the small sign for a neighborhood club: the Harbour Club. And they were pretty sure that they located the right silver Chrysler a block and a half away.

"Wait here," Dale told Rollin. He pulled alongside the club and dashed through the rain to the door. The bouncer was a young kid with baseballs for biceps.

"May I help you?" he asked, holding one hand up.

"I was going to meet someone here for a drink."

"Are you a member?" The bouncer squinted as if it would help him recognize the face or maybe thinking required the energy that normally held his eyes open.

"No. I think the person I'm meeting is a member."

"Who's that?"

"Paul O'Hearn."

"Hold on a minute. I think he's already here."

He hadn't wanted to use O'Hearn's name. It painted him into a corner, but at least he confirmed he was inside.

The bouncer walked into the club. Dale had nothing else he could do if Paul O'Hearn came back to the door, so he ran through the rain back to the van.

"He's at the Harbour Club in Revere, Mr. Tuttle."

"You were supposed to call me every fifteen minutes."

"I'm sorry, sir. We were mobile; we were concentrating on staying with him."

"Don't be sorry, be a professional. I'll be waiting."

"What did he say?" Rollin asked.

"He said good job," Dale said and wondered what to do next.

TWENTY-ONE

Sully arrived at quarter to eight and turned the channel from ESPN highlights to the pay-per-view fight.

"How's the first night going?" he asked Callie.

"Phil's a good teacher," she said, without slowing the flow they had going together, grabbing bottles, pouring drinks, running the register.

"Once the fight starts it'll slow down a little. Let you catch your breath."

"She isn't missing a beat," said Phil. "It's me that needs the rest."

"Go on, Phil," she said. "I can handle it. I don't know what time you got here, but you've been standing for a while."

"I was kidding. I'm fine."

Sully stood at the end of the bar, chomping on an unlit cigar. "I was going to bring over the stretch Hummer to show you. But I got a job for it at the last minute."

"I'll see it sometime, I'm sure," she said.

Sully slid sideways up onto the high-backed bar stool.

Callie reached into her purse and unwrapped a piece of gum. Putting it in her mouth, she held the pack out to Phil. "Want a piece?"

"No thanks."

"Sully?"

"All set."

She put the gum back in her bag and retrieved two of the small devices she was expected to place. The things were each the size of a half-sucked mint, with adhesive backing. She used her thumbnail to scratch the cover off, placing one up under the counter as she bent over. The other one she put in the pocket of her black slacks.

Sully continued. "My limo service is doing pretty well. To the point where I've been looking for a manager to help coordinate the drivers, work in the office, that sort of thing."

"Excuse me, Sully," Callie acknowledged. "Phil, it looks like we're almost out of glasses. I'm going to go gather some."

Phil looked under the bar. There was still a full rack of glasses. She glanced at Sully and held her breath, hoping she had placed the device out of sight.

"You don't have to yet," Phil said to her. "But if you don't mind, the bin is right there."

Callie carried the large gray plastic container as she ducked under the closed bar top. "I might know someone who's interested in the job," she said, putting a hand on Sully's shoulder. "I'll be right back." Truth was, she was trying to think up some name she could give, a friend of a friend. It was only a game she was playing tonight, but her years of experience dealing with men in general made her reflexively avoid letting Sully think he was getting anywhere with her.

She walked into the smoky, dark room and stayed near the wall so as not to get in anyone's view of the television. She gathered glassware, looking for a place to put the bug. Not near the air conditioning unit, preferably under a non-moveable object, like a sill or chair rail. There was nothing in the room, no windows, mostly just folding tables and chairs. Finally she found a heavy metal worktable with a Formica top, covered with empty beer bottles and a few empty glasses; moveable, yes, but at least it didn't fold.

She picked up the glasses and dropped a cocktail napkin. Bending to pick it up, she grabbed the table's edge to steady herself and placed the flat black wafer underneath it. No one seemed to notice. At least, not the bug; she sensed some of them watching her bend over, looking at her ass. She continued to walk around picking up glassware. Some of the tables in the back were tight.

Even in the darkened room, she recognized O'Hearn sitting at the far side of a table, facing the doorway, but with his head and shoulders turned to the right, toward the boxing match.

She walked back to the bar with the heavy bin of glasses. Sully sat nursing his drink, or already had another one. She hoisted the bin to the counter.

"You don't watch the fights?" she asked Sully.

"Some. I don't have any money on this first fight. The main event is the only one that interests me," he said. "Are you a fight fan?"

"I have to admit," she said, setting the bin down by the small bar sink, "that some of the boxers are nice to look at before they start bleeding, but the whole thing is a little boring to me." She turned to Phil and asked, knowing the answer: "Dishwasher?"

"You're it," Phil smiled.

"Two men," Sully said. "Nothing but their wits, strength, and training to try to overtake their opponent. It's the purest sport."

"For those reasons, I can see why some people enjoy it." She ran the water and started washing the glasses by hand in the small sink. "I guess I just prefer my sports to have running."

"Running? That eliminates a lot of good sports...golf... NASCAR."

"Don't forget bowling," she added.

"If someone in that fight starts running," Phil chuckled, "call me in. Dollars to doughnuts it's my fighter."

"Poor Phil," Callie said as she saw the bouncer walk in.

"Everything straight?" Sully asked.

"Yeah," the bouncer said. "You mind watching the door for a minute? I have to check if this guy outside is cool."

"Who is he?"

"I don't know. Says he's a friend of Paul O'Hearn. He's not a member."

The bouncer went into the other room and came back with O'Hearn. They both stepped outside for a moment before returning.

"He must have left," the bouncer said. "Said he was supposed to meet you here, wanted to know if you were inside."

O'Hearn slumped at the bar.

"Everything all right?" Sully asked. "You don't look so good."

Paul O'Hearn feigned a smile at Sully. "It might just be the damp weather." He gave a little cough. "I might be fighting off something."

TWENTY-TWO

Rollin felt his complete reading of the translated, unabridged Israeli Special Forces Training manual as self-proof of his determination. He had honed his skills to be as sharp as possible without ever having applied them to real-world scenarios. Though he had never seen action, he was a mercenary in the making.

Dale was trusting him to get inside the club, and he would.

He told Dale to pull over and park. He would have to walk a ways in the rain, but it was all right, he needed to catch his breath. It was an anxious, shallow breathing. He was going to do it—enter the bar and establish surveillance, light and breezy. He turned his camouflaged jacket to the orange side out and put up the hood, maneuvering so Dale wouldn't see the gun in the small of his back. It was raining hard and his legs got wet as he walked down to the club.

He'd seen Dale get turned away, so he walked past the bouncer and stood to the side with the hood up and his face mostly covered. He lit a cigarette and leaned back under the building's eave as the waterfall of rain running from the roof narrowly passed in front of him. He seldom smoked, but it felt like what he should do sometimes. He found that the nicotine gave him a calming lightheadedness. The image he projected made him feel more pensive, more in control. A man with a goatee came out of the club. He saw Rollin under the eave and ducked out of the rain beside him.

"It's too loud in there to hear," the man said, gesturing with his cell phone.

Rollin nodded and inhaled on his cigarette, not understanding how the splattering rain could be any quieter.

"Having a good time?" the man asked as he dialed on his phone.

"Pretty good," Rollin responded thinking, *for a guy standing in the rain.*

The man held the phone to his right ear and put his left hand over his other ear to block out the rain's ambient hush. It seemed like he was calling home. He said he'd stopped at Home Depot and picked up the hose. He promised to fix the washer in the morning. After the fight he would probably stay and have a couple of beers. Yep, he loved her too, and told her to kiss the kids goodnight for him.

"Marital bliss," he said to Rollin as he hung up.

"I hear you," Rollin said, pushing back his hood.

"The first fight is about to start, the under-card is supposed to be a pretty solid match up."

It seemed he had gotten a break. The guy with the phone thought that he, too, had come out from inside the club. Why wouldn't he have? There was no one outside on this rainy night except them and the bouncer under the awning by the door.

Rollin tossed the last third of his cigarette onto the wet sidewalk and the orange ember hissed in the fat rain. Rollin found himself boldly following the man to the doorway. To give the bouncer the impression they were together, he nervously started a conversation about which he knew nothing.

"You have any money on the fight?"

"Nah, but Troy O'Shea has five grand on De La Hoya."

"He's crazy. Five grand?"

"You know Troy?" the guy with the phone asked as they neared the doorway.

"I know *of* Troy." The bouncer was staring at him as they passed. "I've heard how he makes crazy bets. But I don't know him personally. Just see him around, you know...."

"He's over at the table with Sully."

Rollin was now walking up the several brick steps to the frosted glass door. The bouncer said nothing. He stalled in the entryway, between the inner and outer doors, and shook the rain from his coat by running his hand over his shoulders and down the sleeves. The man with the phone had gone inside.

The sounds of the bar—men talking, the television, bottles hitting tabletops and chairs sliding on the floor, like an orchestra tuning their instruments—were muffled.

He stood stunned with indecision.

He hadn't expected it to be this easy to be right inside the door. But he hadn't known what to expect. He'd gone over it in his head only up to entering the club. He looked back through the inner door at the woman behind the bar, watched as she picked up a gray bin and walked into the semi-darkness of another room. There was only one patron at the bar, a shaven-headed man who turned and glanced at him before returning to his beer. He pushed through the inner door and went to the bar. Now was his chance to settle in. Now he had to be natural.

He ordered a beer, took a sip, and looked around to get comfortable. Except for the Neon Tetra, he didn't stop anywhere unless it was with Dale. Dale was the social one; Rollin was more in his element with the covert end of things. Stalking through darkness was different than walking through a social club where everyone seemed to know each other.

"Excuse me," he asked the bartender. "Where's the men's room?"

"Behind you, right over there." The bartender never looked at him but at the television in the other room, barely visible from such an obscure angle.

He pushed through the door, the word MEN scribbled in black marker inside a rectangle of yellow glue where the original sign had been.

The small mint-green room contained one sink and one urinal, deeply stained with orange-brown rust and mineral deposits. The floor tile was wet from rainy shoes, urine, and spilled beer, the air putrid. He set his beer on the sink. The door didn't lock, so he went behind the bent metal partition to urinate in the toilet—changing his mind once he saw the source of the odor, unflushed. He took his chances for exposure at the urinal. He felt himself stalling as he washed his hands, using the side of his pants to dry them. Looking in the mirror he saw that his hair was wet but not too matted. He pushed his fingers through it to place it just so, letting a strand fall across his forehead, giving himself that devil-may-care look he so wanted. He tucked in his shirt and adjusted the 9mm in the holster in the small of his back, covered by his jacket.

Dale wouldn't have been happy that he was carrying, mostly because it was Dale's gun—the one he kept in the glove compartment.

He walked into the backroom and found an empty metal folding chair near the wall. He sat and feigned limited interest in the boxing on the television while around the dimly lit room he looked for Paul O'Hearn.

Paul couldn't concentrate on the fight as he tried to think what his father or brother would do. But it had been that type of thinking that had put him in this mess to start with, and then Sully walked over and put a hand on his shoulder.

"That guy in the orange coat..." Sully said. "I don't recognize him."

Paul knew Sully had a good eye for things like that. This guy, sitting by himself, avoided looking at anyone, he might be a spotter—a cable company snitch busting up clubs like theirs for illegal pay-per-view screenings.

"The one that looks like a pumpkin?"

"Yeah," Sully said. "I think he might be trouble."

On second glance, Paul recognized him as one of the men that worked for Tuttle doing security detail. They'd never spoken, but it was the same man.

Tuttle was having him threatened and now followed.

Rollin didn't see O'Hearn until the big man's hand hit him in the chest, grabbing at his jacket, at his flab.

"Come on, pumpkin boy—"

Rollin was lifted to his feet and almost out of his chair, the 9mm in the small of his back catching on the back of the metal folding chair. The chair followed into the air, the weight of it pulling the pistol from his waistband before crashing down, the accompanying thud of the gun onto the floor seeming to draw no one's attention.

Rollin stood on his tiptoes to ease the pressure of his jacket from cutting under his arms. And when O'Hearn looked to the floor, Rollin, in a panicked reflex of which he would later be proud, sprayed mace in the big man's eyes.

The grip released and Rollin fell backward on the floor, onto the collapsed chair and next to the 9mm Sig Sauer with walnut grip. He wanted to retreat, to get up and run, but even as O'Hearn rubbed at his eyes, hacking away like a cat with a hairball, he kicked at Rollin on the floor, landing a rib-cracking blow to his right side. Evading a second blind kick, Rollin shot in O'Hearn's general direction before he could consider kicking a third time.

The shot had only been a warning, and O'Hearn heeded it, falling to the floor and rolling out of the way until he hit the wall, his eyes streaming tears and nose and mouth draining snot and drool.

Rollin scrambled to his feet, leaving the gun behind on the floor. He was as disoriented as if he'd just gotten off the tilt-a-whirl and then someone else started shooting. He could only assume the shots were fired at him. There was no mistaking it: this was not the soft *pfsst* and *blatt* of paintballs, it was the real crack and whiz of light armament.

Rollin ran for his life, a man possessed. Dale must have seen him emerge, as he was already speeding toward him in the van.

"Go, go, go!" Rollin shouted, even before he had completely climbed in.

"Are you alright?" Dale asked.

"That was fucking nuts!" Rollin started laughing in a manner that indicated that he had thoroughly enjoyed himself but was glad it was over. He thought of how he had looked at a man and shot, albeit missing—but he still had pulled the trigger.

"What happened?" Dale asked, apparently wanting in on the laughs.

"O'Hearn's in there. And I just taught him who not to mess with." Rollin said and thought all real Special Forces commandos must get this feeling of euphoria.

TWENTY-THREE

When the white van had first arrived at the Harbour Club, no one on the surveillance crews had taken any special notice. It had appeared to be just another patron of the Harbour Club, and the FBI comm team operating out of the back of the Ryder rental truck made no mention of it.

Later, as Chancellor was listening to them relay the quietness of the situation, they suddenly exclaimed: "*What the hell is that?*"

"Come back, Comm One."

"*We have gun shot, maybe two points of origin in the room. A suspect is leaving now…*"

"Let's go!" Led said, hitting both palms against the dash as if the motion would get the car to move.

"Do you have a visual?" Chancellor asked into the headset. "Repeat, do you have a visual?"

"*Negative. The night vision is compromised due to the light in the club. The low lux vision is junk in this fog and rain. It looks like several men are rushing out. How do you want us to respond?*"

"Call the locals," Chancellor said. "But don't let them know why we were here. They'll be bullshit, but tell the chief I will personally bring him up to speed later. I'll follow the van, copy that. You provide assist. We are here to recover the package. If we rush in brandishing badges now we could lose it."

"*Lose* it?" Led interrupted. "Hey, Callie is in there—"

"*Copy that.*"

"Did you see his face?" Chancellor asked.

"*Negative, haven't seen suspect. We had one male run out and get in a white van just after the shots fired.*"

"Was he carrying anything to the van?"

"Negative. Nothing that couldn't fit in his jacket. The van is coming down the hill toward you."

"I'm going to follow," Chancellor stated.

"I'm not," Led said, undoing his seatbelt. It caught in his earpiece as it spooled away. He tossed it on the seat, looking back at Chancellor as he opened the door. "Where is Callie?" he demanded.

"Mr. Ledbettor, please get in the vehicle," Chancellor said as he started the Excursion. "We will send in an agent from Comm One—"

But Led was already running toward the club.

"Comm One, that civilian running up the street is our observer. Repeat, he is not a hostile..."

As one gun had fired and then another, the room lit fully for moments, like lightning on a dark summer highway. A man fell to the floor, people moved away in ever-expanding ripples of fear.

Paul O'Hearn had watched Billy O'Shea turn over a table, taking cover behind its thin, particleboard top as he drew a weapon from his ankle holster. He fired back at the doorway three times and stopped when he realized the pumpkin was already gone.

Paul was rattled. There was no telling what Tuttle was capable of. He knew he'd been followed to the club, not once, but twice. Was he supposed to have been killed?

He picked the gun off the floor and went out the back door; damn if he was going to walk out the front and be shot.

Not without making sure his mother was safe.

TWENTY-FOUR

As the ear-ringing gunshots ended it seemed quiet, despite the panicked voices.

Callie left her purse behind the bar as she flipped up the counter and at Phil's prompting started for the back door into the rain. A steady wall of water fell, more than even the gutters could handle. It cascaded onto her, likely shorting out the microphone in her wired bra.

She saw Phil. "Go," he said. "I'm going back in to see if I can help. I have a little medical training as a corpsman."

"I think I might be giving my notice."

"Stand in line, sweetheart."

To avoid the melee in front of the club she circled the block.

"I don't know if this thing is still working," she said aloud, into her chest. "But I'm all right. I don't know who's still trying to do what to whom out front so I'm going the long way, around the block. In case someone hadn't noticed, it's raining. Helllloooo? Girl could use a ride. The next time the FBI needs my help, don't call unless it's somewhere without bullets. And sunny...let's make it a spa. I will help the FBI with their next spa case. Still don't see you coming. I think I see a man in front of me gathering animals two by two. For cryin' out loud—"

A movement in the shadows and her arm was in someone's grip; she gasped for oxygen revving her heart, flooding her brain. She saw his face as he pulled her behind a garage.

Paul O'Hearn?

"Drop the gun," he said.

"What?" Callie spit out her gum onto the ground.

He looked at the ground. *"Gun,"* he clarified. "Your gun."

"Which gun?"

"Whatever guns you have. All of them."

"I don't have a gun."

"Then why did you say 'which gun'?"

"Because I'm scared."

"FBI agents have guns."

"I don't, I'm not, *what*?"

He held her hair with one hand and ran his other along her spine, her lower back the top of her butt...as he passed around her waist she felt his breath on her neck, could smell alcohol and bar peanuts. He ran his hand hard up and down her thighs, once quickly on each side, in a manner that felt like an airport security check on steroids. She raised her arms voluntarily to show there was nothing there; her top couldn't even conceal her bra now that it was soaked through. He released her hair momentarily and squatted to run his hand up and down the inside of her legs and around her ankles.

Nothing.

"Take off the bra," he said.

"What?" Now she could see the walnut-handled pistol tucked into his pants. "Why?"

"You're wired. I heard you talking on your way down the sidewalk. It's in your bra, isn't it?"

She reached under her shirt, pulling out the small wire and microphone that had been taped there. "Do I still need to take off my bra?"

"No," he said, shaking his head. "Now toss that on the ground and step on it."

Callie did as she was told, smashing the microphone into the pavement, and then she added an extra grind of the heel into the faulty electronics for herself.

TWENTY-FIVE

The light of the club spilled out onto the wet pavement as men started coming out on to the street. Tough guys, mostly...six or seven of them had already exited, forgetting their saunters and struts. They were emerging shoulder to shoulder several deep, their hands on each other's backs, pushing like a conga line's bastard children.

Some ran for their cars and others stood jittery on the sidewalk, waiting for the police, or some other authority to give instructions.

Led could hear his heart pounding in his ears.

Callie was not among them.

He pushed his way against the crowd, through the narrow doorway.

"Callie?" he called, inside. He jumped up onto the bar, landing on his stomach to see the floor behind it.

No one.

He went into the next room, loud with men shouting, the television's continued blaring: *"...attacking Morales with a flurry of punches...he seems dazed and his right eye is swollen shut. Although visibly hurt, he continues to land hard blows..."*

The darkened room moved with the illumination of the big screen, the two boxers colliding with each other's fists. No one had bothered to turn on the overhead lights.

A smallish man with a crown of receding hair stood with his gun drawn, raised at chest level. His pant leg was still caught in his ankle holster as he spoke on a cell phone. Led paused for a second and observed that he was trying to establish some order. He was speaking with the police, yelling into the phone above the room's noise.

A body lay by a table in the back of the large room. Bottles and shot glasses were tipped over, chairs overturned and pushed into piles. Men were stepping over the body on the floor like it was a spilled drink. The man had very few features left that could be considered a face. Most of his right cheek and eye socket had been removed, exposing bright whites and dark, almost black, reds. The center of his shirt puddling with wet flesh.

Callie wasn't here.

He opened the door that read LADIES. The light didn't work but the room was illuminated enough by the light of the bar. Not in there, either. He pushed open the men's room door and checked the stall. He tried the door between the two bathrooms. It was locked. He pushed on it and then moved enough people back so that he could kick it. Part of the doorjamb splintered as the door swung open and slammed against the wall. He lost his balance when the door gave way, almost falling down the narrow stairs. A single bulb illuminated the stairwell.

"Callie!"

No answer, but he still had to look to be sure. He ran halfway down the stairs and looked. The basement was filled with cases of beer, boxes of liquor. An old furnace with obsolete size and corroded joints darkened the corner.

He ran up the stairs and heard sirens. Three men seemed to be taking directions from the man with the drawn gun, who was off-duty law enforcement of some kind. He sent one of the men to meet the arriving officers and let them know he was inside. The other two were told to get the names of everyone who had been present.

The back door was open revealing a short hallway and a small office with a gray metal desk. A man was standing using the telephone. He looked at Led briefly.

"Did you see where the woman went?" Led asked. "The lady bartender?"

The man shook his head no.

The back door opened onto a sidewalk that went beside a garage at the neighboring residence. To the left was the street. To the right was a backyard with a child's swing set. The blue lights on the other side of the building lit up the neighborhood like the Northern Lights of Law Enforcement. The police were corralling anyone they could who came from the club. Some neighbors with umbrellas were coming out to see the commotion, complicating the arriving officers' ability to distinguish witnesses from onlookers.

Callie was not out front. Led stood looking in the crowd. Next to him was a man in a pair of blue nylon sweat pants and a gray T-shirt. He had a dog on a leash, a boxer. In his other hand he held a large golf umbrella. A teenage girl also stood with him. She wore shorts that said SWEET across the buttocks and held her own umbrella. As Led stood next to them, she offered that he stand under a corner of it.

He was sure Callie wasn't inside. He needed to slow down and think...

He didn't see her up or down the street. There was no sign of any van, truck or SUV that could have been a surveillance vehicle from where they were running the Comm One...maybe they had picked her up coming out the back as he went in the front. He wanted to talk to Comm One, to ask them, but he'd left his earpiece and radio with Chancellor. That was stupid. "Shit," he said aloud. "Shit."

The man with the dog and the girl in the shorts both looked at him.

"Officer," said the man with the dog, "I knew it was gun shots. Soon as I heard it. We live right over there."

Led then realized he was still wearing the black bulletproof vest, giving the appearance of a responding officer.

"Keep back, folks," he heard someone shouting. "Let the ambulance in." A red light came up the street, a siren whelping its way closer.

Led turned and started walking back down the hill. A cruiser drove toward him and started to slow, and he extended his arm and waved them on. It worked. They continued up the hill. He jogged down the street, back to the corner where he and Chancellor had been sitting. The empty parking lot, the auto parts store. There, mad at himself, at Chancellor and the whole goddamn situation, he ripped free the Velcro straps, removed the vest, threw it to the ground, and ran for his jeep.

TWENTY-SIX

Paul O'Hearn gripped Callie's arm as he led her around the back of a small white house. The short, one-car driveway didn't have any vehicles in it. He pushed her to the door and told her to knock, to ring the doorbell.

No one answered. No lights came on.

"Good," he said. He nudged her around the side of the house, to a side door. He had her pick up a decorative lawn ornament—a fairy sitting on a toadstool—and used it to rap once on one of the small panes in the door. The gushing rain muffled the sound of the glass falling to the cement floor behind it.

"In here," he said. "Don't touch anything."

Not that she could see anything to touch. It was dark, and she walked with short shuffle steps so as not to trip, ramming her hip into the corner of a workbench in the process. She suppressed the urge to swear.

The only light was the mercury-orange glow of a streetlight out front coming through the panes in the door and a rectangular cellar window deeper in the room.

"Sit," he said. "In the light, so I can see you."

She walked to the geometric shape cast on the floor, squatting so as not to have to sit on the cold cement.

She couldn't see what he was doing. It sounded like he was feeling around in the shadows for something.

"Come get this and sit on it," he said.

She walked toward his voice and saw that he was referring to a five-gallon bucket. It had a cover and looked heavy. She dragged it across the floor to the light and sat dripping, quiet. The night's adrenaline had worn off and no longer warmed her. She felt goose bumps on her arms, heard her teeth chattering. She tried to stop but couldn't.

In the shadows he pulled down something like a drop cloth. He tossed it to her, and she put it over her shoulders. It was rough from dried paint, like a wool blanket studded with wood chips.

Still, it warmed her, some.

Paul stood by the window looking out, half his face in the shadows. She sat still shivering, water dripping from her clothes and forming puddles on the floor, a black shadow on the lighter concrete. In the dark nothing had color, everything a shade of gray, black, and darker black.

The television crews with their telescoping antennas arrived, lighting up the neighborhood with enough white lights for a night game.

TWENTY-SEVEN

Callie!" Led yelled in the dark of the parking lot.

He knew it was futile, but he yelled again, "Callie!"

Only the rain, the nearby traffic, and the distant sirens responded. He jogged along the sidewalk off Route 60, splashing in the potholes and catching the spray of the passing traffic on the busy, four-lane street. Almost two miles he went before returning to the mall, where his jeep was parked.

Only after he was back in the jeep with the key turned did he notice that the steady rain had turned into a torrential downpour. He was soaked through, the back of the seat pushing the cold, wet shirt to his back. The defroster and heater had to be turned on full blast to counter the fogging windshield. In the glove box he found the business card Chancellor had given him. He called the cell phone. It went straight through to voicemail.

"This is Led. I'm trying to find Callie." He strained to control the foreign feel of panic. "Please give me a call back to let me know where to meet everyone."

She might be fine, he thought, sitting in an office, getting debriefed.

But then again she might not be.

He headed to the Holiday Inn, where he had dropped her off over eight hours earlier.

He knocked on the door of Room 214, the room they had used that afternoon. No answer. He stepped back to be sure he had the right room. No light could be seen around the edge of the closed curtain. Maybe they weren't back yet. He waited. He checked his cell phone.

No messages.

He went to the front desk and asked if Room 214 had checked out.

"Yes, sir," said the shiny-faced clerk from behind the counter. "Late this afternoon."

He called Chancellor again but hung up this time without leaving a message. He called Callie's cell phone and listened to her recorded voice, saying she was busy and to leave a message. It somehow almost calmed him.

"Call me as soon as you get this message," he said.

On her home phone he waited for the answering machine. "Callie, it's me. Pick up."

Nothing.

With nowhere to go to wait for her, he went to her condo. He sat in his jeep parked on the street with the motor running. No radio, just the blast of the heater fan and the rain. He started to realize he was cold, so he took off his shirt and twisted it, wringing the rain onto the floorboard. When he put it back on he was given a chill, colder now even than before.

He made a career out of waiting, but nothing like this.

He'd gotten carried away. She was thrilled to have been part of the action, but her excitement made him careless. She was inexperienced and he had been foolish. If anything happened to her...

He wanted to hear her laugh. That was all he wanted at that very moment.

He noticed his mouth guard and thought of her amusement over it. He hadn't used it in months. Now he put it in his mouth and bit down, hard, repeatedly.

Nothing but rain. How he always hated the rain. It made surveillance more difficult. Cameras automatically tried to focus on the water on the windshield, wipers flapping back and forth, drawing attention to an otherwise inconspicuous setup, and people were indoors, leaving no one to speak with.

Rain was only good for following people. In the rain, people were less attentive to what was behind them. Instead they had to concentrate on what was ahead of them.

He sat and watched her unlit apartment.

TWENTY-EIGHT

In the drive-thru lane at Dunkin' Donuts Dale ordered an iced coffee for himself and an iced mocha latté for Rollin, who still looked pale from whatever had just happened. Rollin had been chased out of places before. It's just what happened sometimes when a surveillance went bad. The blue strobe of police lights and the red revolving ambulance lights cast weird images in the night air like a psychedelic shadow puppet show gone wrong. Dale paid at the drive-up window and asked the elderly woman behind the glass what the lights and sirens were for.

"I don't know," she said, handing him his drinks. "Something's always going on around here."

"They attacked me," Rollin said as they pulled away.

"What? *Who?*"

"These guys in the club, they attacked me, they started shooting at me."

"Shooting? With guns?" Dale was flabbergasted.

"They must be dealing drugs in there. Four or five of them, they must have made me for a narc." Rollin tried for stoicism but found himself scattered with excitement. They pulled pieces and I ran—"

"They pulled pieces? Are you alright?"

Rollin remembered his side. "I might have a cracked rib," he said. He lifted his shirt and his white belly poured over his belt. Even in the poor lighting of the van's dome light could see his assailant's red shoe print.

Dale handed him his drink.

"Thanks. Hurts like hell. They had me on the ground...they were kicking me."

"Do you want to go see a doctor?"

"No, I should be okay." He leaned to one side and then the other to test his mobility before holding the cup of iced mocha latté to his side.

"We should probably go talk to the police, you know. Tell them what happened."

"Not if they're running drugs in there. I don't want some drug cartel looking for me."

"Good point." Dale sipped his iced coffee through the large straw, then gave one of his concerned looks to his partner, clicking his dental plate up and down.

Rollin wasn't about to tell him he'd left his gun in there.

Tuttle watched as the news anchor said there had been a tragic shooting earlier in Revere. A man had been fatally shot. The police were still seeking the gunman. At this time no motive was known.

They cut to a reporter standing in the rain under a blue umbrella. The Harbour Club was behind him, across the street in soft focus. People were standing everywhere and uniformed police and firefighters were moving the crowd. There was no way to tell who was a bystander and who had been in the club.

"Only an hour ago the Saturday evening of this local social club was shattered as a gunman forced his way past the doorman and opened fire with a barrage of bullets, killing Walter Dorasi, a local businessman and father of two, who may have been only an innocent bystander here to watch boxing and play cards. Police are still conducting interviews as to what the motives for the attack might have been as they continue to search for the assailant."

A large, sweating man was then interviewed as he waved around an unlit cigar. Yellow words, *James Sullivan, Witness,* appeared below his face. "I don't know why anyone would do this. Walter has done so much for the community. He ran the Sardano Golf Tournament every year to raise money for Dana Farber; he was a ref for youth hockey. He's a great guy, with two teenage sons. It's just a shame."

Tuttle checked the news on Channel 7. It was too much of a coincidence that Dale and Rollin were supposed to be watching O'Hearn at the same club.

But *Walter Dorasi?* What were they involved in? What did they screw up this time?

There was no mention of Paul O'Hearn.

Tuttle needed to call Dale but didn't want the call made from his own phone.

This is a pain the ass, he thought. He had an early tee time in the morning; he didn't want to be out all night trying to reach Dale and Rollin, so without changing from his black and white checked pajama bottoms or Cancun gift shop T-shirt with a picture of a parasailor on it, he slipped on a pair of green hospital clogs and hoped he didn't run into anyone he knew. He didn't know for a fact they were involved, but he had a feeling. Whatever the repercussions were if this episode was linked to those two idiots, he didn't want to find out from a reporter at his door. It wasn't that he feared for his life; he feared instead for his lifestyle being associated with those loose cannons. It could drive investors away from the table.

He called from a payphone in front of a Mobile station.

Dale and Rollin stood outside the van, looking out from the eighth level of the Embassy Suites parking garage into the rain. It was early Sunday morning and no one else was around.

Mrs. Tuttle's minivan had been located on the eighth level. They'd followed her enough to know she would be here. They had planned on working all night anyway and just gravitated back to watching her vehicle out of habit. If they had something to tell Tuttle about his ex-wife's activities, maybe it would be easier to tell him they'd been run out of the Harbour Club.

Dale's phone rang. He didn't recognize the number but answered anyway.

"Hello."

"What are you doing?"

"Mr. Tuttle? We're watching Mrs. Tuttle's car again. We had some problems tonight with the O'Hearn case."

"Yes, Dale, I would say you did. Are the police there now?"

"No. We didn't think we should go to the police. Why? How do you know?"

"It's all over the news."

"Things just got a little crazy, Rollin's fine."

"I don't care about Rollin. Did you find out anything about O'Hearn and where he took those crates before you shot up the club?"

"Shot up the club? O'Hearn was there but people started shooting, so we left. There's something going on there more than a social club, Mr. Tuttle. Organized crime or something."

"Did you fire a gun in the club?"

"No. I didn't even get inside. Rollin got inside and they started to work him over and he ran. They fired a few shots, he said."

Rollin nodded in confirmation.

"Did he shoot back?" Tuttle asked.

"No." Dale was confused; for some reason Rollin was hanging his head. "Rollin, did you discharge a firearm?"

Rollin didn't say anything.

"You two with your games of make-believe, you just imagined yourselves into a murder."

Dale was silent.

"You don't know? You two killed somebody and you're such screw-ups that you don't even know it."

"Know?"

"You shot a man in the head," Tuttle said. "Well, keep my name out of it. I really think you need a lawyer and a new line of work. I don't want anything more to do with either one of you. You were officially fired yesterday. Don't call me anymore. Your last check will be mailed. Don't come near the company."

Tuttle hung up.

"What did you do, Rollin?" Dale's voice cracked. "What did you *do*?"

"I don't know, there were a couple of people shooting. Anyone could have been shot. I didn't know someone was dead, I didn't even know that I hit anyone."

"You were shooting, too?"

"I was going to tell you—"

"When? When we were in the electric chair?"

"It was self-defense, Dale, I didn't—"

"Who? Who did you shoot?"

"I don't know. I was being kicked to death, and I fired a warning shot."

"How?"

"With a gun."

"With *what* gun?"

"With...with yours. With your gun."

"Jesus Christ! My gun? You are a failure, all the training I put you through?" Dale sat on the railing infuriated by the news.

"You weren't there, Dale. He was trying to kill me."

"Then we have to go to the police and tell them what you did."

"No." Rollin could feel his eyes starting to water and was thankful for the poor lighting. "No, we can't. They'll arrest me."

"I'll help you out. Get you a good lawyer."

"Oh, so that's it? We're a team until it's inconvenient for you?"

"You might have killed someone, Rollin. I need a team that sticks to the training."

"You weren't there!" Rollin shoved him, hitting him hard with both hands in the chest.

Dale gave a slight grunt, such force unexpected from his usually quiet buddy. Surprised by the aggression he lost his balance and reached out for his partner's hand too late to prevent himself from falling eight stories to the ground below.

Quiet. No scream, just a thump.

Like a two-hundred-thirty-pound bag of meat.

Rollin felt panic, a twist in his stomach. He looked over the side. Dale was on the ground, near the fenced-in utilities and the pool pump.

He was wracked up pretty good.

Rollin left the roof in a full sprint, stumbling down the stairs and around the pool to the left, where the body was lying partially in the red cedar mulch. He leaned over and listened for Dale's breathing, and then for reasons that were part anger, part guilt, and mostly misguided adrenalin he pinched Dale's bleeding nose and held a hand over his mouth.

All the while looking around, if anyone approached he would act like he just found him. Several minutes or so passed. Dale never gasped or twitched. He was still, wet road kill. Rollin walked back around to the garage. There in a puddle beneath the light he rinsed his hands.

The pink cloud diluted into nothingness.

He walked back to the van and circled his way down and out. At the attendant's booth he presented the ticket. The man inside set down his paperback and stood to ring in the cash.

"Have a good evening," the man said, returning to his book even before Rollin started to drive away.

He went to the Neon Tetra strip club to have a beer and sat at a table toward the back, watching a small blonde on stage slowly running her hands up over her own body. Suddenly he felt his stomach retch. He bent over and threw up under the table on his own shoes. Still trying to catch his breath, he felt the warm vomit wet his socks, sliding down between his feet and his loafers.

No one seemed to have noticed. The loud music and the dancer had most everyone's attention. Not feeling so good, he slid out beyond the other men standing at the bar.

He just wanted to go home.

He got to his car and took off his shoes and socks, tried to rinse them in the falling rain. It didn't work well. He started his car and drove home barefoot.

TWENTY-NINE

There was no telling how long they'd been in the cellar. She didn't wear a watch. If she ever wanted to know the time, she just checked her cell phone. Her phone, however, was still in her purse under the counter at the club.

Most of the retina-searing news lights had vanished, as far as she could tell, probably an hour earlier. Now the last news teams were departing, shutting off their lights, too.

"Are your people still out there?" O'Hearn asked.

"Who are my *people?*" She was no longer scared. In fact she was starting to get mad.

"I don't know. The FBI, Homeland Security, whatever you're called."

"My people are secretaries and auditors."

"You didn't go looking for a job in there because you needed the money. Sully hired you because he thought you'd draw more of a crowd. But you were up to something."

"I don't work for the police or anyone like that. They asked me to help. I was drafted."

"Plea bargain?"

"What? No."

"They held something over you. Drop the shoplifting or check-forging charges…"

"Why would it be that? Why wouldn't it be murder or bank robbery?"

"You're not the type."

"Are you?"

"I can be any type I have to be…people try to kill me."

"They were there for you?"

"I'm pretty sure."

"Then why did they shoot the other guy?"

"Fuck ups."

"They messed up?"

"Don't sound so disappointed."

"I didn't know hit men screwed up like that."

"You think that pro sports are the only profession with a second string?"

"What did you do—finger a mob boss?"

"Nothing that stupid, I stole some stolen property, sort of."

"That doesn't sound so smart either. What are you going to do with me?"

"I don't know."

"Kidnapping is a pretty serious offense."

"I didn't kidnap you! The most I've done is assault you with a dangerous weapon."

"So I can go?"

"Why couldn't you? It wasn't a kidnapping."

"What are you going to do?"

"I'm thinking."

"You could go to the police. Someone's trying to kill you."

"And tell them I stole something, and because of it I think someone has a contract out on me?"

"Give back what you stole."

"They already have it back. Now they want more things that I never had."

"So tell the police that."

"The FBI just watched a gunman come in and shoot up the club. What are the police going to do any different next time? They might hire competent killers next time."

"I'm going to go," she tested. "But good luck."

"Yeah, sure." He stepped back from the door to let her out.

She opened the basement door and stopped. "Do you have a phone on you that I can use? I'm pretty sure my ride left without me."

Led's cell phone vibrated. He was expecting Chancellor. The number was an unknown caller.

"Have you got her?" he answered quickly.

"You sound like you missed me," Callie said.

His heart leapt. "Where are you?"

"Near the club. You think you can pick me up?"

"I'm at your place," he said, starting the jeep and pulling onto the street almost before she finished asking the question. "It'll take me ten, fifteen minutes."

"Don't get in an accident."

"Are you with Chancellor? The son of a bitch didn't call me back."

"No. I haven't seen him all night. I haven't seen any of them since I walked in."

"Stay on the line until I get to you. I don't want you going anywhere. Okay?" He clutched the phone between his shoulder and ear in order to make the left turn using both hands, at a higher rate of speed. "Where have you been?"

"I've been visiting with Mr. O'Hearn."

"*Paul* O'Hearn? Is everything all right? I saw the dead guy. I didn't look close but I thought maybe it was him. Wait—is he listening?"

"He's about two feet away." She looked at O'Hearn. "I'm using his phone. Where are you now?"

"Route 1," Led said. "I'm pretty close to the exit. Does he know about the surveillance?"

"Which one? He knows about Chancellor's crew, and us, and whoever shot up the club."

"I don't know if he's going to recognize me or not. Is he staying until I get there?"

"Well, I have his phone."

"Right."

Callie looked at O'Hearn again. "Do you need a ride?"

"What are you asking him?" Led asked. "It might not be a good idea if he sees me."

"I don't think he's too worried about all that right now."

"Your boyfriend?" O'Hearn asked.

Callie nodded. "It's looking that way."

"Yeah, if I can grab a ride it would be good. I don't know who's watching my car right now."

"Callie—" Led said forcibly into the phone.

"I miss you," she said in a calming voice.

"I miss you, too," he said. "Alright. I'm almost there. Meet me in front of the club."

"We're going to meet him in front of the club," she told O'Hearn.

"No," O'Hearn said. "Have him drive to the far side of the block, opposite the club."

"I heard him," Led told Callie.

And for a while he didn't say anything, but she knew he was still on the phone because she could hear the expansion joints in the pavement chunking out an almost even rhythm against his tires.

"That's probably him over there," O'Hearn said, looking out through the broken pane in the door. "Tell him to shut off his lights."

"He wants you to turn off your lights."

The headlights of the jeep went off leaving only the orange of the parking lights glowing.

"I see you," she said. "We'll be right there."

The rain had almost stopped, with only a few sprinkles falling. Callie opened the front door and got in, leaning over to kiss Led. Led watched O'Hearn in the rearview mirror even as he kissed her with the side of his mouth. She reached and turned on the heat.

"Where am I dropping you?" Led asked as they pulled away.

"Anywhere near Kelly's restaurant," O'Hearn said.

It wasn't far. When they pulled along the sidewalk under the pinkish-orange glow of the streetlight, he watched O'Hearn carefully in the rearview mirror.

"Thanks for the ride." O'Hearn opened the door, but before stepping out put his left hand on Callie's shoulder. "We're cool with everything?"

"Sure, don't worry about it."

"Thanks." He then looked in the rearview mirror, straight into Led's eyes.

Led should have looked away, but didn't. He stared back.

"You got a hell of a girl here," O'Hearn said. And without giving any indication that he recognized Led, he shut the door and walked in between two high-rise condo units facing the Atlantic Ocean.

Led breathed in the moment as he gazed at what others around could not. Cars passed on the other side of the median but the darkened tint on the windows gave no one else the view he had.

"What are you looking at?" she asked.

"A beautiful woman…"

"And? You were going to say something more."

"…with brass ones."

"I'll take that as a compliment. It was supposed to be a compliment, right?

"Absolutely."

There had been no surprise when the commotion eventually erupted with blue lights and ambulances two blocks away at the Harbour Club. As Perkins sat in the shadows he hoped that Paul O'Hearn had not been someone busted in the raid or whatever they had going down tonight. He had expected O'Hearn to run to his vehicle hours ago, but Perkins had the patience of a spider so he waited through the storm of activity and the eventual calm to return. The wet streets were empty for a long time.

It had been an hour or more since a vehicle had driven up the street, but here came another. It was a black jeep and it pulled over a block away, facing in Perkins' direction. *Sure as shittin'*…there was Paul O'Hearn coming out to meet it…*and what the hell? The blonde woman.* The Indian and the blonde were starting to piss him off. No matter who or what they were, they were now an official pain in his ass.

O'Hearn and the blonde got in the jeep and drove down the hill. Perkins discreetly intercepted them two cross streets over and followed them into Revere, most of the time with his headlights off, guiding his way by the ambient lights of the suburbs.

Perkins tried to follow Paul O'Hearn where he was dropped off, but he lost sight of the man as he was on foot and cut between several buildings. If Perkins had a partner to drive, like he was supposed to, he could have jumped out and stayed with O'Hearn. Now he was forced to set up in the general area of the parking lots and hope to see O'Hearn once the sun came up.

He closed his eyes and slept, upright behind the wheel, ten to fifteen minute intervals until the first red streaks of dawn breached the horizon, and then he was ready to work another day.

THIRTY

Paul could hear the television even from outside Rico's apartment. It was almost four in the morning, but the lights were on inside. Rico was a buddy he knew from Local 103 when they had worked in a few of the build-outs together downtown. He still hooked Paul up with some weed now and again.

Paul hoped that Rico hadn't passed out hard, as he was known to do sometimes.

Finally Rico opened the door wide. He wore a black silk robe that hung untied, with the belt dragging off one side, over a white tank top and jeans with the knees ripped out.

"What the hell is that?" Paul asked, grabbing at one of the sleeves and extending the fabric like a bird's wing.

"It's my kimono. It allows freedom of movement. I've taken a few karate lessons, trying to get in shape."

"What you need is a *diet*." He slapped Rico on the belly and entered the apartment.

Rico was almost three hundred pounds but only five-foot-seven. He had several rolls at his chin, the number depending on how he held his head, which was generally back, allowing him to look down the bridge of his nose. Not that he was near-sighted; it was just something he did. When he talked he would point with his chin, as if motioning that something was going on behind the listener. Paul had gotten used to it, everyone did. If they wanted to tell a Rico story, it was easy to imitate the pose. Anyway, Rico's tick was a hell of a lot better than the old Local 103 steward, who used to say "you know what I mean" after every friggin' sentence.

"I don't really have anything on hand."

"No, I don't need to buy anything. I wanted a place to crash tonight."

"The old lady throw you out?" Rico asked.

"She might. I got some issues to resolve."

"That sucks." Rico's attention was held by the television as he sat in his easy chair, nodding. "You want a beer?"

Paul walked over to the kitchen to get a beer from the refrigerator.

"Haven't seen you in a while," Rico said. "So what's happening?"

"Different shit. Work mostly, Cheryl and the kids." He wanted to tell him about the mess he was in, use him as a sounding board. He only had until tomorrow to return something that he didn't have, but it was better to keep his mouth shut. The more people who knew, the more likely something got said to the wrong person at the wrong time. "You still with that Spanish chick?"

"Some. She started to go psycho on me. Wanted me to go to church with her on Sunday, things like that. Now I'm after a little blonde that works for Perrini."

"Nice?"

"I tell you, I would eat corn flakes out of a midget's skull to tap that."

"Not yet?"

"Nope. You making an honest woman out of Cheryl anytime soon?"

"Maybe. It don't seem to be a big deal with her. I bring it up, but she wants to wait," he said, and then added, "Her kids call me Dad."

"That's good."

"Did you stay in tonight?"

"I was over at the track and dropped five bills. The only chance I have of picking a dog to win is if it's fried up and entered in a Korean cooking contest." Rico drank from his beer. "You want me to spark one up?"

Paul wanted to get wasted more than anything, mellow out and relax, but now was not the time. He had to think. He had himself in a mess and wanted a clear head more than anything. "I'm good. I got to grab a few hours of shut-eye. I got a shit load going on tomorrow."

"Not a problem, grab the couch." Rico motioned to the movie on the television. "You ever see this one?"

Paul looked at the television and saw a baby-faced Kevin Bacon on a farm. "*Footloose?*"

"I love this movie," Rico said as he shut off the set. "I'll finish watching it in the other room."

It was a pretty dumb movie, Paul thought, but he kept it to himself. He grabbed the Marlboro blanket from the back of the couch and pulled it down on himself. Rico's place wasn't dirty, but man, his couch was something pungent, somewhere between Cheetohs and antifreeze. He moved his face to the edge of the cushion so that his nose and mouth hung off. He wondered what he was going to tell Cheryl in the morning.

He thought about calling Cheryl, maybe waking her, but without a solid idea of what to tell her, it wasn't the best idea. He shut his eyes hoping for some inspiration to slip in while he slept.

He could hear the muffled sounds of the television in the other room and hear some thumping, like Rico was doing jumping jacks, or dancing along with the movie.

They sat in a small booth eating ham-and-cheese omelets. The ham tasted like it had been packed in sawdust and the eggs were watery. The toast was cold, the butter on top having congealed into something yellow and lard-like.

She said it was the best meal she could ever remember eating. This was the woman who made fun of him for eating at Frizzell's.

Funny how with a change in perspective, even food tastes different.

Callie described the events as she tried to put them in order, summoning forth even the background things: the man walking in, his orange coat. He didn't wear a hat, which was different from the other patrons in their baseball caps and fedoras, the older men protecting their comb-overs from the pouring rain. The gunshots, how they made her jump, the other bartender pulling her down behind the bar before she even knew what happened—running and more shots.

Then out back, where she ran into O'Hearn.

Led sat listening, getting angry with himself all over again for letting her go in there. She looked so much like an innocent girl, sitting there with her damp hair matted from the rain. Her makeup had been washed and wiped away. She was clean faced and looked so vulnerable, her pinched little nose, her lips soft pink even without lipstick, her blue eyes without liner or shadow, still her prettiest feature, with or without makeup.

How had he let Chancellor talk her into going in there?

At the counter was a guy wearing dark blue pants and a matching shirt, like he was either headed to or coming from a nightshift of manual labor. He sat staring at his coffee cup like he expected it to move. A round table in the corner had some drunk kids dumping sugar and salt on the table, trying to make a ketchup bottle stand on edge. They laughed loudly as it kept falling over, crashing into plates and silverware. Two couples in their mid-sixties shared a booth. They wore windbreakers and jogging suits. The RV in the lot was probably theirs.

As Callie spoke about what O'Hearn had said she lowered her voice. He'd told her about the test equipment, how he really didn't feel that he was stealing it, but holding it so that it wouldn't work unless he also got some of the insurance money.

She leaned on the table toward Led as she all but whispered, "Why would someone try to kill him for that? I don't know what the going rate is for killing someone, but it can't be cheap—ten, twenty, thirty thousand. As a point of business it would be more economical to just pay him off. I mean, if he's dead, how are they going to get it back?"

"Obviously they didn't want it back."

"He wasn't sure about that either."

"Why was there shooting? They were trying to kill him."

"I don't know. I wasn't in the room at the time," Callie said as she ate a piece of toast. "I can't wait to find out the answer to that one."

Led let her last comment pass.

The waitress, a hard-looking woman in her forties with a slight black mustache, put the check on the table. "Have a good night," she said.

The bill was $15.38. He put down a twenty and pulled some silver coins out of his pocket without adding up the change.

They drove back to Callie's as the sky turned from midnight black to early-morning gray, outlined in orange.

She came out of the bathroom wearing Led's blue shirt only to find him in his boxers at the edge of the bed, fast asleep. She grabbed his legs and swung them up on the bed, lay down beside him, pulled a bedspread up and over them both, and laid her head on his chest.

Sunday morning came and went as they slept.

THIRTY-ONE

S unlight filtered through the closed vertical blinds. A shaft of light dancing with dust moved slowly across Paul's face and seeped into his slumber, sparking his consciousness. It was already past nine.

Rico's television was still on: two political pundits droning about something.

Paul sat up on the side of the couch, feeling as clouded as if he'd just come off a weekend bender. He rubbed his temples and then tousled his hair to get rid of his bed head, but it still stuck up on one side.

He checked the fridge. Orange juice. It smelled all right, but the carton's opening was discolored a light purple, and the thought of Rico drinking it straight from the carton changed his mind. He grabbed a couple of individually wrapped cheese slices that were in the door. On top of the refrigerator was a bottle of Bloody Mary mix. He poured a glass of that over some ice. Sitting back on the couch he unwrapped the American cheese and sipped the mix...not bad...a little tangy but the cheese mellowed the flavor.

The keys to Rico's yellow Nova SS were on the kitchen table attached to a red rabbit foot key chain. The keys to the Camaro were on a blue one. Rico had made it very clear in the past: no one but him drives the Camaro. If he didn't let the porn star he'd dated and was set to marry drive it, he wouldn't let anyone. Paul wrote a note saying he was borrowing a car; he'd be back with it gassed up in a couple of hours. He grabbed the red rabbit's foot. With the Nova, Rico would be a little more forgiving.

Paul O'Hearn drove and thought about his brother and their plan to steal a little money—more for the thrill than the cash.

They made good coin working. It was a drunken idea that got carried over until morning. Keep the amount low, keep the violence implied and do nothing more than cash a bad check. It had been his brother's idea to switch shirts with him when he got back. Mess up the eyewitness accounts, because though they looked as similar as any brothers, Paul had twenty pounds on Mark. Hell, Mark had made it a point to wear his jacket as he was chatting it up with the roach coach driver that morning. It was a casual complaint that the chicken salad sandwich tasted bad. Cause a scene, just a little one, make the driver of the canteen truck smell the sandwich and give him another one, careful not to overdo it; the driver of the truck was a nice guy.

It went terribly wrong.

The money wasn't the issue as much as what it meant. It had been his and Mark's last adventure together. With the money Paul expected to get when Cheryl won her lawsuit with the city, he could open a bar and call the place Marko's, and the money from the banks would be used to buy one of those big wooden pool tables. For Mark and Dad. That felt right.

He drove over to the Lynnway, got a coffee, and called Cheryl from the only payphone he knew of still around. The FBI could be monitoring his cell.

"Hello?" she answered in a low, strained voice.

"Hi, baby." His tone was submissive.

"Paul? Where are you?"

"I spent the night at Rico's."

"Why didn't you call me? I am pissed."

"I'm sorry. I didn't have time to call you for a while, and then it got too late. I didn't want to wake you or the kids."

"You think I *slept?* I saw the news. There was a shooting at the club, what was I supposed to think?"

"I'm sorry." He was repeating himself. He didn't really have anything else to say. He should have called her sooner. Even though she was mad at him, there was a touch of normalcy; it grounded him and helped him think a little clearer.

"You make me crazy. All I could think about was that day."

That day. She meant Mark, the shooting. That horrible day for both of them: the wife, the brother.

"All you had to do was call, Paul."

"I know."

"Please come home."

"I'm taking care of a few things and got to go over to Ma's. I should be home for supper. I'll probably have you pick me up at Rico's later."

"Is there another woman?"

"You know there ain't. I just have some things to do. I'll tell you about it later."

"I don't know, Paulie, I just don't know."

"I love you."

"Yeah, I know. I love you, too. It's just you make me so mad."

"I should be home for supper," There was silence on the other end of the phone. "Baby?"

He wasn't sure if she'd even heard him before hanging up.

She was upset, but it gave him back some of his focus; he'd been worried about talking to her, dreading it.

He thought of the limerick his brother made up one night after staying out drinking too late. He impressed himself with it and said it often when Cheryl was mad at him.

There once was a girl named Cheryl,
More fun than monkeys in a barrel.
But the red on her head,
That makes her wild in bed,
Fuels a temper that puts all in peril.

THIRTY-TWO

Callie laid back and listened to the shower running as she sorted what had been dreamt from what had really happened the night before. She got out of bed and brushed her teeth.

The sound of the water running made Led pull back the shower curtain. "Morning," he said. "How did you sleep?"

"Alright," she said, spitting out a mouthful of toothpaste. She took off the nightshirt before joining him in the shower.

"Do you need your back washed?"

"Always."

She ran a bar of soap over his shoulders and back. He turned to embrace her in the flow of the showerhead and they kissed as the warmth ran over their heads and down their faces, failing to get between their bodies. He coughed as water got in his nose, and she laughed at the sudden tempo change of the passion. As he took the soap from her, running it over her neck and breasts, she turned, and he ran his hands over her shoulders, down her back and over her butt. She felt the goose bumps tingling her spine as he soaped her legs and moved toward inner thighs when his phone by the sink rang. He ignored it and continued soaping.

"Aren't you going to answer it?"

"That's what voicemail is for," he said, nibbling gently on her still slightly soapy neck.

Then her phone started to ring.

"I'm sorry, love. It's probably Chancellor or Lil' Kim...."

"Go ahead."

She pulled on her robe and sat on the bed.

"Hello?"

"Callie McBride, please." It was a very tired but official voice.

"Agent Chancellor. Where have you been?"

"We've been busy with the situation that escalated last night. I'm calling to ensure that you and Mr. Ledbettor were all set. I just got the message that he was having difficulty locating you."

"That was over ten hours ago."

"I apologize. We're still working the case."

"Did you catch the shooter?"

"That part of the investigation is still open and being conducted by other team members. I don't have any information that I would be at liberty to discuss."

"Did you get what you needed while I was in the club? I placed those things like you said, but it was pretty noisy in there."

"We're still analyzing the tapes. We retrieved your purse from the club. I need you to come in and be debriefed; you can pick it up when you come in."

"Can it wait? It was a long night, I'm only just now getting up."

"Absolutely. We can have you come in on Monday."

"Will you need to speak with Led?"

"That won't be necessary. He wasn't involved in the events of last night."

When she hung up, Led emerged from the bathroom in a pair of jeans and a T-shirt. "What did they say about O'Hearn?"

"Nothing. Ever notice how he never tells you anything?" She stood and ran her hands under the front of his shirt, pulling it back off over his head. "You didn't wait for me."

In a moment they were naked and rolling around on the bed, enjoying the touch of each other's bodies, the culminating intimacy and the fitful sexual conclusion.

Lying together, her head of wet hair on his arm, he sighed and she sensed that something was on his mind.

"What's the matter?"

"At the moment, not a damn thing."

"You sound disappointed."

"No, just expectant."

She went to get the *Sunday Boston Globe* off the porch, pulled it from the yellow plastic bag that had kept it mostly dry. There it was, on the front page: a picture of Walter Dorasi that had been cropped from a family photo, part of a Christmas tree showing behind his head. There was a larger photo beside it of the Harbour Club with the crowd, the uniformed police and cruisers, and an ambulance. The article said that the police had not made any arrests.

"Anything?" Led asked, pouring two cups of coffee, adding cream and sugar to one of them.

"There's an article, but they don't know who."

On page three there was a story about a man who had fallen seven stories to his death. "Look, a private investigator fell. They think he was trying to film something from up on a parking garage when he slipped in the rain. His camera and camera bag were still on the roof."

"Some of these guys think they're Super Sleuth," he said, handing her the black coffee, "running around on the top of buildings."

She reached for the cup while still sitting on the floor, in the sun, in front of the bay window. "Do you know a Dale Foley?"

It took a moment, Dale Foley, yeah, he knew the name. Tuttle's private eye, the one who'd been following him around. That was his name.

"I talked to him two days ago." He took the paper and looked at the article, but it didn't mention much. "He was trying to locate Paul O'Hearn."

"Wow...so do you think this guy was involved?"

"Maybe. He might have been tossed from the roof because he screwed up. Interesting, though, Tuttle had hired him to follow around O'Hearn."

"How do you know?"

"Foley told me himself when I ran into him."

"Does Tuttle know that he told you that?"

"I don't know," he said, handing her back the paper. "Someone tries to shoot O'Hearn, and then the PI that was following him around dies by quote-unquote accident."

"You think O'Hearn killed him?"

"What do you think?" he asked her, but considered the possibility of other forces at play.

"He might have," she said, "in self-defense."

"There's no mention of any guns or anything."

"Should we call Chancellor back?"

"Go ahead," Led agreed as he started to wonder again about safety, not for him, but for her.

She tried and only got his voicemail.

"Don't leave a message," Led said. "We can tell him about it when we go in to see him."

"Listen, Led, Chancellor said he doesn't need to see you. But I can tell him—"

"What?" he asked in disbelief.

"He said you weren't involved enough. Don't get upset."

Led's confidence in getting help from Chancellor faded. "How do they know what they don't know without talking to everybody?"

"I don't know."

Callie sat on the floor with the paper spread around her. Led stood pacing, circling, walking to the window and back as he sipped his coffee.

"No. Both of us are going to see Chancellor," he said. "Dale Foley might have said something to Tuttle about meeting me. I could be in a position of being a witness. When O'Hearn spoke with you, did he say anything about the equipment parts he took?"

"He said he didn't have them anymore. He was going to try to sell them."

"Where—*eBay*? Where the hell do you sell used radioactive parts?"

"He told me he doesn't have any of it anymore. Tuttle took it back. Does that help?"

"He said medical equipment? Not radioactive material, waste, or anything like that?"

"Nope, he said medical equipment; he doesn't know what he took, does he?"

"That or he doesn't have what everybody thinks he does." Led sat down his coffee cup on the bookshelf and got his briefcase. He pulled out the red file folder with the O'Hearn worker's comp case. "I'm going to call him and ask him."

"Voicemail," he said, handing Callie the phone. He pointed to a number written at the top of the folder. "Call his mother at this number," he said. "Leave a message. He doesn't know who I am, but he might call you back. He seemed to like you."

Callie left the message with O'Hearn's mother, who sounded like she was eating potato chips the entire time.

He couldn't relax. As much as he wanted to sit and enjoy a Sunday afternoon with Callie, he couldn't. He needed to go do some research and have a talk with Tuttle. If he told her, she would want to go. She'd been exposed to enough excitement for one weekend.

Led sat up and put on his shoes. "I need to get going," he said. "You have to work tomorrow and I need to be up early for a surveillance in Fitchburg."

"You could stay over," she offered.

"But I need clean clothes," he countered, weakly.

"You can do your laundry here."

"Then I need to go get some dirty clothes."

"I see," she said with a little hurt in her voice. "Are you coming back tonight?"

"I wasn't going to." Lord knows he wanted to, but had to leave before someone looked for him there. He didn't like the idea that Dale was dead and he and Dale had been working on the same file—coincidences didn't just happen by accident.

"You have to work tomorrow and I need to be up early for a surveillance in Fitchburg. I don't want to wake you up as I get ready."

She nodded as he walked over and picked up his bag of clothes, then looked at the clock on the front of her home entertainment system, and it appeared that she was feigning indifference. "I didn't realize what time it really was. I wanted to get to the gym today, anyway," she said, and he really hoped she was just feigning. "And it closes early on Sunday. I've missed a few days and I'm starting to feel the atrophy." She slapped one of her butt cheeks.

"You don't need to worry about that ass trophy," he said playfully, trying to evoke a pun. He gently tapped the other cheek trying to lighten the mood and not have her misinterpret his leaving. He put his arms around her waist and hugged her from behind. She stiffened and slightly pulled away. He should just tell her where he was going, but she would want to come, he knew she would. He'd rather have her upset than in harm's way again. She would have to understand later when it was all settled down.

"I got to go. Don't want to, but got to," he said, still hoping she would just accept it as nothing more than that. "Do you have plans for dinner tomorrow night?"

"I think my calendar is clear," she said in a flippant tone.

"Good. I'll cook us dinner here?"

"It doesn't count as cooking if you dump it out of a Styrofoam container to serve it," she said, still with a bit of an edge.

"I'll do my specialty. Barbecued ribs and corn on the cob." He was happy that she didn't say no.

"I don't have a grill," she said.

"Then I'll bring mine. Mesquite charcoal, my blend of sauce. You have yet to try my tailgate specialty." He got his bag of clothes and gave her a quick kiss before leaving. She kissed him back but there was no doubt that she was still perturbed.

THIRTY-THREE

When Led left, Callie was a little aggravated with herself, since it seemed that she might have misread him. What she had taken as self-reliant and independent might actually have just been a cad. Some time at the gym would help clear her head. She gathered her workout clothes, a pair of light blue satin shorts, a dark blue sports bra, and a large white T-shirt with Capt'n Bob's Whale Watch on the front. The shirt had almost ten inches cut off the original length, so it would come just to the top of her shorts. It kept the shirttail from getting in the way when she sat on the stationary bikes, but she also knew it looked cute. She wasn't going to wear lipstick or eyeliner to the gym like some of the "bunnies" there; sweat and makeup were like baseball cleats and Prada. Nonetheless she wasn't against looking good when it was practical.

She had just put a scrunchie to hold her hair back and was getting a water bottle out of the refrigerator when the doorbell rang.

Her first thought was that Led had decided to stay. But as she approached the outside door she could see it wasn't Led. The opaque sidelights of the door revealed the silhouette of a big man, rounder than Led, head turning to look up the street as he rang the doorbell again. It was O'Hearn. She knew it. She had stared at his silhouette for almost three hours the previous night in the darkly lit basement. She paused for only a moment before taking a breath and opening the door, her curiosity stronger than her apprehension.

O'Hearn stood looking up the street as he started to ring the chime again, unaware that she had opened the door only a few inches.

"You?"

DONAL P. ANDERSON

"You called me," he said, nodding his head.

"But I didn't tell you to come over...or where I lived."

"You left your phone number and I looked it up. May I come in?"

"Why didn't you just call?" she asked suspiciously.

"I might be paranoid, but that happens when people try to kill me. My phones might be tapped. I'm not real comfortable standing out here on the porch," he said, and she decided to allow him into the hallway.

"I was just going to the gym and it closes early."

"Are you alone?"

She hesitated before answering, suddenly remembering about the dead PI, "Only for a few minutes. Led just left for a few minutes."

"Don't be nervous about me. You and your boyfriend are the only ones I thought who might be able to help me."

"Do you know Dale Foley?"

"Who?"

"Led said he was someone Mr. Tuttle hired to follow you."

"The pasty white kid from the bar?"

"I don't know."

"Or is it the bald freak with the garlic breath? I've been meeting a lot of people lately, thanks to Mr. Tuttle."

"Why? Is Dale Foley here?"

"He's in the morgue. He's dead. Last night he died falling off a roof."

"Jesus," he exclaimed as he thought about the night before for a moment and then asked, "You're asking if I had anything to do with it?"

"He was following you."

"Everyone was following me last night," O'Hearn said. "I was with you most of last night and was at my friend's place after that. Who thinks I had something to do with it?"

"No one, but I had to ask."

"Is that why you called?"

"Led wanted to talk to you, knew you wouldn't probably call him back. You told me that the stuff you took was already gone. Were you selling it to terrorists?"

"Terrorists? No. Do I look like a guy that would hang around with Osama?"

"There are a lot more terrorists out there besides him. What about the IRA?"

"They're not terrorists, but, no, I didn't try to sell them anything. What would any of them want with the lab equipment anyway?"

"To make a dirty bomb out of the radioactive fuel cell."

"Radioactive anything is nothing I would mess with. I took the power converter and imaging unit. Nothing that had fuel. Who thinks I have fuel?" He paused and answered his own question. "Fuck me. Everyone thinks I have the radioactive shit."

"So let's tell Chancellor you don't have it."

"Who's Chancellor?"

"The agent at the FBI. The agent I was helping out."

"A friend?"

"No. I just met him. Why?"

"You help out a lot of people you don't know. Why does the FBI think that I took the radioactive fuel?"

"Because it's missing."

"Maybe not. Maybe it's still right where it was supposed to be. Did anyone look? It could change everything."

"Not for Dale or the dead man in the club. Not much is going to change for them."

"It might keep me from joining them. I didn't have anything to do with Dale, or what happened in the club with the shooting, other than trying to defend myself. You have to help me with getting this straightened out. Did your friend at the FBI tell you who told them about this?"

"Agent Chancellor. He didn't tell me how they know. One of their sources, I guess."

"I'll tell you something. I know for a fact that their sources are just someone on the street working an angle, or getting revenge. Not too many of them out there like you, running around being all Wonder Woman with everything."

She liked the image of being Wonder Woman. Not exactly with the uniform of the low-cut top and high-riding 1970 disco shorts, but maybe Wonder Woman with fashion sense.

"Let's go check the warehouse and maybe we can straighten this all out. If the item is there we'll grab it and give it to them."

"You don't think the FBI already checked to be sure it was really missing?"

"The FBI," he said as he motioned her to the door, "maybe not."

"You don't need me to go. Let me call Agent Chancellor in the morning; have him go."

"I have to be the one that gets to it first. To straighten this out. I got more than the Feds after me. And the Feds aren't trying to shoot me at the moment. But things change."

"You can't give bombs to terrorists."

"It's not a bomb and I don't want to give anything to anyone. If it's still in the warehouse, let the two sons of bitches go get it themselves. If the Feds want to stop them, they can," O'Hearn said and looked at her unblinking. "You got to drive me. It's a borrowed car from a buddy. No one will be looking for it."

"I'm going to miss the gym."

"Exercise your compassion instead," he pleaded. "Please?"

And she was reminded of a favorite childhood story, and she felt like the mouse that could chew through the hunter's net that held the lion. She could help, or not, but either way it would be dangerous to be thought of as a mouse.

"All right," she said and he handed her the keys.

Led pulled into the mobile home park. Mrs. Trethway was outside with her cat, a white Persian, on a red leash. The cat walked on the grass at the front of her home. It had its large feather duster of a tail switching back and forth as if it were very bored and very disinterested in being outside. Mrs. Trethway held the leash higher than what looked necessary or comfortable to prevent it from dragging in the grass.

He waved as he drove past, but she only stood and watched. She might not have seen his gesture. Or she might just be back to being the old Mrs. Trethway.

As he pulled in the driveway he noticed that his trashcans were tipped over and a white plastic bag of trash was gutted on the back lawn. Its insides were scattered: mostly take-out containers, a pizza box, a couple of magazines. It seemed that the dogs had been at it again.

He opened the back of the jeep to take out his bag of clothes and the camera equipment. Leaving the hatch open he found the trailer door slightly open. He set the bag and surveillance equipment on the kitchen table and listened. Someone had gone through his modest belongings, opening boxes of CDs and old sweatshirts, pulling the couch away from the wall and leaving the foot locker that doubled as a coffee table ripped apart, the cover from the bottom and old pictures strewn. He carried his clothes into the bedroom slowly, walking through the trailer looking behind the bathroom and bedroom doors.

In the bedroom clothes were scattered even more than usual on the floor. The hard case that contained his compound bow was pulled from the back of the closet and left opened on the bed. He surveyed the damage with clinical acuteness. He had nothing much worth stealing so why and who? When he walked back into the kitchen Mrs. Trethway was standing at the screen door holding her cat. She hadn't knocked or said anything and he was jumpy.

She had the body shape of an apple, so as she stood there wearing a brown knit top that was a little tight, she looked like a caramel apple, one that had started to melt, with the caramel sliding off in soft rolls. She had to be in her seventies. Her hair was gray and thinning but teased on her head to make the most of it, though it closely resembled a ball of dust from under a bed.

"Mrs. Trethway. Hey. How are you?" He was startled and a little edgy but opened the door so she could enter.

She sat her cat down and it lay at her feet. "Mr. Ledbettor, your friend almost ran over Princess Grace."

"I don't think it was anyone I know. I've been gone for a few days." He wanted to release a barrage of profanity over the mess, but didn't want to frighten the old woman. He wasn't really listening much to her as he was closing drawers and cabinets.

"I told him that but he wanted to wait."

"Really?" The information sank in. "Where is he?" He looked out past her to see if anyone was in the driveway even though he had just come inside from that direction.

"He left about an hour ago. But maybe he'll be back. He kept driving past your unit and then sped away, almost hitting Princess Grace. He was not looking."

"Why did you think he was my friend?" Led asked, knowing that few people knew that he lived here, and even fewer would call him their friend.

"Because he said he was. I gave him a piece of my mind for driving so recklessly." She pointed with one hand, reenacting the scolding she had handed out. "He said that he was your friend and asked where you were. He was polite in a smirking way. I know his type. And he never apologized for Princess Grace."

"What did he look like?" Led asked, suspecting to finally find out who might have slashed his tires.

"He was big, with a bald head, like a pro wrestler."

Led was surprised; she hadn't described the pasty white guy with Dale or O'Hearn. "What did you tell him?"

"I told him to be more careful driving through our neighborhood or I would report him to the manager."

"What did you tell him about me?"

"I told him you were probably at your girlfriend's. He asked if she was blonde and thin." She shrugged. "I said I wouldn't know. I've never met her."

"Thanks, Mrs. Trethway," he said as he walked to the door to hold it for her and Princess Grace to exit.

She didn't move. "You will speak with your friends about driving more safely."

"Yes, of course." This response pleased her, not enough to change her expression or mood, but enough to have her walk out the door.

"Bye now," Led said, shutting the inside door as she was setting the cat down in the driveway under the carport and walking her back out to the street.

Led dialed Callie's home phone number and got the machine. "Hey, it's me. Call me as soon as you get this," he said and hung up to dial her cell. It started to ring before he remembered that she didn't have it. It was still in her purse with Agent Chancellor.

He grabbed his bag of camera equipment, tossed it back into the jeep then ran back into the bedroom and closed the hard black case that contained his compound bow. He wished he had a gun. How quickly philosophy changed when you were being hunted. He put the case with the bow and arrows in it across the rear seat.

He quickly backed the jeep out onto the street, threw it into drive and hit the gas. The tires spun in the sand on the street and then caught traction on the black top, squealing as he drove away.

Glancing up in his rearview mirror before turning left out of the mobile home park, there was Mrs. Trethway with her hands on her hips and the cat rubbing up against her legs.

THIRTY-FOUR

O'Hearn said he didn't want to be seen, so at his insistence, Callie got in the driver's side. O'Hearn got in beside her and, kneeling on the floor, lay forward across the bench seat. His head was almost in her lap and she was now conscious of only wearing shorts and a cut-off T-shirt. Her feet didn't reach the pedals. The seat was too far back. She fumbled for a release as she bounced forward trying to move the seat up.

"It's automatic. There's a button on the side," he instructed.

She found the small joystick that moved the seat up and down and front to back. She pushed it and the seat hummed slowly forward until O'Hearn told her to stop and back it up a little. He was pinned beneath the dash. She let him out. She was grateful that he would have to ride in the back.

"Where are we going?" she asked and looked into the rearview mirror at the big man lying fetal over the transmission hump.

"We got to go to my mother's to pick up the key and check on her. Then we'll go over to the warehouse. So first the Charlestown projects."

"Where might they be?" she asked nervously wishing that Led had stayed a little longer, for moral support if not protection.

"Just go toward the Bunker Hill monument. When we get close, I'll tell you where to turn."

She drove as he gave directions crouched down in the backseat. Only once did she get twisted around by turning one street too soon, on a one way, so she was unable to turn around. She was afraid that he would get mad, but he didn't. He sat up and looked around to help get her back on track. Then he had her pull right up next to building two.

"Is anyone outside?" he asked in almost a whisper.

"I don't see anyone," she said, slowly looking around, not wanting to be too obvious.

He opened the door and slipped out next to the concrete wall of the building. "Wait here."

"I'm not sitting out here by myself," she said firmly.

"Yeah, alright. Come on." He didn't wait for her, so she had to jog to catch up.

He tapped gently on door B2. "Mom, it's just me," he said as he turned the key.

"Paulie?" A disheveled older woman sat in a worn easy chair with a lit cigarette. Her complexion was yellowed with nicotine and age, and her face was creased with deep lines, giving her the overall appearance of unwashed linen.

O'Hearn went over and kissed the top of the woman's head. "I'm sorry, Ma." He walked back to the door where Callie stood. "I can't stay. I just wanted to see you."

"Is that man still looking for you?"

"I don't know, Ma. Maybe."

"Let me get you something to eat."

"I can't." O'Hearn hung his head and didn't look at the old lady. "Maybe in a while I'll be back and you can make me a sandwich."

Even Callie could tell he was lying.

"That would be nice," the woman said as she lit another cigarette.

O'Hearn pushed Callie out the door.

"Your mother seems like a sweet woman."

"Used to be..." was all O'Hearn said as he walked quickly between several buildings. Under a stairwell on the first floor in a building that looked like all the rest, he unlocked the gray metal door of a utility room.

"You have a key?" Callie asked.

"I helped wire these when they were being rehabbed. I was still a journeyman. They've never changed the locks."

The small room was rather clean except for some footprints on the floor. A wire cage covered the one light bulb that lit the windowless space. A large, gray-paneled electrical box was mounted on two vertical pieces of channel-lock steel that were in turn mounted to the concrete walls. The panel had thick silver conduit intersecting from all sides. From the panel the conduit was bent in large curves to go through holes in the walls and ceiling, like large roots sent from the trunk of the panel. O'Hearn slid his fingers up behind the panel where it sat off the wall by an inch or two, returning with a set of keys and what appeared to be a key card.

"That's all we need," he said.

"You keep them hidden *there?*" Callie asked.

"Would you have looked for anything there?"

She didn't like the way he patronized her when he said it.

"No," she answered. "But I don't mess with electrical panels."

"Neither does anyone else. If you put something behind 220 volts that requires the power to be turned off at the street to move it, it's pretty well protected. Better than a safe."

"But you didn't need to shut off the power," she said.

"No, not to get the keys," O'Hearn answered. "But I'd have to if I wanted to pull the panel to get behind it."

He shut off the light and closed the steel fire door that sealed off the small room.

O'Hearn was quiet as they drove through to the warehouse. Callie wondered how he could tell where he was by only looking up through the side windows. To her it was a mishmash of brick structures with flat roofs, cluttered with antennas and HVAC units; multi-family homes with air conditioners precariously hanging from upper story windows like metallic tumors, dripping condensation to the sidewalks below; a few trees, light poles, and traffic lights.

When they reached the warehouse, O'Hearn again asked if anyone was watching, and she was ready for the routine; she saw an old red and primer Plymouth.

"There's a car," Callie said and nodded toward it.

"That's always there," O'Hearn said.

They got out of the Nova. This area of the city was quiet on a Sunday afternoon. Like a ghost town. Not a person outside in any direction, just a few seagulls noisily picking at a discarded fast food bag.

The few workers were all inside the surrounding warehouses, picking and packing, only emerging for a cigarette when possible. The red ATM kiosk across the street sat ignored in the big parking lot.

O'Hearn entered his key code on the pad at the front of the building. Callie was surprised to see it still allowed him access. Inside O'Hearn took the key card from his wallet and swiped it through the reader that was in the hallway. He opened the door to the storage bay for Mobile Medi Tech.

There was nothing there; no wonder his key card still worked.

"It's not here, is it?" Callie asked. She didn't know exactly what they were looking for, but she could tell by O'Hearn's face, which was beginning to show panic.

"No..." He looked away in disbelief.

"Maybe the FBI moved it somewhere safer," Callie offered in an effort to calm him down.

"It's not the goddamn FBI that I'm worried about," he said, kicking at the wall and walking silently out of the warehouse.

Callie pulled the doors shut gently as if shutting a bedroom door.

O'Hearn was quiet as they left the area, approaching the Tobin Bridge that dominated the horizon with its green lattice and suspension peaks.

When she turned onto her street, there was a gold Lexus parked on the street. It stood out amongst the Volkswagens and Hondas, but she especially noticed it because of the window tint. It was dark like a limo or the way kids pimp their ride. But this was not a limo, and it wasn't all tricked out over the rest of the car, like a dealer's. She drove by slow, was pretty sure someone was sitting in the front. Not positive, though, with the tint on the windows.

"I think someone is on the street watching my house," she said as she parked around the corner.

"Is it your friend from the FBI?"

"I don't think so. I noticed that the government vehicles were all American made."

"They won't know this car."

"Who is it?" Callie said as she looked in the rearview mirror trying to see in the Lexus.

"I can't look, but it might be a man looking for me."

"Why is he at my house?"

"I don't know. No one knows we've spoken, except your boyfriend."

"Led?" she asked defensively. "He gave you a ride last night."

"I'm just saying. He wasn't too happy about it."

"How would they know where I even live?"

"I found you pretty easy. You aren't exactly living in a spider hole."

"I'm going in to call the police."

"Hold on there, missy. I got to think this one through," O'Hearn said. "He might be waiting to get a look at us when we get out of the car."

"Do you have your phone?" she asked.

"We can't turn it on. It can lead people right to us."

"A little late for that, don't you think?"

"Who do you want to call?"

She turned and looked over the back of the seat at O'Hearn still scrunched up, laying low in the back. "Led," she said.

"No."

"Then I am going to go straight to the police. Right now. This is ridiculous."

"What is he going to do for us?"

"For me? Whatever it takes to get this straightened out."

"Here," O'Hearn said as he handed her the phone.

"Miss me?" Callie asked as Led answered.

"Oh good," he said, sounding excited to hear from her. "Stay at the gym. Don't go home. I'm on my way back there after I look up a few things."

"I didn't make it to the gym."

"What did he say?" O'Hearn asked.

"Don't go back to the house," Callie repeated to O'Hearn.

"Who are you talking to?" Led asked her.

"Paul," she said. "You remember Paul O'Hearn, don't you?"

"Paul?" Led asked in almost a whisper.

"It's alright. For now," she assured Led. "I was just trying to help him with something. We're sitting up the street from my house and it looks like someone is watching my place. And you of all people should know how annoying that can be."

"Why doesn't he want you to go into the house?" O'Hearn asked her.

"Go to the police now. Someone might be looking for me at your place," Led said and she could hear in his voice that he was trying to remain calm and not scare her.

But she didn't scare as easily as she became concerned. "That's funny, because that's the same thing O'Hearn said." Callie wished someone would fill her in.

"Go to the police," Led pleaded.

"Led wants us to go to the police," she repeated to O'Hearn.

"Or call and have them come to you. Either way, but don't screw around," Led said.

"Okay. I'll call the police, but I have to hang up to do it."

"We're not calling the police. Let's go. We are out of here," O'Hearn told her, reached up, grabbed her hair and pulled.

"Ah. Okay," she said to O'Hearn as Led continued to talk to her.

"He won't let you go to the police?" Led asked.

"Evidently not," she said.

"At least pull in the driveway and stay there. Will he stay there?"

"Led is almost here. Can we wait in the driveway?"

"For what?" O'Hearn asked.

"Tell him I will get the car and whoever is in it to leave."

"He will make the car leave."

"No police," O'Hearn stated.

"We'll wait," she said, annoyed with the dramatics of both men and leaned forward to pull her hair free from O'Hearn's grip and started the car.

"Whoever that is, they'll follow me. Once they're gone, go in the house and stay there until I come back," Led instructed as he hung up the phone, feeling that he should have added more.

Carrying the hard case protecting the bow and a dozen arrows, Led walked down the hill, in behind the neighboring multi-family, squeezing between the building and dilapidated stockade fence and into Callie's driveway, unseen by anyone on the street. Callie didn't act surprised to see him walk up beside the driver's window of the yellow Nova. She put the window down and looked at the case in his hand.

"What do you have there?" she asked.

"Hardly a prayer," he said as he looked at the contorted shape of Paul O'Hearn stowed away in the backseat, sheepishly looking out. "Do you have your car keys?"

He got into her car, backed out of the driveway quickly and stopped, being sure to draw attention, before driving away.

It was only a moment before the gold Lexus followed.

Led shut off the radio so he could think as he watched the Lexus try to follow him from a distance; deal with one threat at a time. He hoped he'd made the right assessment of importance leaving Callie with O'Hearn for a few moments. She seemed to have won the trust of the big man. He had come to her for help. Anyway, he was a thief, not a killer; at least, Led hoped not.

He signaled right before cutting left, making an abrupt u-turn and then a sharp right turn past neighborhoods that he knew like they were his own. The countless hours of surveillance on these streets were to his advantage whether he was leading or being led, but the sedan was determined and never fell very far behind.

In the parking lot of the closed shipping terminal Led had time to pull over and open the case and take out the bow.

He hadn't looked at it in years, and had worried about the condition of the string and pulleys; if everything was still sound and the arrows had not warped or the flights detached, as ignored equipment was prone to fall apart. He twisted three titanium-tipped arrowheads onto fiberglass shafts, a setup he had often used to pierce the door of an old jalopy at a fundraiser. It was supposed to look like an accident, that he would miss the apple on the stand in front of the car, but as the arrow pierced the door it would impale an unseen apple that was on the seat behind a closed door. It was a shtick, but when the car door was opened, the crowd always applauded.

Here it was, a bullet ripped past him, and he ducked behind Callie's car. Another bullet took out the windshield and the Lexus was speeding toward him.

He could have shot him, right through the windshield of the Lexus. The white baldhead was enough of a target, but he didn't; to try for that shot would have meant standing completely in the open as the driver shot at him. Not feeling particularly heroic, Led stayed in a crouched position as the car came at him, and then fired an arrow. He was pleased with the accuracy of his shot; the grill swallowed most of the arrow like a hungry cat, with only a few feathers sticking out. He shot again, thinking he might shoot a tire out, but the years of no practice held a heavy influence and he missed.

The car was almost upon him and he had one titanium-tipped arrow left and one big parking lot with nowhere to hide. The driver would be passing by for a kill shot. Led wasn't as ready as he would have liked to be. As he nocked the arrow and heard the car just about to pass, he stood up with the bow raised and followed it within his sight. Led looked in the eyes of the bald man driving as he shot the arrow in the door. With a look of disbelief and pain the driver of the Lexus looked down at his lap, dropped his gun onto the pavement, and swerved to the right.

Led picked up the handgun and tossed it into Callie's car. Although he wanted to shoot the son of a bitch, he decided that getting into Callie's car and driving like hell might be more prudent. The Lexus pulled over and the driver seemed to quickly regain composure because he headed back at Led even faster than before.

Led drove from the parking lot and out onto Route 93, hoping that his excessive speed might draw the attention of a police officer. The Lexus was on his bumper, a bigger motor but one without a way to cool itself as the radiator steamed away coolant from around the arrow in the grille. Moments later the Lexus slowed to the breakdown lane with a blown motor.

He quietly returned to Callie's place.

It worked: he saw that the Nova was gone, which meant O'Hearn had taken advantage of the Lexus' departure in order to make his own.

His throat was dry with the realization that it was possible that O'Hearn had taken Callie with him.

Seeing him on the front porch, she opened the door, and the kiss felt like a homecoming, even though he'd only been gone a short while.

"Who is he afraid of?" she asked. "If the FBI really thought he had nuclear material, wouldn't they pick him up?"

"I'd hope they would, but O'Hearn might have other things to worry about completely unrelated to Mobile Medi Tech. People get involved in a lot, the stolen property could be only one. Trying to tie all the events together, to fit the pieces of different puzzles all together, it might be a mistake." He felt free to think out loud, hearing what his thoughts sounded like in the fresh air. "The FBI doesn't know who has it, but someone does. O'Hearn's involvement was a thread they were pulling at, trying to unravel the outside, to get to the core. The question is, if O'Hearn didn't have this stuff, why does everyone think that he does?" And with that stream of thought he suddenly knew where to get the answer. Tuttle.

True, Tuttle didn't need to steal it; he had a dozen other mobile units. He could take the material from those units, but not without having to account for it. And Tuttle wasn't the type of man who liked to account to anyone for anything.

"Do you have plans?" he asked.

DONAL P. ANDERSON

"Where are we going?"
"To play detective."
"Is that like playing doctor?"
"It can be, if you do it right."

THIRTY-FIVE

The office was in a nondescript, four-story brick structure, a big box of a building with a flat roof and evenly spaced windows that didn't open. The aluminum door was dead center in the middle of the building. It couldn't have had less architectural flair if it had been built with Legos.

Though only a four-story building, the elevator took longer than many in Boston going forty stories. On the black felt marquee was the list of the building's occupants: a realtor, two attorneys, and an accountant on the first floor, the martial arts studio on the second, and an architectural firm on the third. Also on the third was Danko's Information Company. Or, as the marquee put it:

Private D.I.C.

"Cute," Callie said.

"Thing is, the owner doesn't realize his own double entendre. No one has the heart to tell him."

The owner, Al Danko, thought of himself as a descendant of the original 1930s gumshoe. He bought into the television personae, the glamorous job. There was the kitschy spy glass and big eye logo, the scales of justice on the brochure, the graying mustache he pulled at when telling his war stories, the endless barrage of investigative exploits that didn't get any more interesting with third or fourth tellings.

But he ran a good local company, and a handful of clients liked him. Led didn't mind working for him. Truth was, sometimes he forgot that he even had an employer. He was given an assignment and pretty much left alone. That was how the job worked. If he had a question he asked it, but otherwise he just did what he was being paid to do: investigate. There was no clock to punch, no office politics. His office was his jeep. The only reason to stop here was to drop off video, pick up a check, or now——to use the computers for research.

As they got off the elevator the lights were off and the hall was dark except for red exit signs, the sunlight from the windows not having reached the center of the building. He unlocked the office door and held it open for her, switched on the fluorescent lights and sat down at the secretary's computer.

It was time to go on the offensive. He logged on and started to run a background search on Tuttle.

Callie picked up a small bottle of floral-scented hand cream and smelled it. "Who sits here?" she asked.

"Brenda. She's like his office manager."

"We could have used my computer."

He agreed but was concerned enough to get Callie out of her home. The man in the Lexus was disabled, not stopped. All he said was, "I need access to some of the proprietary searches from here."

"I like a good mystery, but tell me what we're doing."

"Trying to find the missing pieces and get us uninvolved."

"You ever see Brenda naked?"

He almost didn't hear her. She hadn't asked him anything about his ex-wife, and now she was asking about the company secretary.

"Brenda?" he asked, caught off guard. "Not really." And as soon as he said it he wished he'd just said no. There had never been anything between him and Brenda.

He continued to cross-reference anything he knew about Tuttle...no property in his name...might be in a real estate trust. His driver's license and vehicle went back to the business address of Mobile Medi Tech. He looked up at Callie, but she wasn't asking any more questions. Which was worse.

"I never dated Brenda," he added.

"That's fine." She looked at the PI licenses hanging on the wall.

"She's not my type. She's quiet...conservative."

Callie just looked at him and smiled. Knowing? Jealous? Caring?

"It was nothing," he said, compelled to go on. "I saw her naked in a magazine once."

"Miss Conservative USA?"

"It was a case I was working," Led said. "Really. It was an assignment from a psychiatrist in San Francisco. This woman, she sounded more paranoid than her patients. She had moved her practice from the Cambridge area to San Francisco."

Callie walked behind him. He felt her warm hands start to massage his shoulders. He relaxed a little, just a little.

"The psychiatrist had opened her new practice in the backyard of another psychiatrist's. If any two people should be able to work out their differences you'd think it should be two therapists, but a turf war broke out over each other's clients."

"There shouldn't have been a shortage of crazy people."

"Just the ones with lots of money. The two got into yelling matches on the telephone, angry letters written back and forth accusing each other of incompetence, childishness."

Led was enjoying the massage, but it was the warm smell of her perfume so close that raised the small hairs on the back of his neck. He paused for a minute.

"And how did this result in you seeing Brenda?"

"My client claimed she was getting harassing phone calls. The calls were guys calling her and talking dirty. After a few of these calls, she started to interview the men who were calling. They thought they were calling a sex line."

"The men actually talked to her when she started asking questions?"

"I thought the same thing. These men thought they were trying to reach a sex kitten and instead they were getting this pushy woman with a nasally voice and an agenda. It had to be a real test even for Viagra at that point."

"Men are motivated when they want to be."

"A couple of the callers said the number was in the back of *Hustler* magazine. She wanted to check the ads of the last three months of *Hustler* and determine if her number had been placed by her competitor to disrupt her business. She didn't trust using a detective agency on the West Coast. She called Danko's...and I got the assignment."

"She was paying you to look at a girlie magazine."

"I didn't say it was a tough assignment; the publisher sent me a couple back issues.

"You throw yours out?"

"It was far more tedious than I would have expected," he said, ignoring her jab. "I had to look through even the small block ads, not just for the phone number, but for the all those letters' numeric equivalents. They all were 900-BIG PINK or 900-HOT SLUT. Anyway, in one of the amateur photos was a picture of our conservative Brenda, naked, upside-down on a couch. I didn't recognize her at first. It wasn't a position I'd ever seen her in."

"Did you ever mention to her that you found the photo?"

"No."

Callie kissed the back of his neck. She was wonderful, but somehow he felt that she had just administered a polygraph. With a random question about someone who meant nothing to him she had calibrated the baseline.

"As far as the psychiatrist's phone number, if it had been placed in *Hustler*, it wasn't in the issues I checked. Speaking of magazines," he said, and, picking up the phone, called a subscription service for *Golf Digest*.

"This call is being monitored for quality assurance. This is Tara, how may I help you today?"

"I have a problem. I want to send a gift subscription to a colleague, Richard Tuttle. I think he's already getting the magazine but I want to renew it for another year. He's going through a tough time, I thought it would be a nice gesture."

"Do you know his address?"

"He's in Massachusetts, Manchester by the Sea or Marblehead, somewhere like that."

"No problem, sir...would it be Richard Tuttle at 213 Cranston's Bluff in Marblehead?

"You know, I'm sorry, I'm not sure if that's right. I'm going to check with someone and call back. I don't want to send it to the wrong address."

"That's alright. Is there anything else I can do for you today?"

"No, thank you. You've been very helpful. If a supervisor is monitoring this call, give this woman a raise. She's great."

"Thank you, sir."

He hung up.

"Never would have thought that would work," Callie said.

"It usually doesn't."

THIRTY-SIX

Rollin awoke that morning in the same twin-sized bed with the wagon-wheel headboard he had been sleeping in since he was eight years old. Facedown with one of his arms stuck through the headboard's spokes, he had a pounding headache and an acidic taste in his mouth. From the small refrigerator his parents had allowed him to keep at his bedside, he retrieved a cold can of Mountain Dew, alternately sipping at it and holding it to his forehead.

With his parents out for their Sunday dinner, he had time to pace freely about in his white skivvies. He was starting to feel frenzied as he recalled the events of the night before. They had seemed as far removed from real life as the plot of a video game, but now were starting to haunt their way back into the day.

Paul O'Hearn had recognized him and would eventually tell the police. They would be looking for him. He would be wanted for murder and he didn't have the resources to hide. Standing in his underwear in his parents' living room he didn't feel very gangster-ish. Maybe it was best to just go back to work at Radio Shack, pretend none of it happened.

He showered, dressed, and drove to the mall, but what if the police were already there waiting for him? He called in sick from the parking lot.

Without thinking anymore about it, he drove home and got his father's .38 Chief's Special revolver, put a towel on the floor, and shot himself.

The wound was in his side, where it was fleshy, where he was pretty sure there were no organs as important as his heart or lungs. The searing bullet stung like a hot, rusty pickaxe had gone through to his back. With his ears ringing from the blast, his eyes watering from the pain, he realized what he'd done: shot the dresser of drawers that had been his grandmother's.

He peeled the round, red-and-gold NRA membership decal from his mirror and put it over the hole so his mother wouldn't see it.

The searing wound seemed to get only hotter. He took short, controlled breaths to mitigate the pain and to keep himself from passing out. He checked his wound. He was bleeding, but not as much as he thought he might. He picked up the towel and held it to his abdomen.

The hardest part was done. He did it, and now all he had to do was claim he'd been shot at the Harbour Club and fired back in self-defense.

He was feeling pretty resourceful. He could handle himself.

But they would look for the gun that shot him...so he wiped it down with a dirty sock and wrapped it in a T-shirt. He would drive over to the Harbour Club and toss it in the bushes; they'd find it eventually...

The club looked benign except for the yellow tape across the door that read "Crime Scene—Do Not Cross."

His father had always bragged about that gun. That it was untraceable, and in case there was trouble, no one would know he had it. He hoped it was true but never knew what kind of trouble a mid-level manager at a metal fabrication plant could ever expect to have. He only slowed down to throw it out through the window. It fell somewhere in the orange mulch beneath a large rhododendron.

He was satisfied with his plan but unsure if he should check himself into an emergency room yet. He needed to be the victim here. He needed to react naturally as he was told someone had died in the gunfire. What would be most natural? If he went to the hospital too soon his wound might look too fresh, his alibi wouldn't fly. He looked at his side. It was wet, but he didn't know what it was supposed to look like if it had happened the night before. No, he would wait. He was glad to have mostly stopped bleeding. He was sure that the hot throbbing of the full abdominal piercing would ease once he took some aspirin.

He'd baked a great idea, now he just needed to add the frosting.

He needed to get some collaboration for his story. Dale would have been ideal. And he was feeling bad about that...but he needed to stay focused on the task at hand. Dale was no longer an option. Mr. Tuttle knew about the club but didn't know particulars. Rollin decided that he would go to Mr. Tuttle's and ask if he'd seen Dale. Act all surprised about Dale's death. He would tell him he hadn't seen Dale since he dropped him off at his car and told him to go to the hospital; maybe Dale told him he was going to talk to O'Hearn about shooting his partner, his buddy. Maybe Paul O'Hearn even had something to do with Dale's death. It wasn't a lie. O'Hearn was the whole reason for all of this mess.

All he had to do was believe in his story, he figured, just like Tuttle would. Most of the time people like Tuttle believed other people like Tuttle.

The wound in his side felt like a bad cramp, but the pain somehow helped. It kept him from thinking about Dale.

Rollin by habit parked by the garage where Mr. Tuttle always made them park, off to the side so they didn't leak oil or antifreeze onto his precious cobblestone driveway.

As he got out of his car his knees folded like a cheap lawn chair, and he fell. He checked his side, too tender to touch and throbbing, a dull ache. But not bleeding. He dismissed it; he hadn't eaten all day, he told himself, it was just low blood sugar. He sat by the car tire and rested for a minute.

He was still sitting, leaning against the side of the car door when he heard another vehicle approaching. It was a familiar looking black jeep. He watched by looking under his car. He could see the feet of the driver, in black cowboy boots, and the passenger, a woman, in open-toed sandals with red painted toes. He didn't need to see the face of the driver to know it was that other investigator Mr. Tuttle had hired. Maybe this was even better. He let out a hard breath, pulled himself to his feet and walked around to the kitchen entrance, where he knew a key was hidden under the third landscape brick.

As he unlocked the door he thought how Mr. Tuttle often had him and Dale go into the house when he wasn't around, for errands having nothing to do with security. Dale never minded, but it bothered Rollin that he was an errand boy, a delivery boy. Moving furniture, delivering lawn statuary, and most recently moving crates from storage to the office at Mobile Medi Tech—these weren't protection services. He was further reminded of the last menial errand by the two black fingernails on his left hand from pinching his fingers beneath one of the heavy crates in the back of Dale's van.

Unlocking the glass door he went into the kitchen. He was eager to establish his alibi but also curious to the point of jealousy as to why this other investigator, Ledbetter, was there.

Feeling a little lightheaded, he took a wine glass from one of the cabinets and filled it with ice water from the refrigerator door.

THIRTY-SEVEN

Tuttle had returned earlier from playing eighteen holes with two doctors from Brigham and Women's Hospital and a pharmaceutical rep from Eli Lilly. Lunch at the clubhouse had included a couple gin and tonics, and after being in the sun all day he needed a nap.

It had been 5:38 according to his Invicta Diamond Lupah watch. He loved his watch.

He took off his shoes and stretched out on the moss-green leather sofa flicking through the channels. The Sox had won and he watched a few highlights before changing to a Discovery Channel program about shipwrecks and sunken treasures.

He was asleep when the knock came at the door. A banging, actually.

Someone not using the doorbell.

He looked out into the driveway and observed a black jeep. Thinking it was the landscapers, he answered the door a little perturbed. "Yes?"

Ledbettor stepped forward into the entryway, invading his personal space. Tuttle took a couple of steps backward. The investigator was with a woman, who stood behind on the front porch.

"Oh, I didn't recognize you, and I don't believe I've met your secretary."

"I knew you wanted an update when I found O'Hearn." Led was looking past Tuttle into the other room.

"Yes, of course. Come in. I didn't expect such personal service, but what do you have?"

"Nice place," Ledbettor said, motioning for the woman behind him to come inside.

"Thank you, I've been working on it since I bought it over three years ago. The work never ends. This green marble in the hallway is from the same quarry as the marble in Trump Tower. I just had it installed. So what brings you and this lovely lady out on a Sunday evening? I thought you were finished with that job."

"I was, but then I did a little extra. I felt I was missing something. I knew he wasn't as disabled by the accident as he said he was."

"Good."

"I found the proof I was looking for, but I also found something else you might be interested in."

"Oh? And what is that?"

"He was stealing from your company."

"He *was*?" Tuttle found himself still shaking off his nap, lagging just a little in his feigned surprise.

"Yep," Ledbetter said. "Stole two components for one of your mobile medical machines. Aren't those things worth thousands?"

"Oh, yes. Wonderful." Tuttle was having difficulty creating his own excitement. "Do you have proof?"

"Absolutely," Ledbetter said. "But I didn't tell the police."

Now no longer faking his excitement, Tuttle asked, "You didn't call the police?"

"No. The insurance company isn't going to press charges. I thought you might want to pay a reward, so I came straight here. It seemed more of a business matter."

"Yes, certainly." It wasn't easy concealing his relief that the police weren't involved. "I need to get a drink. Can I offer you anything?

"I'm good," Ledbetter said. "Thank you."

"No thank you," said the woman.

They followed him down the long, wide hallway into the kitchen with two large stoves and a ceiling covered with hanging stainless steel and copper pans. Tuttle opened the glass door of the refrigerator and took out a juice bottle. He took a moment to think as he poured the juice over a cup of ice.

He didn't see Rollin's empty glass still on the counter.

"A reward was going to be offered," he said. "I was talking it over with my corporate attorney and we were going to offer a thousand dollars, as we were hoping to recover the items."

"So you knew they were missing?"

"We knew something was missing, but we hadn't taken a full inventory."

"A thousand dollars seems a little low for recovering such expensive equipment."

"Considering the trouble you saved us," he said, raising his glass, "I can juice it a little."

"Exactly how much are we talking about?"

He walked into an adjoining room and removed a check register from the top drawer of the credenza. "Who am I making it out to?"

"Asher Ledbettor." The investigator looked expressionless as he glanced back at the woman. "You don't want to see the equipment?"

"Of course I do," Tuttle said, ripping out the check and handing it over. "Where is it?"

"In the back of a Lexus on Route 93."

Tuttle was confused. He looked at the woman. She was silent.

Ledbettor continued, "Funny thing about it, though…"

"What is that?"

"O'Hearn didn't take everything he could have. He only took the imaging unit and power supply."

"Maybe he did take everything," Tuttle said, "and sold it?"

"Not likely. He has a fused disc. He never would have been able to carry anything over fifty pounds. He grabbed just the two pieces and left the rest behind."

"Unless someone else helped him."

"Thought of that, so I checked the security camera."

"There *isn't* a security camera at the warehouse," Tuttle said, his voice deepening to regain authority. He wasn't sure he could trust this man.

"I know. That surprised me, such a high-tech entry system and no camera. But I checked with the bank across the parking lot. Its camera points in that direction. O'Hearn only carried out the two pieces," Ledbetter said, finally accepting the check. "But you have them recovered now."

From the corner of one eye, Led saw a dark shape move. "If you're handing out checks," came the voice from behind him, "I'll take one too."

It was the pirate from the van that had been following him, the pudgy one. The dead one's partner. His pallor was a dull primer-gray and sweat was beading on his forehead and beneath his nose.

"Are you alright?" Callie asked, staring at the mostly dried blood, soaked through his white shirt.

"I've been shot," the man said. "While at the club last night. Mr. Tuttle, they tried to kill me, and I shot back in self-defense."

The tone of Tuttle's voice revealed his vexation. "You're *bleeding*; did you walk anywhere else in the house?"

"I only came in through the kitchen."

"Do you want us to call you an ambulance?" Led asked, more as small talk than sounding concerned. He watched the man cautiously, looking for signs of a weapon.

"I don't need an ambulance," he said. "I've been like this all day." He paused before adding, "Since last night."

"You need to go to a doctor," Callie said in a motherly tone.

"I need some money," the man said to Tuttle.

"If you don't have insurance," Callie pressed, "they'll still treat you."

Led knew he and Callie should leave now, but he wasn't finished with Tuttle.

"No, lady, I don't mean for the doctor." The man looked confused, turning to Tuttle. "But, yeah, I'm going to need some money for that, too. Have you seen Dale?"

"Dale?" Tuttle said. "What are you talking about? You two were together last night," Tuttle said. "You didn't read about it in the paper?"

"I slept in and then I've been trying to get in touch with Dale."

"Why didn't Dale take you to the hospital?" Tuttle asked. "I spoke with him last night and he didn't mention anything about you being shot."

Led could see the bleeding man growing confused, wiping his forehead with his forearm. "Where's the gun you used?" he asked.

"Where I can get it again if I need to use it," he said, grimacing in pain.

"All right, buddy," Led said. "Let's get you to a hospital."

"But I don't know what happened to Dale, he dropped me off and went to check on Mrs. Tuttle, like we always do."

"The paper this morning said he fell from the parking garage," Callie said with condolence in her voice.

"Dale is dead," Tuttle added.

Rollin's eyes were red and irritated from pain or from the sting of sweat that ran down his forehead.

"I think you should call an ambulance," Led said to Tuttle. "Or the police."

"Why don't you two drive him over?" Tuttle suggested. "He obviously doesn't want an ambulance."

Callie seemed like she was considering it.

"No," the man said.

Led sighed, just a little.

"I am really upset about my best friend and I'm not feeling too well about being shot. So if I could just get paid for what you owe me and Dale I will get going."

"You want me to pay you *Dale's* money, too?"

"What, he's dead so you should keep it?" the man asked, growing visibly angry. "He and I were partners, and you owe the partnership two weeks' pay. Dale's gone, so I'm the managing partner now."

"You weren't with Dale when I was talking to him last night?"

"Stop asking questions. Just give me the money so I can go."

"I agree with him," Led said. "Pay him and let him go."

"When I talked to Dale, he made it sound like the two of you were still together, and he didn't mention you being shot."

"Just pay him so he can go," Led said.

"Give me my goddamn money!" Rollin lashed out, less like a wounded animal and more like a child throwing a tantrum, grabbing a steak knife from a butcher block in the middle of the kitchen.

The knife was small but sharp.

Led put his arm out across Callie, trying to force her back. She took one step before stopping. The man didn't approach them; he stared at Tuttle for a long, silent moment. Tuttle stared back.

"All right," Tuttle said. "I suppose it's fair for me to pay you Dale's share."

He wrote out a check and ripped it off, sliding it across the green granite countertop.

Without saying anything further, the man snatched up the check, took a darting glance at it, too quickly to have focused. Then, staring back at them with dull eyes, he backed slowly toward the door, exaggerating the potential of being stopped by any of the three, who were more than glad to see him go.

Once at the doorway he threw the knife back across the floor and slammed the kitchen door.

"That was interesting," Tuttle said. He walked to the window and looked out as the man drove from the yard. "I suppose I should call the authorities."

"We have to get going too," Led said. "I would say that you're all set with Paul O'Hearn. Despite his supposed hand injury he gets around fine."

"Well, that is good news." Tuttle took a big gulp of juice, and the ice in the glass slid down onto his face, splashing his nose. He lowered the glass and wiped his face with the palm of his hand.

"I am not the adjuster on this," Led said, "but I bet they cut off his comp checks. And you're going to save on your comp premium."

"As Ben Franklin said, 'a penny saved is a penny earned,'" Tuttle quoted.

Led put his arm around Callie and said, "'All you need is love.' John Lennon."

THIRTY-EIGHT

With his arm around her waist they walked down the brick walkway back to his jeep in the cobblestone driveway.

"Tuttle is still standing in the doorway watching," he whispered in her ear. He didn't need to tell her that, but wanted to say something as he leaned in close to her. And it was true: as they drove past the brick pillars that marked the end of the property, Tuttle stood in the open door like a statue in a presidium; a statue with a cup of juice.

"I think we can tell your buddy Chancellor who has his radioactive boxes," he said, playing it nonchalant for full effect.

"We can?

"Tuttle."

"*Tuttle*? Why do you say Tuttle?"

"I think he's behind most of this," he said, taking a pack of gum from the center console. "When I started thinking about how it was adding up, Tuttle was the only answer."

"Chancellor never even mentioned him."

"Chancellor doesn't mention much. You want a piece?"

"No thanks. But this was O'Hearn's employer?"

"Chancellor didn't ask us about Tuttle because they probably aren't having much trouble following him around." He put a piece of gum in his mouth and rolled up the empty wrapper into a tiny silver ball before tossing it into the ashtray full of loose change. "He lives his life a little more in the open than O'Hearn."

She stared at him. "I wasn't sure what you were talking about back there—about the radioactive material."

"I told him that O'Hearn didn't take it."

"But if Tuttle is the one who knows where it is, then he already knew that."

"Exactly, and that's why he had me following around O'Hearn. Tuttle likes to get insight for all his negotiations."

"He was negotiating with O'Hearn?"

Led felt himself relaxing for the first time in two days. He was enjoying Callie's interest. "Tuttle knew O'Hearn didn't have it, and O'Hearn knew he didn't have it; so he probably knew Tuttle still did and has been blackmailing him since."

"But you can't prove that," she said as she leaned forward, her elbows on her knees.

"No, but Tuttle doesn't know I can't prove it. He's under the impression that the security camera on the ATM machine across the street shows what O'Hearn took. And *only* what he took."

"What video? There's no video."

Led gave a slight smile. "So I stretched the quality of the evidence a little…he doesn't know what's on the camera, but he *does* know what he's been up to. His own paranoia will fill in the hows and the whens."

"Why did you bother?"

"For his kids. He's going to be busy for a while explaining himself to the FBI. But maybe he'll keep from getting himself killed," Led said. "And for you. The sooner this mess is cleared up the sooner we might be able to have a third date. One without someone being shot."

"You think I'm going to give you a third date?" she asked, smiling. "So where is the radioactive material?"

"I think it's still around, and it might suddenly reappear; misplaced is all it is. Right now, Tuttle is trying to figure out how he's going to explain that the equipment wasn't on the wrecked mobile medical unit when he put in a claim that it was. This wasn't a planned theft, just a fraud of opportunity. He's slick, though, and he'll come up with something. Probably just pay some fines. That is, if there was even any law broken for losing track of radioactive medical material."

"And the shooting?"

"I can't solve everything," he said. "I have to leave *something* for the police to do."

"So you're not concerned about the other people hired by Tuttle? Like the car that was in front of the house?"

"Well, we aren't going home yet. But if the chubby guy with the bleeding gut is any indication, there's nothing to be concerned about."

"I hope he's all right," she said.

Rollin first only saw her from behind and wondered if she was a desperate housewife contemplating an amateur review, or a lesbian lover of one of the strippers. She was a little older than most of the girls but was aging a lot better. And before he could create more fantasies about the woman, he recognized her. Unsure at first, he now realized that it was Judith Tuttle–Mr. Tuttle's not-soon-enough-to-be ex-wife. Sitting there nervous at the bar trying not to look at the naked girl dancing in front of her. She appeared to only be comfortable talking with the waitress. The men in the bar did more than sideways glances as they stared over at her; dressed in a slim fitting dark blue jacket with matching slacks and wearing a cream colored camisole she was smartly put together and fit enough after three children to still attract attention even in a strip club.

He didn't think that she would know who he was. She had driven past him a hundred times as he and Dale sat outside of her home under the orders of her domineering husband. Rollin picked up his beer, pulled his jacket closed over the mess of dried brown blood that covered his side, and walked over to her table. He was emboldened with several aspirin and beer, lowering his usual anxiety of talking to women. Besides, he knew her. It was like they were old friends. He sat down in the empty seat to her right, and she immediately leaned left but stared at him.

"Hi," was all he could think to say.

"Hello," she said. "I'm waiting on someone."

"You never come here."

"No, I don't," Judith said, visibly uncomfortable speaking with him, she glanced to see if a bouncer was going to assist her, not sure what the procedure was in a place like this.

"Who are you waiting on? Maybe I can help you find them. Judith, I know a lot of people," Rollin lied, thinking with Dale gone he now knew even fewer.

"Do I know you?"

"I don't think so. You might say I'm an acquaintance of your husband."

"You know Richard?" she asked as she shifted back closer to him to be heard over the loud dance music. "So you are—how do they say it—connected?"

"I suppose I am."

"Then you are who I'm looking for. I want to talk to the mob."

"The mob?"

"Yes, but it isn't easy. I had no idea where to go. It's not like they have a website."

"Actually they do, but you need to know where to look."

"Really?"

"What do you need the mob for?" Rollin asked, expecting her to say she wanted to hire someone to kill Tuttle. For a small sum, he would consider it.

"I want to make a deal with them."

"They don't make a lot of deals with people."

"I understand, but the FBI is asking questions about my ex-husband's business dealings because they think he's involved with racketeering, gambling, and money laundering. Maybe they're right, or maybe they're wrong, but they think he's in bed with the mob. They think I'm stupid and don't know that if they bust him they take everything we got." She paused and wiped the mouth of her beer bottle with a napkin and took a swallow.

Rollin sat and listened. He was getting excited about the possibilities. He could have a reason to work with the big time.

Judith continued, "But if the 'family' is his partner then they might want to transfer the company to me. Let him take the fall. I get to keep what we got. The Feds get an arrest and the 'family' doesn't lose the money they have tied up in Mobile Medi Tech."

"You thought this out."

"I took my time."

"Do you want another beer?"

"No, thank you," she said as she sat as if waiting for him to say or do something.

"What?" he asked.

"So will you talk to them for me?"

"Absolutely."

She took out three bills, all hundreds and handed them to him. "I suspect they know where to find me when they want to talk."

"At the hotel in Revere," he said, feeling a little cocky.

"That's right," she said as she stood and stared at him, obviously trying to figure out how he knew her.

"From your lips to the mob's ears."

"Thank you," she said as she shook his hand with an over-emphasized grip, and the pain streaked down his side, overpowering the aspirin and alcohol.

Perkins left the car on the side of the road. He'd come back to get Uncle Charlie's equipment and report it stolen later, easier than explaining the damage. He called an associate and caught a ride to the Neon Tetra as it was the nearest joint to have a beer to ease the throbbing of his leg while he waited for another ride that would take him back to his facility in Middleboro. He had broken off the shaft of the arrow but knew not to try to pull the head out. It would cause more damage than leaving it in. He would have Uncle Charlie's physician cut it out tomorrow. It hurt, but it was no worse than the several knife or gunshot wounds he had collected while working personal security. He thanked his ride, which left him in the back of the Neon Tetra. Slowly, he walked across the parking lot.

Rollin backed out of the parking spot and saw Perkins walking across the lot, recognizing him from Perkins' website. He was the founder of War and More, a paintball facility in Middleboro. Rollin had wanted to go there for a while for training by a real VIP protection professional. Where Rollin might have been intimidated meeting this man before, he was now in possession of information that the mob would want. He would be able to ingratiate himself with the right people. Perkins knew the right people; his website hinted at the protection services that he had provided in the past to several defendants of Federal racketeering charges. Rollin couldn't believe the way his luck was changing. He could hardly wait to tell Mr. Perkins what he knew about Tuttle's wife and the FBI. That would be huge. But as he sped across the parking lot to intercept Mr. Perkins, he gave little thought as to what Mr. Perkins' reaction might be at being framed in the headlights of an oncoming car speeding across the parking lot.

Unable to run with half an arrow broke off in his leg, Perkins pulled a gun from a shoulder holster and pointed it straight at Rollin. Rollin, almost drained of all his blood anyway, half ducked and half collapsed beneath the dash to avoid being shot.

The car drove out of control, eliciting shots from Perkins through the windshield.

When the police arrived they found Rollin's car melded with a dumpster. A large, bald, rumpled body was pressed hard between the two and a gray, pudgy corpse was lying on the floorboard beneath the airbag. There was little need for an ambulance, just a coroner and some good theories about what had happened.

THIRTY-NINE

Callie flipped through the radio pre-set buttons, stopping only for a few moments to decide that a song didn't hold her interest. She started her second rotation through the channels looking for a nugget of entertainment.

"I still don't understand why O'Hearn would blackmail Tuttle," she said. "He seemed like a nice guy when I talked to him. I guess you never know people."

"He had a brother die rather harshly," Led said without interpretation. "Shot by police, mistaken identity."

"That's horrible."

"Somebody robbed a bank in broad daylight. Their best ID was that it was a white male wearing a Red Sox shirt."

"That doesn't narrow it down much in Boston."

"Something like that can fester," Led said, stopping her on a Tom Petty song.

"Wouldn't necessarily make someone steal, though," Callie said.

"No. But it could kick in an attitude of what-the-hell-life-isn't-fair-anyway. Most of the time what people do is for no reason at all. People make up reasons after the fact. Don't you think that people do things because of opportunity more than reason? Maybe O'Hearn had the opportunity and then he came up with a reason afterward."

"Did they find the money?"

"The article I read didn't say. In any case, it wasn't relevant to the worker's comp case."

"Makes you wonder," she said.

"About what?"

"O'Hearn."

"How so?"

"What if he was the guy that stuck up the bank?"

"I would hope the police checked that out," he said a little more patronizingly than he had intended.

"Probably," she said, ignoring his tone. "But if he did take it, I know where he would have hidden it."

"How would you know that?"

"Investigative reasoning," she said. Now she had his interest.

"Where?"

"Behind an electrical panel."

"That doesn't narrow it down much."

"No, but he did hide a key behind the panel in the utility room. He was bragging about how sly a place it was behind a panel of 220 amps. He said the power on the building would have to be shut off to get to it."

"You couldn't hide much behind an electrical panel. And if you did, you couldn't get to it too easily."

"Not unless you were an electrician," she said, smiling at Led.

"If he took it, you think he hid it at his Mom's?" He was thinking hard now, his eyebrows askew and left eye squinting.

"I don't think so. Maybe behind the panel he was working on at the Harbour Club."

"You don't know that he even took it," he doubted. "Or had anything to do with it."

"Call it woman's intuition," she said. "Aren't you curious?"

"We couldn't keep it, though. Even if we found it."

"I know that. The money's not the point."

"We just have to get someone to let us into the club," he said, warming to the idea.

FORTY

Paul had run out of ideas.

He was in a bad place—people following him, looking into his business too closely. He had shaken the wrong tree. There was no fruit to fall, only a nest of hornets. He thought about killing Tuttle. Not that he ever would, but he thought about it. He had called Tuttle and was going to threaten him, but only reached the answering machine and didn't bother to leave a message.

He hadn't checked in with Cheryl and it was getting late. He'd said he would be home for supper. He needed to let her know he was just finishing up and would be home later, but he didn't know *how much* later. Hell, he didn't have a clue as to his next move. For now he would take the car back to Rico, maybe stay there a while as he thought it out.

He called Cheryl from the phone at the bowling alley, which was mostly dead with only three lanes being used, but still loud.

"Hey, baby," he said.

"You're still not home and haven't been in two days."

"I'm busy with a few things. I've had to be away working for a few days before; you make it sound like I've never been away."

"I knew weeks in advance when you were going to be working. This weekend you just didn't show up. If you got some whore you're seeing, you can just stay away."

"Jesus, Cheryl. There's no whore. There's nobody. I just got some things going on that I can't talk about right now."

"My sister says you're seeing someone." He could hear her starting to cry, sniffing back tears. "I don't want to believe her, but what am I supposed to think?"

"Bridget just likes to get people going. Tell her to get a job."

"This is not about Bridget. If you can't tell me what's going on then what are we doing together?"

"I love you," he offered.

"Paulie, that's not enough. You keep saying that, but it's not enough. Bridget says you're only with me waiting for Mark's settlement money."

"Bridget is a bitch," he said, out of frustration. He immediately wished he hadn't.

"You don't do nothing but keep avoiding coming home. Goodbye."

"No—don't hang up. I'll come home so we can talk it over. I'll tell you what's going on. It's nothing. It's work. It has nothing to do with another woman or anything. I'll tell you and then you can tell Bridget to piss off."

"Where are you?"

"I'm not far. I'm just down to the alley. I'll be there in about fifteen minutes. Alright?"

"Alright," she sniffed. "I'll listen."

He walked out to Rico's car and drove down the street to the Christie's Mini Market. Sunday evening there wasn't going to be anything else open. From the counter he bought two of the red roses that were enveloped in cellophane in a bucket of slick water sitting between the Slim Jims and the Chap Stick. He realized that he hadn't eaten anything all day so he bought an energy drink and a bag of pretzels.

He finished the drink in the car in front of the house looking at his teeth in the rearview mirror to be sure he didn't have pretzel dough stuck in them. He would need all his charms to calm her down.

He walked to the front door and peeled the orange price tag off of the cellophane surrounding the roses, stopping for a moment to try to get the pieces of the sticky pricing tag from his finger and thumb. He didn't see the two men approach until they had already grabbed his arms; the flowers dropped to the ground. He was bigger than both of them but they were efficient in their moves, in getting the handcuffs on him, and reading him his rights. He was a little relieved when he realized it was only the police grabbing him.

They said he was being arrested for questioning in the murder of Dale Foley.

"Who the hell is Dale Foley?" he asked. Then he remembered: *that guy who works for Tuttle.* He thought of his mother: *I hope she understands.*

As he was led down the steps he saw Cheryl and her sister, Bridget, looking from behind the shade of the second-floor window. He wondered if she had told the police he was coming or if they had been waiting on their own.

FORTY-ONE

Callie saw Sully waiting outside the Harbour Club, sitting in his limo with the front door open and one leg out on the ground. Once they parked he turned the key in the ignition to shut the radio off. He got out of the limo, shut the door, and set the alarm.

"I used to think this was a safe neighborhood," he said as he walked over to meet them.

"Sully!" she said, as if they'd known each other for years.

He smiled and gave her a big hug—and a somber nod to Led.

"Sully, this is Led," she said. "My...partner."

The two men shook hands.

"I was glad to hear you were alright," he said, putting a hand on her shoulder. "What a scene last night, I barely slept. Poor Walter Dorasi. He was a good man. It was a waste. I still don't understand." He shook his head and looked down the street at nothing in particular. "So what can I do for you, little lady?"

"My partner and I are investigators. I took a job here to check on Paul O'Hearn."

He squinted as he looked at her and then over at Led; she was unsure of his reaction to her new identity.

"But...Paulie? What's up with Paulie?" Sully asked with skepticism. "Is he in trouble? He ain't been the same since his brother died."

"We don't know. But I would like to look in the basement."

"Why? There's nothing down there except supplies."

"O'Hearn was doing some work down there," Led said. "We'd like to see what it was."

Sully scowled at Led for just a second before turning to Callie. "I don't see why not. What harm can you do?" He smiled at her. "You're like one of Charlie's Angels. Maybe you could use me on some cases?"

"Maybe," she said realizing that Sully was fine as long as he could find an angle to work himself into the action.

They entered the club, which smelled of stale smoke and skunked beer. Wide yellow plastic tape was still strung across the access to the function room.

Callie walked in behind him. "It's okay that we're in here?"

"The police pretty much wrapped up this morning," Sully said, motioning to the other room. "But I still wouldn't go in there."

"Remind me to take some more of your cards, Sully. I know a few companies downtown who are always looking for a good airport limo service."

"I appreciate it. So what are you checking on Paulie for?"

"Insurance," Led interjected. "Just an insurance claim."

"Nothing to do with what happened last night," she added.

"Well, that's good. I would hate to see Paulie in any real trouble."

Sully clicked the switch at the top of the stairs and walked into the basement first. The foundation was old brick that had been patched several times with splatterings of cement and mortar. The floor was powder-dry dirt. Wooden pallets were laid on the floor with cases of beer and liquor boxes stacked on them. The two naked light bulbs on the ceiling cast everything in multiple shadows.

"All that rain last night and this basement is still dry," Sully said, sounding impressed, looking into the corners. "It can get a little wet down here in the spring if the ground is still frozen, but otherwise it's a pretty good building."

"This the panel that Paul put in?" Led asked.

"He put it in a week or two ago. We had a sixty-amp fuse box before. A private club, so we were grandfathered in with some of the new codes, but it was a good idea to replace it before we lost the building. People were getting stung and it wasn't blowing fuses."

As Sully went ahead of them, Callie felt Led's breath on her ear, heard his hushed voice. "If you're right about where he would hide something, and that is a *big* if, then this is not the place we're looking for."

"What were you looking for?" Sully asked.

"A big panel that Paul installed."

"Paulie doesn't do much electrical work anymore. He retired from that when his brother died. You know about his brother?"

Callie nodded.

"When his brother died he took it hard," Sully said. "He went to work for that guy in Wilmington."

"Richard Tuttle," Led offered.

"Something like that. He works as the main gofer as far as I can tell. Lives with his brother's widow. It's kind of messed up."

"Does he do any electrical work for Tuttle?" she asked.

"He could, I guess. If something needed electrical. He still has his master's license."

Callie saw Led giving one last look at the small panel in the basement, secured straight to the bricks. "Do you know where all those buildings are?" he asked.

"No. Never asked. I've known Paulie for years, but mostly just through here, you know?"

"We should go," Led said to her, raising his eyebrows.

She picked up the cue. "We're all set here Sully. I appreciate you meeting us."

"We ever going to see you back?"

"I don't think I'll be bartending anytime soon, but I might stop in to say hello. I'll be sure to pass around your limo cards."

"You are a sweetheart. And keep me in mind for any spy work you have. I think I would be pretty good at it." He put his hand in the small of her back and walked in front of Led to the stairs. Looking back over his shoulder, he said, "It must be nice working with such a good-looking partner."

"I don't know," Led said. "You'll have to ask her."

"*Nice*," she said, not stopping her ascent up the wooden stairs.

On the street she gave Sully a hug. Led shook his hand and they both took some business cards. Sully told them good luck. It was insincere by all, but it seemed like the thing to do.

Driving down Route 60 they didn't say anything to each other for several miles after leaving Sully. Thinking.

"We aren't headed home?" Callie asked.

"Not yet. If that's alright." Led was still stalling, expecting to see the bald driver of the Lexus at any point.

"What else am I going to do on a Sunday night? Iron?"

"O'Hearn started working for Tuttle after his brother died," Led thought out loud. "He gave up a good paying profession as an electrician."

"Do you know how much Tuttle was paying? Maybe it was more."

"I doubt it. You saw how cheap he tries to be, but I've spoken with the man a few times and his charms are few. I don't see anyone working for him because they like him. Money would be the only reason."

"What if O'Hearn was working on one of Tuttle's buildings three years ago and put the money there? And then went to work for Tuttle to have access to the building when he needed to?" she asked.

He had been thinking the same wild idea. "You might be stretching things a bit, but at least it's a possibility."

"What building, though..." she wondered, without much hope in her voice. "And where?"

"Well, that's where we're going. The office building in Wilmington where Tuttle's office was built three years ago."

"And O'Hearn worked on it?"

He shrugged. He was only guessing.

He could hear the excitement in her voice as she said, "The timeline matches up. We can't get into an office building as easy as the Harbour Club. There's no Sully to call."

"No, but I wanted to drive past it again just to get an idea."

When they neared the building Led saw blue and red lights flashing, with six or seven vehicles parked in no immediately recognizable order. Two large white lights on a trailered generator made backlit silhouettes out of the people walking around.

A state police car blocked the parking lot. Led slowed and pulled up next to the trooper, who held up his hand to stop them, rolling down the window.

The trooper leaned over slightly. "I'm sorry, sir, but you can't enter this complex at this time."

"What's going on?"

"There is a crime scene investigation is all I can tell you."

"That's Lil' Kim!" Callie said, recognizing the woman who had wired her bra twenty-four hours before.

"Ma'am, you can't get out of your car."

"That's a friend of mine," Callie said, rolling her window down all the way in order to lean out. "Kim!"

The woman looked up and did not give any gesture of recognition, although she did walk over to Callie's window.

"I could use some sleep," she responded with a slight smile. "I want to apologize. They briefed me this morning. I was your handler and I lost you. I'm glad you're okay."

"It got crazy real fast. No one could have seen that coming."

"You made it home okay?"

"In a roundabout way. Agent Kim Clark, let me introduce you to Led."

She looked through the passenger side window. "Nice to meet you."

"So what's going on here?" Callie asked.

"We're just following up on a lead."

"Is Chancellor here?" asked Led.

"He's over on the other side of that HAZMAT vehicle."

"Can we see him?"

"Hold on," she answered, looking at the state trooper and over to the vehicles in the lot. "Let me check."

Led saw the officer standing with his thumbs hooked into his black gun belt. "Think the Sox will take the ALC?"

"Toronto's the team that could come out of nowhere," the trooper said, rocking back on his heels. "But the Sox will have the wild card at least."

"Not worried about the Yankees?"

"I'm a Sox fan. I'm always worried about the Yankees."

Agent Clark gave a wave to the trooper. "I guess you're all set," he said. "Pull the vehicle over to the side there."

They got out and walked over to the large white truck with HAZMAT on the side. It resembled an ambulance. Three people in yellow space suits were talking with Chancellor, and so were the two men in tweed jackets and polo shirts.

"We were looking for you two."

"And here we are," Led said.

"You don't know anything about a George Perkins?" Chancellor asked.

"Never heard the name before that I can recall," Led said honestly. "Should I?"

"He died about an hour ago in a car accident."

"Why does a car accident involve the FBI?"

"The driver worked for Tuttle."

"That connects to me how?"

"Oh, I didn't say that it did, just that Perkins had one of your business cards in his pocket."

"I give out a lot of those cards," Led said. "The idea is to get people to pass them around. It's good for business."

"I figured that." Chancellor said. "But he died with an arrow sticking out of his thigh."

"An arrow?" Callie asked.

"Piece of it anyway. We found a Lexus on Route 93 full of arrows and two pieces of the Mobile Medi Tech mobile medical unit in the back."

"Really?" Led asked, as if surprised that he had some of the units.

"The driver of the car that killed him had been shot by a self-inflicted wound in his side."

"A pasty white guy in an orange jacket?"

"Yes, you know him?"

"No, but he was at Tuttle's earlier. I was surprised he was still alive then. Maybe the other guy shot himself with an arrow?"

"Both of them are dead," Chancellor said.

Led paused as if pensive and serious about the information. "Sounds like a game of cowboy and Indians gone bad," he said and winked at Callie.

She glared at him but only for a moment, and then smiled at Chancellor. "Maybe it was a suicide pact."

"Yeah, maybe," Chancellor said very sarcastically, not for a minute believing their naivety.

Chancellor introduced the two other men. "These are Agents Vasquez and Boutwell. This is Mr. Ledbettor and Ms. McBride. Look at them quickly while they're standing still." He turned back to Led. "Why are you here?"

"Out for a drive," Led responded. "Why are you here?"

Chancellor hesitated for only a moment. "We got a tip that the material we've been looking for was put back at Mr. Tuttle's office."

Surprised that Chancellor was telling them anything, Led pressed on. "Did *he* put it there?"

"I doubt it. He doesn't strike me as the type to do any heavy lifting. I think the source that called probably helped move it. That's why he knew where it was." With his hands in his pockets, looking a little relaxed Chancellor asked, "So what are you doing?"

"Go ahead and tell him," Led said to Callie. "If we're right we're going to need help getting to it anyway."

"What's that?" asked Chancellor.

"The money," she said, "from the bank."

"You never mentioned it," Led interjected, "but it was something that came up while I was researching O'Hearn. His brother was mistakenly shot as a robbery suspect."

"I'm aware of it."

"What if it was O'Hearn who hit the bank?" Callie asked.

"He was investigated. He had an alibi and no direct evidence connected him to the crime."

"We got a hunch he took it and we know where the money is," Callie said. "It's in this building."

She took two steps toward the building before Chancellor grabbed her arm. "You can't go in there."

One of the men in the yellow suits and bootie shoe-covers stepped forward. "Actually we're clear now," he said. "There's no trace of any contamination. You can go in if you want."

Chancellor released her arm. "All right, where are we going?"

"To the utility room," she answered, "wherever that is."

With a master key at the bottom of the stairwell, Agent Clark opened the gray utility room of phone lines and power cables. The power panel was divided into four, one for each floor, mounted to a grid of channel lock.

There was no way by looking at it to know if anything was behind it.

"Doesn't look like anything," said Chancellor.

"Behind the electrical panel," Callie said, pressing her face to the concrete wall in an effort to look behind it. "Does anyone have a flashlight?"

With a small mag-light that Agent Clark handed her, she tried to look again but saw nothing but dead flies and cobwebs. "We need to remove the panel."

"You can't touch that. We'd have to get a warrant and kill the power and have an electrician come in. How does she know something is back there?"

"We don't really know it's there," Led said. "We *think* it is."

"You could x-ray it," Vasquez said. "You have HAZMAT out there; they have a portable x-ray gun on the truck."

"That'll be easier than trying to justify the cost of an electrician and going through the trouble of pulling it," Chancellor said. "I don't want to do a Geraldo here."

Led realized at that moment that Chancellor was actually going to listen to them.

"All right," Chancellor told Vasquez. "Get them in here to check it."

As they waited for the device to be retrieved from the truck Chancellor continued in his official mode of questioning Led and Callie as Agent Clark took notes. Callie did most of the talking. She explained how Paul O'Hearn had appeared to brag about being able to hide anything behind a panel. The hardest part was convincing Chancellor that they didn't have a plan for when they arrived; she conceded that she was hoping Led would think of something. Chancellor couldn't accept that they were just going to see what they could make happen, as if by asking them the same questions several times, he might uncover their true intent.

One of the HAZMAT team, still wearing the yellow suit but without the gloves, returned to the utility room with a handheld, cordless power tool with a seven-inch screen sticking out of it. The metal arm curved like a caliper to measure the distance as he stood in front of the panel.

Everyone except the HAZMAT man stood out in the hallway until he responded,

"There you go."

Led, Callie, and Chancellor returned to the utility room to look over the tech's shoulder at the small screen.

"See right there," he said. "There's something in the wall."

"Money?" Callie asked.

"There's a depression with something other than concrete in it," said the technician. "That's all I can tell."

"Let's get it out and see," Led said to Chancellor.

"Not that easy. It won't be until tomorrow before we get the warrant and the contractors in here to remove the panel."

Callie couldn't believe it. "You're just going to leave it there? Aren't you dying to know if we're right?"

"Of course, but we have to follow procedure and the law. For tonight, we'll leave an officer here."

"Not Lil' Kim," Callie said. "She needs some sleep."

"We'll get a state trooper to lock it down," Chancellor said. "You two should go home and get some sleep, too."

"Providing that's the money there," she asked, "what will happen to O'Hearn?"

"He's already in custody. We picked him up for the questioning of Dale Foley's homicide. We'll keep him until we get behind that wall and see what's there. If it is the money from the bank, depending on the prints we find, we'll be real curious about what Mr. O'Hearn has to tell us about how it got there."

"Is there a reward?" Led asked.

"I'm sure there's something, but I'll know more tomorrow."

Resigned to accepting that nothing more would happen on this day, as enough had happened already, Callie and Led got in the jeep and drove off.

He looked at her sitting beside him, beaming in the streetlights, in the headlights of passing cars.

She seemed to sense that he was looking at her.

"I'm not going to be able to sleep," she said.

Led thought about her as if she was far away even though she was sitting beside him. She had heart. Not the valentine, romantic, in-the-middle-of-the-chest heart. She had the heart that sits low, on top of the stomach, pushing on the guts until they are all in agreement to bull ahead with the faith that she could handle any pitch thrown.

"I want to ask you something," she said as she looked over at him. "I'm thinking about tomorrow and how I don't want to go to work because I don't want to leave you. Crazy, huh?"

"I know. It would be great if we still had the whole weekend. It would be nice to have a few days to spend in bed eating Chinese, watching movies. So what was your question?"

"Would you like to spend more time together?"

"That would be nice," he said.

Since the divorce he'd never imagined getting tangled up emotionally again. Relationships, he figured, were things he was just not good at. Like working on cars: he wished he was, but the mechanics of it all eluded him and so he didn't dwell on it.

Right now he felt as if he could rebuild a jet engine. How hard could it be?

"So you're not worried that working together will be too much—that we'll get on each other's nerves?"

He shook his head out of bewilderment.

"I don't think so either."

He sat quiet. He had to. What was she talking about? His simple brain, quick to solve a fraud case, was having trouble adding this one up. He remembered sitting on lawn seats at a Jimmy Buffet show once. He'd been talking to someone and did not see a Frisbee until after it hit him in the side of the head. This was the same feeling. But then at least that orange Frisbee lay at his feet, letting him know what had hit him.

"What about your job?" he asked.

"I don't mind pushing papers, but I don't love it. This weekend, on the other hand, I loved. What we were doing was like real-time anthropology, studying people as the ruins fell. Solving mysteries. Like Shaggy and Scooby."

"As long as you have a realistic concept of what the job involves..."

"We immersed ourselves in someone else's life for a short period of time and got paid for it."

"I'm not sure what we'll get paid and that reward money would probably only come with a conviction."

"So we do insurance cases, missing kids, divorce, it doesn't matter, whatever will pay the bills. Let's start our own agency, you and me."

"We'll probably starve trying to get clients."

"So we eat a little macaroni and cheese. I'm a girl of simple needs. Are you worried I'll be better than you?"

"You already are. So what'll it be? McBride and Ledbettor, PIs?"

"I like Led and Callie, Co.," she said.

He felt the euphoria of possibilities again, the comfort of promise. "That sounds like a plan."

FORTY-TWO

Martinez got out of the county jail and learned that his partner was dead, but it took him almost six months to become motivated to do anything about it. He had never been much of a thinker. He was the doer. And he was going to do in the man responsible, not out of some great vow of vengeance, but out of boredom. He had snorted, drank and screwed away almost all the money Uncle Charlie had given him as severance and now he found himself with time in a semi-sober, edgy state of pissed off.

It was in the john at one of the pubs where he found himself spending most of his days and all of his nights that he sat and read a Boston Herald someone had left on the back of the stool. There on page three was a story about the Led & Calico Detective Agency. And there was a picture of Asher Ledbettor; and it mentioned him and a Callie McBride solving the bank robberies six months earlier and that he was a former competitive archer.

And the details of his partner Perkins dying with an arrow in his leg and run over by a car all came together in his mind as sweetly as if he had just been handed a psychotic schematic. Martinez now had something to do. He would kill Asher Ledbettor.

After a month, Led gave up the lease on the trailer and moved in with Callie. They talked about the future. She someday wanted to have employees and Led didn't. They were a big responsibility that would always have to be worried about. Callie said that a company is all about employees and security. They agreed to wait and see.

For a two-person agency, they were doing well. Led took the cases in some of the tougher neighborhoods, not that Callie wasn't willing. He still wouldn't let her go to where he said wasn't safe, and since there were enough other cases for her, she accommodated his chauvinistic impulse. But as she sat cramped in the back of her vehicle she pondered the anonymity of the inner city cases he worked versus the nosiness of suburbia that she was left with. There were times when she thought that Led might actually be conning her, leaving her to deal with maybe not the most dangerous cases, but certainly the more tedious.

And it was on 93 North, headed towards a case in Somerville, that Led saw Fatima drive past him. Not knowing if it was still an open claim, he followed her to Mobil Medi Tech. He took video as she went inside and then searched the glove box of napkins, catsup packets and sundry business cards to find Agent Chancellor's number.

He had not spoken with Chancellor since the wall was drilled and Paul O'Hearn's cache of stolen money recovered. The money had totaled over $100,000. Seems that Paul and his brother had robbed more than the local savings. They were tied to six robberies from Maine to Rhode Island.

Led didn't consider Chancellor a friend or even contact, but he should still take his call, and might be able to shed a little light on the current status of Mobile Medi Tech.

Chancellor not only took his call but also was down right gregarious as he asked how Callie was and freely recounted what he knew about Tuttle and his company.

Supposedly Judith Tuttle had tried to reach the mob through a man she had first met in a strip club. After a week she was incredulous that no one had contacted her, so she went to the dog track still trying to find organized crime. There she spoke to a Marlon Brando look-alike who she was sure must be able to put her in touch with the right people. Despite the man's appearance, he was a retired Polaroid executive and a grandfather who notified the police. "Judith Tuttle eventually was telling one of our undercovers everything she had already told me," Chancellor explained, "but this time she thought she was telling the other side, so now she, too, was a conspirator. It might have saved her marriage. I guess being indicted together actually brought them closer.

"When Tuttle failed to make his projections and the Venture Capitalist called in his loans, he turned over his stake of Mobile Medi Tech and is doing eighteen months on tax evasion. Judith was put under house arrest but neither one provided enough information to do anymore than take the mob's name in vain."

"So who is running the company?" Led asked.

"Some secretary they promoted."

"Tuttle's?"

"I don't know. Maybe." Chancellor said, "You know her?"

"No, she just seemed like maybe she was running the place even when Tuttle was there."

"Why your interest in Mobile Medi Tech again?"

"I followed someone there and was surprised to find it still in business."

"Fraud lives on." Chancellor chuckled.

Actually it didn't. Once Led called Randall Crawford at the insurance company, he found that Fatima had dropped her claim. It was a closed file. So he drove on towards his case in Somerville.

Martinez parked behind the blond woman he had followed from the detective agency, and she was watching him in her side view mirror as he got out and approached her. He watched her watching him, seeing only her nose and left eye in the mirror.

At the window he politely tapped on the glass and gave one of his full teeth grins of niceness.

"Excuse me," he said. The blonde rolled down the window and Martinez reached in and grabbed her by the throat pinning her head to the backrest. He unlocked her door and pulled her out gasping, her eyes slightly bulging. She fell and stood quickly because he never loosened his grip; like an angler of men *and* women he let his catch thrash around a little at arm's length enough to be worn out and starving for oxygen before he pulled her in close and walked her back to his car. No one was paying any attention. There were only the two men on ladders at the roof next door with their backs turned, installing gutters.

He never felt so good as putting an arrogant woman where she belonged. It was nothing against the woman. He loved women. It was a boast in action against all the men who were too weak in her life, who were too soft to do what he was man enough to do. Because she was good looking, weak men let her get her head filled with ideas. Let her think that she wanted to be like a man, not seeing the beauty of being the woman. The men that created this idea in her head were not men; they were boys willing to be castrated for the sniff of a pair of panties.

The woman sat still, gasping a little but not playing it up. She was actually trying to hide her fear of him.

"You like to play with the boys?" he asked her. She set her jaw a few times to stretch the muscles in her neck that he had bruised. That was her answer.

He drove to find Asher Ledbettor.

With her cell phone he scanned through her contacts and found nothing under Asher, but there was Led. "This your boyfriend?" he asked her. When she ignored him he punched her hard in the side of the head and she slumped in the seat.

It was a lugubrious picture of Callie bound in a trunk with a text message, *Brng Ur Bow Tonto, No 911. @ 3 pm Old Fanning Farm Bogs, Middleboro.*

Led's first reaction was anger at himself, and he hit his hand into the dash to send pain through his brain of fragmented thoughts. Who? Why? Was she all right? Should he call the cops or do as was said, and go alone?

He couldn't afford to get it wrong.

It was 1:36 p.m. He didn't have time to think. He drove to the condo, got his bow case and rushed back to the jeep. He had almost an hour drive in traffic. He would think along the way.

Led didn't decide to call Chancellor until he was taking the exit for Middleboro off of Route 24. Chancellor dropped into his monotone voice of procedure and training as soon as Led had said what the problem was.

Led lied about what time he was supposed to be there, giving him an hour to resolve the problem or exacerbate it. By the time Chancellor arrived it would either be over or it was going to need some big gun support to clean it up—or at least write Led's obituary.

The bright light had awakened her. She found herself bound at the wrists by a small band dug into her flesh and rubbed against the bone. She could only breathe through her nose; duct tape was over her mouth. In the moments that it took her to assess her current state, the silhouetted man had shut the trunk again. Her face hurt, her head pounded and she was in total darkness. He'd taken her photo. That was what he was doing with a cell phone: her cell phone. Was she kidnapped for ransom? He had clearly confused her with someone with money. If all her friends and family pooled their resources there might be enough to pay for a three-day bender in Sheboygan.

She laid there, hurting but afraid enough to feel she should do something, no matter how futile. At any rate, it would keep her busy enough to stop thinking about the possibility of her own death occurring very soon.

There wasn't much room to move, and with her hands behind her back all she could do was roll around. She kicked off her sneakers and with her bare feet felt around the darkness of her automotive coffin for anything—a bottle of water, a cell phone, or a gun would be nice, but right then she would settle for sharp edge of anything on which she could cut her wrist constraints. With her toes she had found a nub of something, above her. She peeled the carpet lining back enough to expose the end of a screw. It barely stuck through the sheet metal, but it was sharp. It was awkwardly above her and even after she rolled to her knees she was still too far away from it.

She put her bruised face to the bottom of the trunk and arched her back, going up on her toes: a human tripod. She felt for the point of the screw as her face pressed into the coarse nap of the industrial carpet. She worked her body down a little in an effort to line her wrists up with the screw, but the car took a high-speed turn and she lost her balance and tumbled back to her side.

Before she could try again, her efforts were further impaired by the unevenness of rural roads where the bumps and turns changed her status of cutting loose from not likely to impossible.

She heard the tenor of the pavement change to a baritone rumble and gravel crumble of a dirt lane. Where he was taking her she could only guess. What did he want with her? She knew not to dwell on the demented reasons of her abduction—she skipped straight to accepting that it had happened and no one else knew where she was.

At the paint ball range was an old equipment shed, a few picnic tables and a refrigerator. Martinez was glad to find a few cold beers. He wondered what would become of the property once the taxes were no longer being paid. Shame, too. It was quiet and relaxing for a little while, but too much of it would drive him nuts. Martinez preferred the isolation of the city, where his skills were more practical. But this was a good place to have a beer and dump a body.

After his second beer he walked to the trunk of the car and popped it open. The blond squinted at him. Ledbettor would come after her—most men would.

And then in the relaxed country setting, he had a sadistic idea. He would make Ledbettor shoot his own girlfriend.

This was going to be fun. A little righteous vengeance. He took a sheet of wafer board from in back of the shed and looked around for something to use to draw a target. Not finding anything more practical, he took a couple of paint balls and stepped on them, turning the instep of his black Italian leather loafers florescent pink. Then, with nothing more than a stick dipped in the splatter, he drew three concentric circles and put a big splotch of paint in the middle. He stood it up. It was a target, a little oblong and with paint running in streaks, but the idea was there.

He dragged the target out to the mound of gravel near the driveway and tried to lean it to stand, but the bottom slid and it fell over. He got a shovel from the shed and made a shallow trench to stand the base of the wafer board in. Then he propped the shovel's handle behind it to provide additional support from behind.

He dragged the woman from out of the trunk well and pushed her to the ground behind the sheet of plywood.

Martinez was excited. It would be hard not to tell someone about this. Hell, he wished Perkins was there right then to congratulate him for such perfect revenge.

"I told you I'd take care of it," he said out loud, as if the deceased Perkins were looking down—or up—at his exploits.

Then he got another beer and sat on an overturned milk crate next to his target.

Led drove down the dirt access road to an area of overgrown bogs and briars. There had not been a house for a mile or two; only an out-building or pump house along the edge of the canals signified any sense of human interest with the reclamation of the upland bogs as they transcended to meadow and woods.

There ahead was a dark blue Lincoln Town Car parked by a metal machine storage shed. In the trunk he imagined Callie lying frightened and waiting for him.

The man in the suit coat and wrinkled white shirt stood as Led approached. He held up a handgun, something semi-automatic, big and chunky, black and militaristic; it was clear what Led was expected to do.

Led stopped two car lengths away from the Lincoln and got out. He thought of running to the trunk of the car to spring Callie, but only hypothetically. In reality he knew he needed to move slowly and take directions until he could find out what was going on.

"Where is Callie?" he yelled to the man with the gun.

"You bring your bow and arrows?"

"Like you said."

"Get them."

Led felt inclined to walk with his hands slightly raised so the schizoid with the gun would not misinterpret any move. With the case removed from the passenger side, he set it upon the hood of the jeep, opened it and removed the compound bow and six arrows. He stood with it at his side as he turned back to look at the man by the gravel pile.

"Do you know who Perkins was?"

"Give me a hint," Led said.

"He was my partner and you killed him."

"You've got me confused for someone else."

"You shot him in the leg. Then he was run over."

"*That* guy." Led realized who he was talking about, the stalker who had tried to shoot him six months ago. It was no surprise that he would have a partner that was a speed freak with a gun. "Shouldn't you be after the person that ran him over?"

"He's already dead. You're still here."

And *here* was where Led intended on staying, but where was Callie? He asked again.

"She's around but a little tied up at the moment."

Led scowled at the obvious attempt to be witty. "She better be alright. For your sake." He tried to feel as tough as the words.

"You talk pretty brave."

"What do you want?" Led asked, looking around trying to determine if they were alone.

"I want to kill you, but I want to be fair about it."

"That's considerate."

"I will give you a chance to kill me, too."

Led pictured some kind of one-on-one war game throughout the old paint ball facility, and started to consider his options for cover until he could get to the trunk of the Lincoln, get Callie and get out of there. "Sounds too good to be true."

"You like shooting people with your bow and arrows—so you will use those."

"Of course." Led considered the distance—about fifty feet—that separated them and wondered if he truly could shoot this man while looking him in the eye, given the opportunity. Then he glanced at the trunk of the Lincoln and knew he could kill this man without any further thought.

"So this is how it goes, Mr. Ledbettor. I will shoot at you—" and he fired a round from the handgun that cracked the quiet air surrounding them. The bullet sprayed up dirt several feet away from Led, who flinched but otherwise stood stalwart.

The man ducked behind the sheet of graying wafer board with its poorly drawn bulls eye. "Go ahead shoot. It's your turn."

Led knew the ability of his arrows to surprise with their penetrating velocity. He tried to imagine where the large man might be behind the board, where he might have contorted himself to hide. Would he kneel, crouch or lay down? Where was his head, the bridge between his eyes?

Led drew his bow until the cams reduced the draw weight, and he thought about jumping back in his jeep and pulling up beside the Lincoln. Maybe he would have a chance to release the trunk. He should have told Chancellor to be here by now—he wasn't going to be able to distract the psycho for another forty-five minutes, which might just as well be forty-five days.

He sighted and at full draw shot the target, guessing a vital organ might be pressed against the lower right.

The arrow sank deep into the board, all the way to the red feathery flights.

The razor sharp tip grazed Callie's cheek. She could feel the cold burn of air touching filleted flesh and the warm sting of blood, no more than a thorn bush would have caused; but she squirmed with the unexpected sensation and the probable outcome of the situation. And she felt the gun of her oppressor placed to her temple.

"Don't ruin my game," he said in a low forceful whisper. The man in the dusty suit then stood up and addressed Led.

"Too bad, you were so close. Let's try again." He shot the dirt in front of Led, closer this time, but still without the accuracy that would be expected from someone so homicidal.

It didn't add up. Led casually cast the arrow into the ground beside the target, missing it by five feet or more.

"You are no fun." The man stood up from behind the target, anger starting to sound in his voice. "And fun is the only reason I haven't shot you or your girlfriend already."

Led had another arrow ready when the man stood, but he did not have it drawn. He wasn't sure he could pull back the string and release before he himself was shot. But if he at least stopped this man, Chancellor would find Callie in the trunk when he arrived. He hoped.

And as Led looked the man in the eyes and saw the gun point at his chest, he was a little surprised, but not disappointed, to see Callie rise up, gripping a shovel with the familiarity of a Midwest farm girl.

In one seamless motion she leaned in and swung with the precision of a medical professional. It appeared that the blade of the shovel separated the man's vertebrae C1 from C2. His eyes rolled up to the top of his head and he flopped facedown in the gravel as if someone had just hit his off switch.

Led ran over to needlessly kick the gun away as Callie peeled the tape from her mouth.

"Looks like I got my dark past," she said unsympathetically, looking at the dead man on the ground.

"And just in time," Led acknowledged.

They sat and shared a beer, and waited for Chancellor.